LAWS of the BLOOD

PARTNERS

SUSAN SIZEMORE

ACE BOOKS, NEW YORK

LAWS OF THE BLOOD: PARTNERS

An Ace Book / published by arrangement with
the author

PRINTING HISTORY
Ace edition / November 2000

All rights reserved.
Copyright © 2000 by Susan Sizemore.
Cover art by Dave Dorman.

This book may not be reproduced in whole or in part,
by mimeograph or any other means, without permission.
For information address: The Berkley Publishing Group,
a division of Penguin Putnam, Inc.,
375 Hudson Street, New York, New York 10014.

The Penguin Putnam Inc. World Wide Web site address is
http://www.penguinputnam.com

Check out the ACE Science Fiction & Fantasy newsletter
and much more on the Internet at Club PPI!

ISBN: 0-441-00783-X

ACE®
Ace Books are published
by The Berkley Publishing Group,
a division of Penguin Putnam Inc.,
375 Hudson Street, New York, New York 10014.
ACE and the "A" design are trademarks
belonging to Penguin Putnam Inc.

PRINTED IN THE UNITED STATES OF AMERICA

10 9 8 7 6 5 4 3 2

ACKNOWLEDGMENTS

So, I'm standing in the Roy Wilkins Auditorium at a Queensryche concert I almost didn't attend 'cause—well, Chris DeGarmo's not with the band anymore and I haven't yet fallen in love with the new CD, but they've been my favorite band since the mid-80s and I simply can't miss 'em even if I should be home working on this late-autumn night. So I'm there. It's not supposed to be stadium seating, but I've sneaked up pretty close to the stage. Great view. Good crowd (who says metal's dead?). Delighted to be there. Band's as good as ever. Inspirational. I've been having this writer's block problem—me, who *never* gets writer's block and doesn't even believe in it. The vampire book set in D.C. just isn't working, and I'm going nuts. Then Geoff Tate starts talking to the audience, something about free will and do you agree this person has the right to do this or that and everyone's agreeing with this politically correct spiel. Until he gets to, "What if a vampire decides to take a bite out of your throat? Does he have a right to do that?" and the band goes into my all-time favorite Queensryche song, "Walk in the Shadows," which is from *Rage for Order*, the best album of all time—and the subconscious inspiration for The Laws of the Blood. And suddenly, the writer's block is gone. Poof. And Char is there, a shy, quiet Enforcer girl from Seattle with a demon extermination problem, and I've got to get home to start writing her story while inside my head she's humming "The Lady Wore Black." Thank you, Geoff Tate, Michael Wilton, Scott Rockenfield, Eddie Jackson, Chris DeGarmo—and Kelly Gray. Once again, I couldn't've done it without you.

But the book is still dedicated to
Ginjer Buchanan—
the good, the patient, the wise . . .

Prologue

SEATTLE

"DO YOU WANT to live forever?"

"Not particularly."

"Fool," the Disciple said to the tourist and walked away, his arms wrapped tightly around his thin body. He shouldn't have bothered stopping to talk to the man with the camera.

It was cold for the time of year, but the Disciple didn't wear a coat. He hadn't shaved that day or changed clothes. He looked homeless and half mad, but that was nothing new in Pioneer Square. And it was what the Prophet required of his missionary to the world, to go searching in this humble, helpless guise. The Disciple had a gift for seeing into the hearts of those chosen to understand the word. The tourist was ripe for saving; the Disciple could feel it. It hurt him to know that he'd lost a soul, but he was in too much of a hurry to turn back and work at persuading the stranger to come with him.

Tonight his task was to find a very special pair. Someone to act as a Vessel and channel for what was to come, and someone for the Angel to love. A shudder of pride and pleasure and hunger went through him as he continued his quest. Which would they be?

The place was thick with humanity tonight. They were crowded onto the benches beneath the trees, strolled arm in arm across the brick paving, spilled in and out of the shops and restaurants.

The Disciple didn't like Pioneer Square, but that was where he'd been sent tonight. He didn't like the way it smelled. He walked around and around the square, with the stenches changing every few feet, so strong they were almost solid. The reek of pizza spilled out from one building, beer from the next, sickeningly sweet candy from another. The aromas of hot yeast and grease and flour turned his stomach, and he had to stop and hold his breath for a while, but he kept doggedly on. He couldn't understand how or why anyone could stand to taste anything that smelled as much of decay as cooked vegetables and meats. He was sent here often, but he never got used to it. People were drawn to the food like flies. Some of them were worth saving to serve the Angel; he had to always keep that in mind—and that he was happy to serve.

You went where the Prophet sent you or the Demon ate your brain. If you wanted to live forever, you had to do exactly what you were told. The Disciple was glad only the Demon was allowed to eat brains. The Disciple himself lived for the sweet taste of the transcendent flesh and blood of the Angel of Life. Serve the Angel, and you lived forever.

He stopped just inside the fancy ironwork bus shelter on one side of the square, barely protected from the sharp wind. He knew he should continue his quest, but he had to think about the Angel for a while to give him strength.

In the end, and as he should have trusted it would happen, the ones he sought came to him. He did not have to find them. The Disciple hugged himself with joy when a couple pushed past him into the bus shelter. He turned to stare at them, and they stared back, surly at first, but with growing fascination. The man was tall, young, wiry, and looked to be as mean as a snake despite the conservative suit and haircut he wore. His eyes held no great intelligence, but they shone with cunning—and the Gift. This one would be the Vessel of Eternity. The girl was young and close to pretty, and that was all she needed to be.

The Disciple drifted closer to the couple. The man put his arm tightly around the girl's shoulders, but his eyes never broke contact with the Disciple's. The Disciple said to him, "Do you want to live forever?"

Eternal life was not something he could offer the girl.

AUGUST

ARIZONA

The flamethrower worked better than anything else he'd found. Napalm would probably be the best, but Haven hadn't been able to get his hands on any recently. The ATF had raided his primary sources of supplies in a sting operation a few weeks back. Haven had a fondness for alcohol, tobacco, and firearms but no love at all for any law enforcement agency that regulated anything on local, state, or federal level. The forces of law and order didn't love him, either, but they did want him. Or would have, if it wasn't believed he'd been killed five years before.

"Reborn a little, but not killed," he murmured into the coolness of the desert dusk. He and Santini were two hours late getting to the site they'd scouted out the previous night, but Haven didn't think the upcoming fight would be much of a problem. Darkness was okay; a daylight raid might be noticed by the workers in the nearby copper mine. Even if his targets were stronger at night, they wouldn't be expecting company. Haven didn't care much if they were. He smiled a little. He was actually looking forward to a fight.

Beside him, Santini yawned, scratched, and said, "Reborn." He fingered the gold cross he wore around his throat. "Right."

Santini was one of the survivors, one of only four out of twenty, who had lived through the horror that had made Jebel Haven what he was today. Santini had been a drug-dealing, hard-drinking, whoring biker before Haven met him. He still was, but he never failed to show up to help out when Jebel Haven gave him a call. Sometimes Haven had to bail him out or break him out to get him to the firefight, but the biker's expertise and commitment were worth the trouble. This time, though, Santini had been hanging around Baker's office when they got the tip about the nest two days ago.

Tonight would be a simple cleanup operation. They'd gotten most of this nest already, and the survivors had run to the desert for cover.

Haven looked up at the starry sky, then shifted his gaze downward to the dark hole in the cliff side where the cave was located. Their hiding places were easy to find if you knew what to look for. Funny thing about that, you'd think they'd have more sense. That they'd at least hunt out new holes after the old ones were burned out again and again. They were stupid, true, most of 'em, but they could be tough. He'd run into a few that had given him plenty of trouble, but this wasn't going to be one of those ugly fights.

Too bad; Haven lived for the rush of righteous vindication that came with the really spectacular kills. Those were getting few and far between. Part of him hoped that maybe what he and Santini and Baker did was having an effect on culling their numbers. A part of him suspected he was being played for a fool. Hope was not something he was comfortable with. The suspicious part of his nature had the upper hand most of the time.

What was he missing? There was a growing itch in the back of his mind that told him he was going about this all wrong, that it wasn't as simple as it seemed.

He took a drag on his cigarette and tried to think only of what he and Santini needed to do in the next couple of hours. Had to go in, flame the nest, drive in a few stakes, chop off a few heads, get back to the Jeep and out, well away before dawn.

He tossed the cigarette to the ground and smashed out the butt with his heel. Checked his weapons and equipment again, glanced at Santini while the biker did the same. "Ready?"

"Yep."

At first, Haven had enjoyed the hunting, but lately all the fun had gone out of his current occupation. Somebody was going to pay for messing him over soon. But sooner than that, he was going to get Baker to teach him how to use a computer. Maybe holes and caves weren't the only places to look for the sons of bitches. Maybe he'd try the Internet. If Baker could use it how hard could it be?

Haven was almost bored when he said, "Let's go kill some vampires."

Chapter 1

PORTLAND

"GOT A JOB for you."

Char didn't know whether to be pleased or worried when the man behind her in line whispered in her ear. She recognized his voice. Normally, she would have felt the approach of one of her own kind, but her senses could be forgiven for not picking up any scent of Istvan the *dhamphir*. Once she knew he was there, the trick was not shaking in her shoes. She didn't know if Istvan was officially the chief of all the Enforcers, but he was certainly in charge. She supposed that gave him all the clout he needed to order her around. As far as she knew, no one had less seniority than she did. And seniority aside, Istvan had the biggest fangs and baddest attitude of all. He scared anybody in their right mind to death.

"Didn't know you were in town." She was quite pleased that her voice didn't shake when she spoke.

"I'm not."

And who was she to question that? When a fingertip touched the side of her neck, Char managed not to scream, though she shuddered as she squeaked, "What?"

"The Council has decided to kill Jebel Haven. You're it."

The Starbucks was crowded on this rainy autumn night, but Char was certain no one but she had heard the *dhamphir*'s words. She wished she hadn't.

She whirled around to protest the unfairness of such a dirty job being given to her, but of course the *dhamphir* was no longer behind her or anywhere in the coffee shop. The dead traveled fast and all that hyperbole. Where he'd come from she didn't know, where he went she didn't care—as long as it was somewhere far away from her. The woman who was behind her in line gasped as Char bumped into her, and Char stepped aside rather than offer excuses or apologies. She moved to the back of the other line and indulged in a bit of sulking while waiting to order her latte.

Why me? she wanted to howl into the night—though it would disturb the other patrons who'd come in out of the cold rain if she were to make a fuss. She did not go around disturbing people. Okay, occasionally she had to kill them, but she hated the idea of upsetting anyone she didn't have to. No reason the patrons of Starbucks should be burdened with the knowledge that she'd been ordered to commit a murder. The floor was wet and the windows steamy; the place was full of warm bodies and the rich scent of coffee. Jazz played on the sound system, barely audible over the buzz of conversation. The lines waiting to order stretched all the way to the door, and every spindly chair at every tiny table was full. Bodies brushed against hers, and the sound of laughter filled her ears, only serving to emphasize to Char how alone she was in the night. She liked to think of herself as serving and protecting. But then, she supposed, so did Jebel Haven.

Jebel Haven could not possibly be his real name. Come on, was anyone really going to be named something as wildly heroic as that? She knew all about Jebel Haven, or at least as much as was possible to learn from a long way away from the man. She'd made a point of following his career, which was probably why she'd been picked to eliminate him as a threat to the Strigoi. She could argue that she didn't see why he was a threat, but arguing with the Council would get another Enforcer sent after her, and eventually Jebel Haven was going to kill a strigoi, and mortals simply couldn't be allowed to do that. That was the Enforcers' job.

Jebel Haven was a good name for a crusader; Char gave him that. She was of the opinion that if you were going to be a superhero, you needed a cool name to go with the gig. Problem was, comic book writers had grabbed all the good hero names long ago. You had to do your best with what was available. Char wasn't *exactly* her real name, either, but Charlotte McCairn just wasn't a very good name for a vampire, especially not an Enforcer, a Keeper of the Law, and a daughter of the Nighthawk line. She went by Char, as in burnt and blackened. Like charcoal rather than simpering, silly Char, pronounced Shar—bleah! She'd considered calling herself Cairn for a while but figured that at some point someone would call her Rocky, and she'd have to kill them.

Kill them. What an awful thing to joke about. One did, though, easily, and such casual references to murder made no sense. Committing murder was serious business and should be treated with respect. And handled strictly by hardworking professionals such as herself. Except that Enforcers were supposed to be involved with executions rather than indiscriminate violence . . . which brought her thinking back to Jebel Haven.

Char put murder out of her mind for a few minutes more until she picked up her order and left the coffee shop. Her original plan for the evening had been to settle down in a quiet corner and watch the world go by for a while. She had a copy of today's *Oregonian* with her in case there was no one interesting in the place to strike up a conversation with. If she didn't make direct contact with humanity, that was okay, too; just being out among people was a relaxing pastime sometimes. She knew she spent way too much time reading books and working with databases. Pity Istvan had put a hard, abrupt end to any semblance of normal, ungeeky, civilized behavior for this late-autumn evening in Portland.

The rain had slowed to a cold drizzle by the time Char stepped outside. She took some pleasure from the moist air while she walked. She walked a long way and eventually found that she was in her favorite spot in her favorite park. And what a symbolic and sentimental choice her subconscious had chosen, the place being a memorial to fallen war heroes. Truth was, she hoped it was the smell of witch hazel and roses that led her to the Garden of Solace, even though the scents were faint at this time of the year. Her sense of smell had become keener since she'd become a Nighthawk. Her wits, however—well, she worried about them a lot.

For one thing, Char now realized that she'd forgotten about her latte, though she still held the cold cup of coffee in her hand. She dumped it onto the ground and thought of libations and sacrifices and muttered, "Oh, come on, it's only a Grande from Starbucks, Char." Besides, the goddess, if the goddess had ever existed, would prefer blood to coffee. Char didn't, but it was a little late to mention an aversion to the stuff at this point. Blood had its place, of course, and could be delicious under the right circumstances. But *never* in her wildest dreams had she ever suspected she'd crave the taste of another living being's heart.

"I was a vegetarian once, you know," she said, though there was no one around to hear her. Char did that a lot—talked to herself. Came from being alone too much, she supposed. Of course, she'd never been very good socially. Being a vampire had helped her natural shyness for a while. Then she'd changed into a Nighthawk, and nobody wanted to hang out with her anymore. Nighthawks didn't have a lot of friends. Probably because they ate them under the right circumstances. That tended to put people off.

Speaking of putting things off, long, lonely walks in the mist weren't going to help her forget her troubles or that she was now Haven's trouble. Char sighed loudly. There was nothing she could do but to go home and consider the best way to kill a man. And what she needed to pack for a trip to Arizona.

Home was not a nest, with a household and companions and all the other trappings of strigoi society. She knew some Nighthawks lived perfectly normal lives, but she wasn't up to it, not yet. Maybe never. She hadn't been involved with anyone since Jimmy left, not in any emotional way. She was pretty certain she was a one-vampire woman who had ended up a lone hunter. But that was all right, because Enforcers needed to focus on the job rather than having personal entanglements. Char knew her destiny was to be more like the scary, psychopathic Istvan than Marguerite, Portland's other Enforcer. Portland's real Enforcer, actually. Char was allowed to hang around because she didn't have anywhere else to go. Or she hadn't until a few hours ago. Now she had somewhere to go and didn't want to go there.

"On so many levels," she murmured, noticed that she held the key to her apartment in her hand, and wondered why.

Char focused her attention and realized that she was staring at the dark, blank wood of a door and that she was home, at least in the physical sense. She shook her head, annoyed at being so out of it tonight. It was a good thing no one had attempted to assault her on her evening ramblings, or they would have ended up a tasty, wholesome snack before she'd been able to stop herself. Thinking of people as snack food showed how undone she was by Istvan's appearance once more in her orderly, quiet life. Not that she'd actually gotten a look at his appearance, per se, not this time, but the *dhamphir*'s taking an interest in her was no more welcome this time than the other times she'd communicated with him. Been communicated at by him? Yes, that said it much better. The last time he'd talked to her, he'd told her he didn't think she was up to acting as an Enforcer yet, and she'd readily agreed. Now it seemed he had changed his mind.

Of course, she had to go out into the world sometime and prove her mettle. She knew that, but she had enjoyed her two quiet years doing research and compiling data on subjects relating to the strigoi. It was useful, important work that she'd taken far beyond the strict parameters she'd begun with. Highly classified, as well. In fact, she strongly suspected only she and Istvan knew about it, that it was his idea. They would both be in big trouble with the Strigoi Council if they—whoever *they* were—ever found out about it. In fact, she suspected one of the reasons Istvan wanted the information was so that he could find the Council. But why he wanted to do that since he was their voice and hand, at least in North America, Char quite firmly refused to think about.

Besides, she didn't like the idea of leaving town so close to the holidays. She had an invitation from Marguerite's nest for Thanksgiving. She didn't get invited out often. And then there was Hanukkah, Christmas, and Blessing of the Knives coming up. "Maybe I can put off killing Haven at least until after Blessing Day."

With that thought in mind, Char unlocked the door and went into her dark apartment. Of course, she needed a better excuse than multicultural merrymaking if she was going to put off carrying out a direct order from the Strigoi Council.

Char had barely turned on the living room light and taken off her old blue raincoat when she realized someone was about to knock on the door. A tight knot formed in her stomach, and her hands balled nervously into fists. Natural shyness warred with predator instincts, and the result was that her diamond-sharp claws pierced bloody indentations in the tough skin of her palms. The knock sounded, low and fast and frantic.

"Coming," Char called to the vampire in the hall. She snatched a tissue from the box on the coffee table and wiped her hands, then stuffed the Kleenex in her pants pocket before turning the handle. The tiny cuts were already healed, her claws safely retracted, but the scent of blood lingered on the air. Not such a bad thing, she told herself, in the home of a hunter. She was still blushing when she opened the door. A woman stood outside, a thin, pale wraith of a woman. At least that was the impression Char had at first sight. The woman was actually short, matronly, and comfortably plump, but Char could tell that the stranger's spirit was worn thin with worry. "Yes?" she said to the other vampire.

The woman looked up and down the empty hallway, then pointedly at Char. "May I come in?"

The legend about vampires having to be invited into human homes was not true. However, no right-thinking vampire would enter another strigoi's home uninvited. To do so was a gross insult, a breach of territorial rights that led to the sorts of dominance games Enforcers actively discouraged in this modern age. To enter an Enforcer's home uninvited was tantamount to offering yourself as the Enforcer's next meal. Sort of like being a self-delivering pizza.

Char grew queasy at this thought. She stepped back and said, "Please come in."

Once the stranger was inside, Char took the woman's coat, made room enough for her to sit on the living room couch, and said, "Can I get you anything? Coffee? And you are?" she added almost as an afterthought, trying to sound cool and in control as well as polite.

The woman dismissed Char's courtesy with a slight smile. Then she turned a worried expression on Char and said. "My name is Helene Bourbon. I need your help."

A ripple of emotion went through Char that was so strong she had to quickly sit down in the chair across the narrow coffee table from the couch. She sat on a pile of paper and books, of course, but she ignored that. Help? Someone actually needed *her* help? She was thrilled. Excited. Happy. Terrified. Definitely terrified. Puzzled. Why would anyone need her help? This was the opportunity to aid her community that she'd been hoping for and dreading with equal zeal.

"This is an eventful night," she said and found that she was rubbing her forehead. She even tried the old nervous habit of pushing her glasses up on her nose and then remembered that she hadn't had to wear glasses for years. Yes, she was shaken. First Istvan and now Helene Bourbon putting in appearances to shake her out of her quiet, circumscribed life. "I've heard of you, Ms. Bourbon," Char said to her visitor. "Your nest is down the coast."

"Near Yachats. And I'm too old to be comfortable with being called Ms. Of course, I was never anyone's Mrs. And Lady Helene does sound a bit silly these days. Never mind." The woman made a sweeping gesture, as though waving away her own facetious words. Char had noticed that Helene Bourbon had been looking anywhere but at her, but then the woman made an obvious effort to make eye contact with her. She said, "I'm nervous about being in your presence, Hunter."

It shocked Char that a vampire would be afraid of her, but that *was* supposed to be one of the perks of the job. She knew who Bourbon was, some of the woman's past as well as her present occupation and address. She wasn't a lady in the heraldic sense of the word, and she wasn't one of *those* Bourbons, but she never actually *claimed* to be. Char thought everyone was allowed at least a little vanity. So, rather than reveal that she had secret knowledge, Char asked, "What brings you to Portland?"

Any sign of nervousness disappeared in the woman across from her, and all her concern rushed back. "I've come about my missing nestling," she told Char.

Chapter 2

TUCSON

"I'VE COME ABOUT my son," the woman said.

She stood just inside the doorway, with Baker behind her.

Haven almost said, *Lady, this isn't a detective agency*. Then he remembered that, technically, it was. It was Baker's office. Baker was a retired cop, now a PI. It was also Baker's desk, which would make any missing-person problem the woman had Baker's business. But from the way Baker was looking at him, it wasn't. *Ah, hell*.

The first thing Haven did was put down the gun he'd picked up when the door opened unexpectedly. The woman hadn't seen the weapon he held just below the top of the desk, which was piled with books and papers. The second thing he did was save the file the way Baker had taught him and turn off the computer.

Then he waved Baker and the woman into Baker's office. Baker was some mixture of Native American, black, and Irish and said he got his stubbornness from all three. He was big and brown and bald and ugly but about as soft in the heart as he was hard everywhere else. Haven had liked the man even in the days when they'd been playing hide-and-seek across the Southwest. Baker had been intent on returning Haven to prison, Haven had tried to kill Baker a few times, but they'd put their differences aside in the service of a higher purpose long ago.

It was because of the reproving look Baker gave him that Haven stood when the woman came toward the desk. Baker'd been trying to civilize him, but Haven preferred to ignore the niceties most of the time. Being polite to a distraught woman seemed like a halfway sensible idea, though if Baker hadn't been there, Haven would have followed his first impulse and told her to get out.

Baker closed the door and leaned against it. The woman stopped in front of the desk and said, "My name is Brenda Novak, and I'm with the FBI." By the time he had the Glock pointed openly at her, she'd sat in the chair across from the desk. She looked at him steadily— at him, not the gun. The worry hadn't left her expression, but she wasn't worried about him. "I know who you were," she told him. "And I don't give a shit. I know— something—about what you do now, and that's why I need you to help me find my son."

"What do you know?" Haven asked. "Who told you?" How many was he going to have to kill to keep his secrets quiet? He glared at Baker. "I doubt you told her anything," he said to his partner.

"He didn't," Brenda Novak answered. "I found him." She spared a quick glance over her shoulder at Baker. "Not an easy task." She brought her attention back to

Haven. "Easier than finding Danny, though. Searching for Danny has led me down some strange roads—and I'm an FBI profiler; I know strange intimately."

He'd read about profiling. It was like a kind of officially sanctioned ESP. The government had these people who looked at pictures of crime scenes and predicted what killers would do next and how to catch them. Crazy people got profiled. Haven wasn't crazy. He kept the gun aimed steadily on the woman and said nothing.

"I realize telling you about myself is dangerous," Novak went on. She shrugged. She had the manner of someone with nothing to lose. Jebel Haven understood the look of a spirit at the end of its resources. He knew you had to get there before you could get beyond it, into the realm where he lived. Or you got to the end of the road and you gave up and died. He didn't have any sympathy for the ones he'd known who'd given up. He didn't have much sympathy for those who'd died trying, either.

Baker crossed the room. He put his big, meaty hands on the back of the woman's chair. "Put the gun away, Jebel. We're going to listen to what the woman has to say. It's our kind of business," he added when Haven flicked his gaze to his partner's for a moment.

Haven wanted to think that if this was some sort of trap, Baker would have smelled it. He trusted Baker, and he hated trusting anyone. He didn't like it, but he sat. He put the gun down, but not away. He left it on the desktop, with his hand close to it. "What are you talking about?" he said to the woman.

"About finding my son," she said. "That's the only thing that interests me."

"You're with the FBI, and you have a missing son. Kidnapped?"

She nodded.

"The Bureau takes care of its own. Your kid's missing, your own people are looking for him."

She made one of those sounds that was a little like a laugh but without any amusement in it. She was a good-looking woman, fortysomething, worried, but keeping it together. "The Bureau does not really deal with "X-Files" cases, Mr. Haven. We don't even use the term *profiler* in the department, though that is the common— well, the polite—term for what I do. I work for a conservative government bureaucracy. We do indeed take care of our own, but no one wants bad publicity. The Bureau would hang me and my son out to dry if he was caught."

"Caught?" Haven asked. "I thought you said he was kidnapped. Feds are responsible for kidnapping cases."

"Only if the victim's transported across state lines," Baker put in.

"There are federal rules and regulations about what the Bureau is allowed to investigate," Novak said. "I think my son has been kidnapped. I also think he is involved with a cult of murderers. If it were not for the fact that my son might have to face charges on several counts of murder, I would happily turn over my suppositions—I can't call anything I have proof—to the Federal Bureau of Investigation. And some of the conclusions I've come to lead me to believe . . ." She sighed.

"What I suppose—suspect—I don't even want to say out loud." She smiled grimly. "I do not believe in supernatural evil. I already know what the human race is capable of without any help from Satan. There are nut cults out there. They brainwash vulnerable young people. There are some people who use a delusional belief in unearthly evil to do any vicious thing they want. But my son . . . I don't want to believe that my son . . ."

"Is a serial killer?" Baker asked. He put his big hands on the woman's shoulders.

"I suspect he is involved with a serial killer." Her words came out in a sharp, distinct rush, but she didn't look like she quite believed what she said. Haven noticed that she didn't try to shake off Baker's comforting touch.

Haven had no interest in serial killers. "What do you mean by supernatural? What does that have to do with your son?"

And how do you know about your son's involvement, and what does that have to do with us, and how did you find out about us? He had a lot of questions for this woman, though he didn't want to ask them. He didn't get involved with people; he had other things to do. Baker took on PI work sometimes. That was okay, it helped keep him in contact with other cops without anybody asking funny questions, and it helped pay the bills. Baker didn't like it when Haven and Santini committed armed robbery in the name of the cause.

Haven already regretted showing even a slight interest in the woman's problem by the time she answered.

"Do you believe in vampires, Mr. Haven? I think you

do," she went on before he could issue the standard scoffing denial: No one believes in vampires. She was the one who gave the scoffing laugh. "I'm not sure if anyone ever really did, except maybe the folklorists who listened to the lies Balkan peasants told them for the price of a few beers. I don't think you're a gullible person, but I do know that you killed a group of teenagers who were involved with a blood-drinking cult last year. They *thought* they were vampires."

The little shits deserved what happened to them, even if they hadn't been the type of vampires he was used to dealing with.

"Those teenagers murdered at least two babies that I know of," Novak went on. "I don't mind what you did to them."

Not to mention all the dogs the nut cult butchered to drink the animals' blood and eat their hearts. He'd followed the trail of animal mutilations looking for his usual prey and come across the wacko kids instead. Would have been a waste of valuable time if he hadn't taken down the little murdering bastards.

"The case was kept quiet. The local police were happy to avoid a media circus," Novak said. "Your version of rough justice gave the appearance of being a tragic accident. Looked like those kids got drunk and their car stalled on the train tracks. The cops didn't look any deeper than they had to, but I did."

He supposed the woman had proof, and she was going to use that proof to blackmail him into helping her find her son. He didn't mind that sort of coercion, it was better than Baker looking at him sincerely and talking about helping people.

A silence stretched out for a couple of minutes, then Novak said, "Something happened to you about five years ago, Haven, that changed you from a worthless piece of repeat offender shit. Officially, you died." She glanced up at Baker. "Something turned you from an honest cop into this scumbag's partner. The pair of you and some of your friends have been playing vigilante against satanists and other cult crazies ever since."

Haven and Baker exchanged a look, but neither of them tried to deny what Novak said.

"What I know about you comes from my own research," she went on. "You were always too small-time to be a blip on the Bureau's radar, Mr. Haven."

"Thank goodness for that," Baker said.

Haven didn't like the humor he saw in his partner's eyes, but he ignored it. "That's me," he told Novak. "Small-time. I hunt crazies," he admitted. "For my own reasons. You want me to hunt your crazy kid, is that it? Bring sonny home to mama before the cops track him down and put him away. And you're doing this for love rather than the fact you're scared of losing your career." Bright spots of color appeared on the woman's cheeks as Haven went on. "Glass ceiling at the Bureau's hard enough to break without a complication like having a serial-killing kid in your personnel file."

"Enough, Jeb." Baker squeezed the woman's shoulders. "You stung him," Baker said to Novak. "So he stung back."

He could tell that she was more angry than offended.

Haven didn't care, just as long as he got a reaction. He already knew she was going to make him work for her, and he would take whatever price he could get in turn.

Novak opened her purse. Jebel Haven stilled the instinct to pick up the pistol. He was not surprised at what she took out and slid across the desk to him. "There are several copies of most of the information on that," Novak told him as he picked up the zip disk.

"Information about me."

She nodded to his statement.

"But this is the only copy that also has everything I need to know about finding your son."

She nodded again.

Short of killing the FBI profiler here and now and risking her information about him being passed on to unfriendly eyes, there wasn't much Jebel Haven could do.

He rubbed his jaw. He needed a shave. He turned on the computer and popped in the zip disk. "What's the kid's name?"

Chapter 3

"HIS NAME IS Daniel," Helene Bourbon told Char.

Char had gotten out the bottle of red wine she'd picked up for Thanksgiving and poured the nest leader a glass. Helene held her second glass between her hands. The first seemed to have helped her to relax a bit in an Enforcer's presence. Char didn't take any of the wine herself but enjoyed the dark, fruity scent the liquid gave off.

"Daniel what?" Char asked? "Who is his blood-parent?"

Helene's shrug was slight but eloquent. "I have no idea on either count. Word has gotten out that my nest is the place for the difficult ones. He's not the first that has been dropped off and left for me to cope with." She sounded sad and resigned and a little resentful.

It occurred to Char that Helene Bourbon had not deliberately set up her nest on the Oregon coast as a retreat and shelter. Sometimes the role you ended up with in life just *happened*. For example, Charlotte McCairn had never intended to become a policewoman. And no one, as far as she knew, ever intended to be a vampire. She hadn't intended to continue being an archivist after her change to a Nighthawk; inertia and shyness kept her at that task. Since she was a Nighthawk, it was obvious that she was *meant* to be a hero, even if she didn't feel like one.

She needed to start thinking like one. Or at least like a cop. "Who left Daniel with you? Did he know who made him? Where he came from?"

Helene rolled the wineglass between her hands, then set it down on the table. When she sat back on the couch, Char's cat picked that moment to come in through the window Char always left open for him and to leap on the nest leader's lap. The nervous woman jumped to her feet. The cat was flung. Fangs and claws came out on strigoi and feline alike.

"Lucien!" Char snatched up the hissing cat. "Helene!" she snapped at the woman. The command in Char's voice surprised everyone involved. Even the cat stopped trying to claw her and looked up with something resembling respect. Char cleared her throat. She opened her mouth to apologize to her guest.

"Apologies, Hunter." Helene Bourbon said, voice shaking. She ducked her head contritely. All evidence of change disappeared from Helene's features, and she slowly sat back down. "I was startled."

Char tried not to show how taken aback she was at the automatic respect her position garnered from the older vampire. Her mouth felt funny. Then she realized she was showing *that* face, the one that had scared *her* witless the one time she'd made herself look at it in the mirror. She made the hunter's mask fade away as quickly as possible. Once she was back to normal, Char tried to make her nod imperious, though Helene was deliberately not looking at her.

Char tried for gracious calm when she said, "Apology accepted." That sounded like the right sort of thing for an Enforcer to say. She kept a firm hold on the bad-tempered tom and sat back down. Lucien's sleek fur was pure white; Char ignored that it was also wet from the rain at the moment. She concentrated on Helene. "Tell me all you know about Daniel."

"I think he's from Seattle," was the first thing the nest leader told her.

Those few words held layers and layers of meaning. Char worked her fingers through Lucien's wet fur while she thought about the implications. The cat relaxed and seemed to grow heavier in her lap. He began to purr. "How old is your Daniel?" she asked after a while. "In mortal years."

Her guest answered reluctantly. "Late teens, I'd say. Young, but not as young as the ones—"

"Some of them were around sixteen or seventeen." Legends were growing up around the Seattle affair, but Char had the truth from the source—his version and as much as he'd been willing to tell her in one short phone call. As disturbing as it had all been, Char at least had the consolation that Jimmy Bluecorn hadn't been involved. Helene gave Char a curious look, which reminded Char that she wasn't the one who was supposed to be explaining things. "Go on," she said.

"My guess about Daniel from a few things he said is that he was one of the victims that were changed rather

than destroyed. That is one of the rumors, that several
of those abused children were salvaged to become strigoi."

"I've heard that rumor," Char answered, rather than
confirm or deny. Istvan was not merciful; everyone knew
that. *He* would never turn anyone into a vampire. "But
baby strigoi don't generally say anything that makes
sense."

Helene nodded. "Sex and blood. That's all the greedy
little monsters can focus on. It's always so nice to get
them beyond that stage and be able to treat them like
people." Helene laughed, her expression softened with
fondness. "As much like people as any teenager can be,
that is. Getting them to realize that just because they're
vampires doesn't mean they don't have to clean up their
rooms and take out the garbage is quite another challenge. Then there's teaching the little monsters that the
Laws aren't just words but survival tools and getting
them to believe that the consequences are fatal if they
don't obey them. Daniel was almost ready to—" Helene
cut herself off and took a deep breath. "But you want to
know about Daniel's disappearance, and here I am giving a demonstration of why everyone on the coast thinks
I was made to adopt their unwanted brats."

Char was glad she didn't remember the infant stage
of her transformation, at least not the first and most difficult change from mortal to strigoi. From strigoi to
Nighthawk—that transition was terrifyingly memorable,
but at least it didn't take as long. Depending on how
long a person had been a companion, the period of ad-

justment for a newly made vampire took anywhere from several months to a couple of years.

"Daniel's adjustment has been difficult?"

Helene nodded. "He's very disoriented. He's restless. He's wandered off before. No one died that time," she added. "Thank the goddess for that."

"I see." Char didn't, but the words sounded both comforting and ominous, which seemed like a useful mixture for an Enforcer.

Lucien abruptly took it into his furry head to jump off Char's lap. The tomcat bounded across the coffee table, spilling a pile of books in his wake, and settled once more on Helene's lap. This time the nest leader reacted to his presumption by rubbing his head.

While the cat's loud purring filled the silence, Char gathered up the disturbed books, set them on the floor, and glanced at the clock on the VCR across the room. Plenty of time before dawn, but the night seemed like an unusually long one. First the Haven assignment and now someone coming to her rather than Marguerite for help. It never rained but it poured, as her great-grandmother used to say.

She wanted to ask why Helene had chosen her rather than Portland's official Enforcer, but she could guess the main reason. Oh, Helene Bourbon would make some excuse about how Marguerite couldn't be expected to leave the city or how a missing person's case would be good experience for a young Nighthawk just getting her claws bloodied. Truth was, Helene thought that Char wouldn't come down too hard on her for having lost a nestling. And she assumed Char was more likely to return the lost cub to her rather than kill him if he'd betrayed the Laws.

Truth was, those suppositions Helene Bourbon wouldn't voice were probably quite true. Char was a wimp, and she knew it; it didn't even bother her unless someone tried to use her. Like now. And right now it didn't bother her because hunting for a lost nestling was not only a very important duty, it was an excellent excuse to put off killing Jebel Haven for a while.

She could let him do his work while she pursued justice and protection for her own kind. "Do you have any idea where I should start looking for your nestling?"

Helene nodded. She picked up a leather bag she'd set beside her on the floor. She took a folder out of it and handed it to Char. "When Daniel disappeared the first time, he wandered north. I asked him where he was going when I caught up with him, but all he would say was, 'The underground.'" Helene stopped petting Lucien for a moment and got a complaining yowl and her hand batted with a paw for her temporary neglect.

"Which underground?"

The strigoi had called so many places the underground over the millennia that Daniel could have been referring to almost any cave, cellar, basement, subbasement, crypt, vault, archaeological dig, or hidden room on the planet. Then there were the passageways, subway tunnels, and sewers, not to mention all the revolutionary groups, freedom fighters, criminals, and paramilitary types whose underground existence attracted vampire attention, usually as food sources. And, of course, there were cemeteries. Vampires used to live in graveyards. In fact, all those huge, overdecorated marble and gilt Victorian mausoleums had been terribly popular dwellings until Stoker's book attracted tourists and ruined real estate values. These days, urban graveyards attracted druggies, Goths, and television crews filming documentaries with titles like *In Search of the Supernatural*. These days, a cemetery was the last underground place a sane strigoi would head for.

A young vampire that had recently been a sexually abused mortal teenager might not know any better. Or—

"I think we both know which underground," Helene said, interrupting Char's thoughts.

A tense knot formed in Char's stomach. "Why would he return there? Because it's all he remembers," she answered herself. "Poor baby." *And if you know where he is, why don't you go find him yourself?*

Before Char could voice the thought, Helene said, "I have no proof and no trail, only those newspaper clippings in the folder."

Newspaper? Publicity? About a vampire? Char said a bad word. She quickly reached inside the folder and pulled out a handful of clippings. "Oh good," she said with a sigh of relief after reading through several pieces of newsprint. "It's only a serial killer." Not that reading about a mortal who preyed on mortals was anything to rejoice about, but the last thing she wanted to see was any hint of a reference to vampires in the media.

"Most of the stories are from the *Post-Intelligencer*." Char looked up at Helene. "I noticed that." She hadn't planned on bringing it up, though. "Where did you get these?" Char asked.

"A friend in Seattle sent them."

"There are no strigoi in Seattle." Maybe a few lonesome strigs, but the nearest nest to Seattle in Washington state was in Carnation.

"The friend is not one of us, exactly," Helene said. "There was a companion who lost her lover in the massacre, but she survived, after a fashion. She lived on the streets and in shelters until she began to recover from the loss a few months back. Now she runs one of the homeless shelters."

Char nodded. "Della."

"You know her?"

"Of her. I keep track of things." Char didn't say for who. Della was a loose end but a harmless enough one. Mortal still, but an ally. Strigoi weren't supposed to have mortal allies outside of slaves and companions, but the Law and reality weren't always quite in sync.

Helene said, "I called Della a couple of weeks ago to ask her to look around, see if she could pick up any word on a narcoleptic kinky sex addict anywhere in town. She sent me the clippings."

"Nothing about the word on the streets? Nothing about why she thinks your boy might be involved with a serial killer?"

Helene shook her head. "Maybe being cryptic makes her feel better. Della's a friend, but an angry one."

Justifiably so, Char thought. "Wait a minute. You called her two weeks ago?" She looked through the clippings again. Some were over a month old. "How long has the nestling been missing?"

Helene's hand stilled on the cat's head. She looked down. "Since August, Hunter."

Char was on her feet. "August!"

Lucien jumped off Helene's lap and stalked away. Char moved around the coffee table and pulled the older vampire to her feet. "What do you mean, August? You do know that it is now late November, don't you? How could you have misplaced a nestling for three months?"

"Maybe I didn't want to find him!" the woman shouted back.

"He's your nestling!"

"I never invited him in."

"But still—"

"Maybe I'm tired of taking in other people's mistakes!" Helene cut her off. "I'm sick of being the Mother Teresa of bloodsucking monsters."

Well, yes, Char could see how someone could get tired of being imposed upon. The woman obviously had a conscience that had eventually acted up about the missing boy, or they wouldn't be holding this conversation. But somehow Helene Bourbon's diatribe did not sound completely convincing.

"Then why come to me now?" Char asked. "Why not pretend you've never heard of this lost kid?"

Because the nest leader suspected Istvan was the one who left Daniel on her doorstep, and she didn't want to face retribution from him? Or was it more complicated than that? Char doubted she'd learn the complete truth from Helene Bourbon. Vampires were secretive by na-

ture and justifiably paranoid about dealing with Enforcers.

Char realized she was holding Helene by the woman's
jacket lapels. She was also fighting down the urge to
shake the woman like a terrier with a rat. This was really
a quite unacceptable urge. She'd already let her emotions
get out of hand far too much this evening. She dropped
her hands and stepped back. She wanted to be alone.
She wanted the world to be the same as it had been a
few hours ago. Then, she'd *fantasized* about excitement
and about people coming to her for help. Reality, as
usual, sucked.

"You better go home," she told Helene Bourbon.
"Your nest needs you."

Helene made a small, imploring gesture. "You'll—"

"Look into it?" Char felt the weight of the mortal
death she didn't want any part of. Haven was a lucky
man tonight, even if she was stuck with going back to
her hometown to give him some extra time. Home for
the holidays, she thought; just what she needed, when
everyone she loved was dead or gone. "Yes," she said
to the nest leader. "I'll look into it."

Chapter 4

SEATTLE

"Putz," the witch said, and spat on the sidewalk in front of his feet.

He stepped over it and kept on walking. The Disciple didn't look at her; she had the fire of eternity strong in her eyes, but her voice rang in his ears. Even worse, he felt her fire burning into his back as he walked quickly away. He knew when she went back inside the building and slammed the door, though he was halfway down the next block when she did it.

The Disciple had tried to kill the Witch once, not long after he'd found his own key to eternity. Her cold laughter still rang in his head when he thought about it. He didn't want to save her, he didn't want them to know about her, he wanted her gone. He wanted to be the only Disciple. He was strong, but she'd beaten him and laughed while she did it. She knew about living forever, but she didn't want anything to do with them. They'd want her, though, he was certain, if they knew about her. So he kept one secret from those he worshiped, afraid they would look into his heart and read it someday.

He stopped for a red light at the next street corner

and waited there after the light had changed and changed again. Traffic and people swirled around him, unnoticing in the night and the fog. A cold wind whistled up off the bay, and gulls circled and cried overhead, their racket loud even over the traffic noise. He concentrated on the sound of the birds, on the icy daggers of the wind, trying to make himself believe that his shivering was from cold, the ringing in his head from too much raucous noise. It was a way to control the bout of fear triggered by the glaring Witch.

He never used to be afraid of the ones he served. At least no more fear than was right and proper at being allowed to look upon the face of gods. He used to take what was given with reverence and joy and humility, and go out into the street to use his gift and bring back other converts. He'd been happy in the knowledge that he served and would serve forever. Then he had sought out the serpent they'd told him to find, and the serpent became the Vessel. The Vessel was more important than the Disciple.

The Disciple still served, but he was no longer special to the Demon and the Prophet. He wanted to live forever, but what if they decided to take the Angel's gift from him? The thought formed sometimes, like now, and blew through him like the November wind. It left him shaking, like now. He couldn't enter the sanctuary while the fear gripped him. The Demon was attracted to fear.

It was all the Witch's fault that he was having a panic attack. He needed to turn his fear into hate but not by thinking about the Witch directly. It would not be wise to call up any specific images. So he stood at the stop light a while longer, making himself hate all women until he was good and angry. Then he smiled and crossed the street and went into the building that looked like a warehouse on the outside. But inside, it was heaven and hell on earth.

It was dark inside, of course, but warm. The Disciple didn't notice the warmth at first because there were three of the Angel's slaves squatting near the door eating fast-food hamburgers and fries. The scent of the cooked meat and greasy potatoes gagged him and sent a wave of dizziness through him that nearly brought him to his knees. He shouldn't have worried about fighting down his fear on his own when all he needed to do was step inside and have everything but nausea driven out of him. The trio were laughing and talking among themselves. They were covered in bite marks, scratches, and bruises, and happy as clams about it, the little sluts. They didn't take the ceremonies with the seriousness and gravity the sacrament deserved. But, then, they were slaves; they weren't going to live forever. The Angel took their blood and their bodies, and that was enough for them. They gave the Prophet everything else, bringing him everything they earned or stole. They were only slaves, but his was a greater calling, and he paid them no mind as he passed though he heard their sneering comments behind his back.

He went up the two flights of metal stairs and through the small rooms that had once been connected offices but now led inexorably, door by door, to the innermost sanctuary, to the Holy of Holies where the Angel slept. The Angel never looked upon the sun. The Prophet said

the sun could not bear it. The Disciple knew only that
he needed to be near the Angel who gave him life. It
had been too many days. He was growing weak. If he
didn't feel the touch of the Angel soon, he'd be driven
to the abomination of having to taste and swallow the
same earthly swill as the slaves gobbled downstairs.

Pain twisted through his guts at the thought of being
forced to eat like that. The spasm was so sharp that it
drove him to his knees only a few feet away from the
sanctuary door.

It was the Vessel who found him there and nudged
him with his foot. "Pitiful."

The Disciple looked up, then was caught by a fresh
wave of dizziness as the Vessel reached down and
hauled him to his feet.

"Come on. You're wanted." The Vessel pushed the
Disciple before him into the sanctuary and shut the door
after them. There were no windows in the sanctuary.
Scarves had been draped over the long strips of fluorescent overhead lights, softening and diffusing their harsh
white glow. The Prophet and the Demon were there,
sitting on the altar, arguing, as usual. The Angel slept in
the wide bed in the corner, a girl on either side of him.
Whatever was said or shouted would not disturb him
now.

"We need more deaths," the Demon said as he banged
a huge fist down on the altar. "At least one a night until
the Night of Knives. Then a hundred must die all at
once."

"We can't," the Prophet answered. "You know we
can't. My way is simpler. Using the Vessel—"

The Demon sneered. "We must. Your magic isn't strong enough to perform the Ceremony using only a Vessel with what we've been doing."

The Prophet drew himself up angrily. "My magic is strong enough for anything!" He pointed at the Angel. "We have all we need right here. I brought him to us."

"We need a huge store of energy. Only death brings us the energy we need."

"We'll have enough with the Vessel."

"No we won't."

"You're a glutton. You only want to feed."

"Weak mortal."

The Prophet laughed. "You're as mortal as I am—but uglier."

"And hungry. But it's your weakness that we have to counter."

"Neither of us will be mortal much longer. We have the secret and the key. You need patience."

"You need power."

The Vessel moved forward as the argument continued, to stand before the Prophet and the Demon. The Disciple inched closer to the bed, alert and listening, but his rapt gaze was on the sleeping Angel's beautiful, bloodstained face.

"What about tonight?" the Vessel asked. "Do we do one tonight?"

"Yes," the Prophet and Demon said together.

The Vessel laughed. "That's all I care about." He rubbed his hands together. "Doing it."

"You! Get over here!" the Demon called.

The Disciple reluctantly left off worshiping the Angel

and came to kneel before the Prophet and the Demon. His knees sank deeply into the thick Oriental rug before the altar. He bowed his head as much to avoid looking at the Demon as to show respect.

"You look like shit," the Prophet said.

"He's starving himself to death," the Vessel said from behind him. "Idiot."

"We need you." The Prophet's voice was kindly. He reached down and touched the Disciple on the shoulder. "You need the Angel's blood, don't you?"

The Disciple dared to raise his gaze from the patterned rug. "Please let me taste eternity tonight."

"You're going hunting," the Demon said. "And watching the Vessel's back during the sacrifice."

"He'll pass out on me if he isn't fed first," the Vessel spoke up. The Vessel had no qualms about speaking to the Demon. The Disciple would have been grateful for the Vessel's words if he didn't hate him.

The Prophet touched the Disciple's cheek. "It's not so long until sunset." He smiled. "You can greet the Angel when he wakes."

"We need the Angel for the ceremony," the Demon protested.

"A light snack won't hurt him," the Prophet answered. The Vessel snickered.

"Light snack." The Demon's harsh laughter rang through the sanctuary. The Demon's huge foot shot out. The kick took the Disciple high in the chest and knocked him halfway across the room. He was too weak to rise. The room spun faster and faster. They all laughed. Before he passed out, he heard the chuckling Demon say, "He's light enough, all right."

It wasn't that far between Portland and Seattle, not in actual miles. You got on Interstate 5 and drove for a while and there you were. Psychologically, though . . .Physically, Char hadn't been to Seattle since the CD on her car stereo was released. *Empire* came out sometime around 1990, right? That was a long time ago, in human terms at least. Even in strigoi terms, she'd been through two lifetimes in a little over a decade, which was not only unusual, it was desperately unfair.

"For a tender, ladylike person such as myself," she said, though she had to shout to even hear herself over the heavy metal music filling the car. Her plum-colored Cavalier was not in the best condition, but the sound system was good. Jimmy Bluecorn had installed it himself.

Jimmy. Jimmy and Seattle were inseparable, and he was the reason it had taken her two days to work up the gumption to go home and face the places that would be empty without him. Finding Daniel was important, but searching Seattle was going to be one long, constant, wrenching reminder. If nothing else, it would be a reminder that she was not good at shedding past lives the way snakes shed skins, like proper vampires were supposed to. They used the owl as their symbol—some sources said it had something to do with Athena, others said it was a medieval adoption of—well, never mind the research. The point was, Char thought a snake sym-

bol would be a more appropriate heraldic emblem for
her kind than the owl.

Jimmy liked owls. He'd even gotten involved in the
whole tree-hugger save the spotted owl controversy.
He'd said it was his duty to protect his people's totem
animal, but she knew he just liked raising hippie hell.
Jimmy had taught her a lot about raising hell and having
fun and—

Sometimes weeks would go by without her thinking
of Jimmy. Sometimes longer. "Decades," she said now,
knowing it was a ridiculous lie. But if she couldn't lie
to herself in the privacy of her own car as she drove
down a mountainside at sixty miles an hour in a blinding, cold rain, what was the use of living? What was the
use of living, anyway, without Jimmy? She'd been asking herself that even before the change came and he'd
had to leave her.

"Decades," she said again, with no bravado this time.

Decades meant a lot to mortals. They were used to
mark off the passage of brief eras and gave them artifi-
cial symbolism in this age of instant history. In human
terms, she guessed she was an '80s woman, though as a
vampire, her significant changes had come in the '90s.
It certainly looked like the upcoming century was going
to try its best to be more eventful than she liked, as well.
She was a superhero now, Char reminded herself. She
should welcome all opportunities for adventure.

"I want to go home."

One of the reasons she'd settled in Portland was that
Marguerite, who was Enforcer of the City, had let her.
But mostly she'd stayed after Marguerite had helped her

make the transition from strigoi to Nighthawk because it was such a nice, peaceful place. Seattle had a cryptic, edgy quality to it, clinging to its steep hills over the deep, dark bay. A lot of things, bad and good, had spilled into the water around Seattle, and the psychic residue remained. Portland was a city for roses and walking in the rain without constantly feeling the need to look over your shoulder. The wide, powerful river washed it clean, took its bad moods out to sea.

Portland was a good town for pedestrians, too. She rarely drove these days and wished she could have taken a plane rather than renew rusty driving skills in the heavy interstate traffic. Vampires couldn't fly. This had nothing to do with the fact that they didn't have that particular supernatural power, which they didn't, but because it was forbidden by Law. Unless they booked passage on the Strigoi's private airline, which cost an arm and a leg. Sometimes literally. But the airline was for long journeys, and booking passage required the approval of the Council or a very large bribe to the companion who actually ran the three-airplane private charter operation. Char had neither the money nor the clout to make plane reservations. Besides, she was in no hurry, and she did own a car.

She packed a few things and her laptop and left Portland two nights after the visit from Helene. She could have left sooner, but there was the matter of psychological distance to deal with before she could make herself head back to the place where her life had begun and ended.

"Not ended, changed," she said over the cranked-up

roar of the car's stereo speakers and the constant swoosh-splat of the windshield wipers turned to the highest setting. She wiped away tears the way the wipers did rain and was glad she was alone—well, she was generally glad of that—as the skyline of her hometown filled the view before her. The sky was laced with lightning as well as city lights. To her left was the huge expanse of Boeing Field, as was only right and proper since the song rattling the inside of the car was "Jet City Woman," which was close to being her favorite song. "At least from the good old days," she said and gave yet another in a series of melancholy sighs.

She didn't plan to keep this mood up for much longer. She couldn't afford to and knew it. Nostalgia was a dangerous thing. Sentimentality even more so. She didn't indulge in either very often, but this return was bound to bring out the memories and the longing. For what? The good old days? There was no one left from the Seattle of her happy days, not among the immortal population, at least. The bad ones were dead and the good ones gone. As for the human she'd been as child, teenager, and college student in this same city? She didn't cry for the girl who had been Charlotte. She didn't think about her mortal family very much these days. Char missed—

"The exit," she snarled, and she quickly shifted the car over two lanes slick with icy rain to get into the correct lane for exiting the interstate at the next street. She could double back easily once she turned onto the city streets. She might not want to go back, but at least she had a place to stay. Jimmy had sent her the keys to their old place when he took off for Alaska. He'd promised in his note that he'd had it redecorated and performed a banishing spell himself before he left. Technically, there should be no residue of *them* left in the condo at the top of a Capitol Hill street. She knew that there would be nothing familiar but the shape of the rooms, the view from the tiny balcony, the surrounding buildings.

"The sky, the earth, the sea, and my memory of thee," she quoted, but Char didn't know what fool romantic poem or song she quoted from.

Jimmy liked poetry and music. Loud music, sexy music, rhythm-section-driven guitar-hero rock and roll music. She'd tried to get him interested in classical music, but Jimmy said he'd been there when it was invented and it wasn't classical to him. He also said Seattle stopped being fun when grunge caught on outside the local clubs, and he should have moved on when Pearl Jam got a big recording contract.

Char knew that Seattle stopped being fun when Jimmy was no longer there. "But that's all right. I'm not here for fun." She had a job to do.

The car pulled into the three-stall parking lot behind the old mansion that had been subdivided into a trio of condominiums without her feeling like she had any control over where the machine went. It was like it knew its way home even after so many years.

Char turned off the engine and wiped her eyes. She knew she would not let herself cry anymore. She would run in out of the rain, go into the place that no longer had Jimmy's magic attached to it, and she would unpack.

"There's no magic here," she said. "Just a job."

After a good day's sleep, she would start looking for Daniel. How hard could it be to sense the presence of a vampire in a town where no vampires were supposed to live?

She got out of the car and looked down the hillside and up at the building, letting the rain and fierce wind pour and pound over her. She glanced up at the storm-split sky. Lots of lightning tonight.

The cold and the wet and the lightning didn't bother her. The weather was a strong, powerful thing, but it was natural and right. The storm was a part of the city. The magic all around, though . . .

She'd been wrong about there not being any magic.

Char felt the dark surge of it beneath the power of the storm. Not Jimmy's kind of magic, oh no. Evil. Dark. Vicious and barely controlled. Someone somewhere was conjuring, preparing to channel—

Char stepped out into the center of the alley behind the building. There was a low fence on one side of the alley overlooking a hillside garden. She looked over the fence and down toward the center of the city. It was so very dark in the heart of town. She was cold, but not from the weather. Her nerves strung out tautly, her mind and heart ached, but not with her own old, well-known pain. A new sorrow filled Char, and a fear that was beyond bearing but not her own rose to a pitch that nearly made her scream.

She tried to tell herself that what she experienced was the residue of recent events in Seattle. That she was feeling the deaths of the strigoi Istvan had executed. But

Char knew what she sensed had nothing to do with her own kind. Or so she hoped, prayed. She hugged herself close and couldn't help but mutter an old prayer learned in mortal childhood.

It didn't comfort her one little bit when the fear and agony rose up all around, exploded through her, and crashed down like all the water in Elliot Bay coming down like a tidal wave.

Char clutched at the fence to keep from falling, but her hands slipped, and she went to her knees. It was not the blinding flash of nearby lightning or the crack of thunder immediately overhead that sent the worst shock through her. It was the sound of the woman crying out, "Help me!" as she died that sent Char over the edge into darkness, falling face first into the icy stream of water running down the alley.

Chapter 5

"MY MOTHER ALWAYS said I'd end up in the gutter," Char said when she came back to her senses and found herself lying on the ground in a freezing stream of water. Her mother had never actually said any such thing, but a quip seemed the appropriate way to distance herself from the situation.

She sat up, soaking wet and shivering, pushed hair out of her face, then wiped water out of her eyes. She pulled herself to her feet. Char had to hold onto the fence for a while to get under enough control so that she could make her way up the back stairs and into the building.

She was so shaken that she barely noticed her surroundings once she entered the third-floor condo. The place smelled of dust and felt unused, and the psychic emptiness was fine with her. What was important was that there were towels and soap in the linen closet and plenty of hot water gushed out of the showerhead when she turned it on. She stripped out of her wet clothes as quickly as she could and stepped into the shower. She was so glad to feel hot water running over her chilled body that she almost forgot feeling the woman's death for a few minutes. Almost.

She had killed mortals, of course, several times and without any qualms. She was no angel; she was a vampire. She had killed a vampire once as well and had taken pleasure in the act, though she'd been quite disturbed about it later. She had the slim consolation of knowing that each death she'd brought about had been deserved. The mortals had preyed on other mortals. She had served all of humanity by ridding the world of them. The vampire's death had been decreed necessary by the Council, and killing him had completed Char's transformation into a Nighthawk. The world needed Nighthawks—Enforcers—to keep the strigoi and mortal worlds safe and separate. Each of those deaths had been accompanied by magic. Vampires and Enforcers were made by magic. Spells had to be cast as well as blood exchanged. She preferred to think of the process that was called magic as an advanced method of energy manipulation, but however you defined it, magic was all about power. You had to get energy from somewhere in order to manipulate reality. A human mind gave off a lot of energy, especially when experiencing strong emotions. Terror, and the release of death, were very powerful sources of energy. Char knew this in theory and in practice, and she preferred theory.

The death she'd felt earlier tonight had not been theoretical, and it had been accompanied by ritual magic.

"Maybe." Char shuddered with the memory but held onto a shred of hope that she'd mistaken what she'd

sensed. It was possible; she was out of practice and out
of touch. The death had been real. The woman who had
died had been psychic enough to shout for help. And
asking for help at every level with every conscious and
unconscious resource at your command was a logical
way of reacting at the instant of death.

"The woman was murdered." Char shuddered again
and shut off the tap at the exact instant that the hot water
ran out. That wasn't any magical talent, she told herself
as she grabbed a towel. She'd used this bathroom every
day for several years, and old habits were hard to forget.

"Murdered," she said again and looked in the mirror.

She had a reflection, of course. Sometimes she
thought it would fade, but that was on the days she was
feeling particularly like a nonentity, particularly sorry for
herself. It had nothing to do with her being a vampire.
A great deal of the bad publicity that stigmatized her
kind could be traced to other magic-using entities, but
vampire was a catchy, sexy term that people remembered. You could hang just about any evil and ridiculous
behavior pattern on vampires. True, there were some entities that couldn't cross running water, some that reacted
badly to all forms of alum. There were all sorts of be-
haviors, all of them restrictions that came about due to
the type of magic that had created the entity. Vampires
took the rap for all of them. Fortunately, no one *really*
believed in vampires—strigoi spent a great deal of time
and money seeing to it—so it didn't really matter.

Magic mattered, though, and murder. The woman
who had died could have been a vampire. Char had felt
her strength as she died and knew what a waste the

woman's murder was. It was a tragedy on several levels. For one, the poor woman would now never have any chance to explore all she could have been. For another there was a vampire out there who would never be able to take her as companion. The strigoi community was too tiny to sustain many losses like that. A predator population should remain small, but . . .

Char shook her head. She was letting herself sink into the comfortable security blanket of layers and layers of facts and data and analyses when she should act!

Act on what? Do what? Char ran her fingers though her hair and wondered just what she was supposed to do. A mortal had died. It had felt funny—wrong—evil.

But had it felt like a vampire was involved? Had it been Daniel? Would even a young vampire kill someone so gifted? Wouldn't instinct have prevented him from destroying one of his own kind? Vampires didn't kill each other. They had mortals and Enforcers for that. But would an abused kid in need of sustenance recognize a potential companion when he didn't yet have the ability to focus on one lover? Maybe he had good reason to hate vampires. Or maybe he had the gene or whatever it was that turned normal vampires into Nighthawks.

Had Daniel just killed a mortal without permission? Never mind explanations of why. If Daniel had committed the murder, Char's job was to deal with it. If it had been a mortal that had killed the mortal woman, well, she would like to deal with it if there was time, but finding Daniel came first.

But what if what she had felt out in the storm was magic?

It wasn't an if, she just didn't want to believe she'd gotten hit in the face with a really ugly conjuration the minute she arrived back in town. Not that it had been aimed at her . . .

But maybe it had. She blinked at her reflection. "Don't be paranoid," Char said to the mirror. "No one knew you were coming." *Except Helene Bourbon.* "I never told her I'd go to Seattle. I just said I'd look into it."

She finished toweling off and walked into the bedroom. She'd left her suitcase in the car and had no intention of going out to get it now that she was warm and dry. She'd slept naked in this house before, she thought with a bittersweet pang. Fortunately, neither the bed nor any of the bedroom furniture was the same. Jimmy had done quite a thorough job of redecorating. It crossed Char's mind for the first time, as she settled into bed a few moments before dawn, that maybe the vampire who had made her had been as devastated by losing her to the Law as she had been.

Or maybe he'd just been bored.

Which was a hell of a depressing thought to fall asleep on.

"Good morning."

"It damn well better not be morning," Haven answered as he came out of the bathroom, voice rough with sleep, mood as bad as usual. Worse. "Hell of a dream," he said and took the coffee Santini cautiously held toward him. Weak stuff made in the little coffeemaker that came with the room, but fresh and hot. Haven took a look at the digital clock on the nightstand. It was morning, all right, but edging close to noon.

He'd turned off the light around three A.M., after having had one drink too many while reading more information on Danny boy and serial killers than he ever wanted to know. He'd been in prison, he'd heard talk, but crazy mass murderers were kept out of the general prison population. They didn't stay out of his head when he closed his eyes last night, though. The details of the murders occurring in the Seattle area turned his hardened stomach and freaked his brain into a rare nightmare.

The dream had been very real. He distinctly remembered hearing her voice, jumping out of bed, and running into the rain. He remembered standing on the sidewalk, a cold stream of water rushing over his bare feet, and staring up the empty street, knowing that she was up on a mountainside. She was calling to him, but she was already dead—dumped like a slab of meat—her soul torn in two, drained out of her, eaten. . . . Then he was there, in a clearing in the deep woods. He could smell the pine. The wet cold froze his bare skin. Then reality shifted again, and he was yanked backward, back to the sidewalk outside the hotel, then back into his bed. He sat up as she called out for help—to him. She looked him in the eyes from miles away and begged *him* for help. Her eyes were green. One moment they'd been alive with terror and impossible hope, looking into his. The next there'd been nothing in them, they'd been like bits of green glass.

When he woke up, he knew he'd dreamed it all. The memory chilled him, tore at him, pulled him out of thoughts of his past and awareness of the present. He'd been asleep through the horror. He knew damn well he'd been asleep, that he'd seen the desperate woman in a dream, that there was nothing he could have actually done to help her. But he knew he'd failed her, all the same. He could still hear her screaming over the sound of thunder.

He gulped down the coffee. Burned his mouth, too, and the stuff boiled relentlessly down into his empty stomach. It felt like he'd swallowed hot coals for a minute, but the agony finally got his head back into the real world.

When he could breathe again, Haven threw the cup away, but Santini caught it before it hit the hotel room wall. "Want some more?" he asked, grinning.

Santini had that manic look in his eyes all of a sudden. The one that told Haven he was bored and restless and ready for anything. They'd been cooped up in the cheap hotel near the airport for two days while Haven did some research. Once upon a time, he'd been the impulsive type. Sometimes he still went off like a madman. He felt like doing that now, after doing nothing but reading for hours on end. He wanted to find the woman in the dream—and he knew *that* was crazy.

"Walls closing in?" he asked the biker.

"Got a job for me?" Santini asked back, eager as a rabid hunting dog on a scent.

"Known body count is six, four unidentified. Go find out who they were."

"Seattle's got a big homeless population," Santini

said. He rubbed his bearded jaw. His grin widened. "Want me to go undercover?"

Sometimes Haven wondered why they bothered talking at all; they always thought along the same lines. He answered with a brief nod.

Santini started toward the door but turned back when he got there. "What are you going to do?"

"Go hunting," Haven answered. He didn't try to explain that he wasn't going to be able to do anything else until he found out about a woman who didn't exist and a murder that hadn't happened. "Up in the mountains," he added. That was where the imaginary woman hadn't died.

"Which mountains?"

Santini was right, the city was surrounded by a glut of mountain ranges; a good part of the state was vertical real estate. Haven shrugged. "I'll know the place when I find it."

Santini looked at him strangely. Santini always looked at everybody strangely, but he didn't say anything else before he left.

Chapter 6

"SORCERY," CHAR SAID, tapping her fingertips on the painted iron railing. The word left a bad taste in her mouth that a sip of cream-laced SBC couldn't wash out.

She didn't want to think about last night. She didn't want to think at all, actually. In fact, she found being in this house surprisingly comforting. Melancholy, too, but the familiar street, view, shape of the rooms, didn't conjure up quite as much bitter sorrow as they had last night.

"Conjure," she mumbled, and cradled the warm cup between her palms. "Rituals."

She'd found coffee in the freezer but had had to make a quick trip out for groceries before she could settle down to a late breakfast. After she'd eaten, she took her coffee mug with her out on the balcony to think. The night was clear, the view from the condo balcony as spectacular as she remembered, but the wind coming down from Canada had the bite of winter. The house seemed as much of a haven as it ever had.

"Haven," she said, and sighed. She particularly didn't want to think about Jebel Haven. Which meant she needed to concentrate on why she was in Seattle, and she had to consider that last night's mortal sorcery might somehow be involved.

"Would rather chalk that up to being a coincidence." The coffee was stone cold, which led her to believe that she'd been mindlessly watching the view longer than she thought. What did she think this was, a vacation? She turned around and went back inside.

She'd left her laptop on the kitchen table. She sat down and turned on the computer. That Char didn't want to think about sorcery wasn't unusual. Witchcraft was hard to look at straight on, difficult to confront. Magic was something that *happened* to vampires once, maybe twice in their lives. It was something they *performed* to change long-time lovers into strigoi. Not every vampire did that, and most of the ones who had children didn't make them very often. Other than the rituals of change that continued the community, the strigoi sanely and sensibly left magic alone as much as possible. Last night, Char'd been caught in a blast of the stuff, and the immediate aftershock had made it far easier to consider.

Now that her head was clear, Char would much rather brave the world armed with logic, technology, and her highly enhanced psychic abilities than deal with spells, potions, incantations, and all the other volatile and dangerous ways of harnessing energy.

She wasn't much for doing something as simplistic as turning on the television in search of local news. No, she checked the websites of the Seattle newspapers instead. She found no new missing person reports and no grisly tales of bodies drained of blood or victims having their hearts ripped out. She saw no lurid headlines about

ritually slain fresh corpses, either. Not that she looked
too hard for such evidence of magic. She was in town
to find a missing baby vampire. Her supposition was that
the young vampire was being used by a serial killer as
a form of accomplice or even as a murder weapon. She
had no trouble imagining a mortal madman getting off
on watching an uncontrolled vampire attacking his victim. Infant nestlings were more interested in sex than
anything else, but under really sick circumstances, the
sex could go too far.

Of course, the only evidence she had that Daniel was
involved with a group of linked murders were the newspaper clippings a justifiably disgruntled but not necessarily rational mortal had sent to Helene Bourbon. That
was no proof at all. Char knew she might have to talk
to Della, but she wanted to look around on her own first.
No use bringing a mortal into the mix if it wasn't necessary. No matter what Della might have been once, her
connection to the strigoi was now tenuous and dangerous.

Technically, Char supposed, Della shouldn't be allowed to live. Char also supposed that if she didn't actually have to see Della, she wouldn't have to make any
Enforcer-type decisions about the woman. But where
was she supposed to start an investigation without en-
countering Della?

That brought her back to sorcery, of course, which
she wanted to think about or deal with even less than
she did with a widowed companion.

"No, it doesn't."

What was the matter with her? Char shook her head

violently as the computer screen faded in and out of focus. Sometime in the last few minutes she'd gone off-line and was now staring at the laptop's screen saver. She stood up and pushed back the chair. She made a sharp gesture and began to pace from the kitchen, across the living room, out onto the balcony, and back again. She tried to wrap her thoughts around something that was obvious, but it slipped and slid and slithered away from her every time she got hold of it. She was not being lucid and logical, and she knew it.

She wished she'd brought Lucien along with her. At least then she would have company. She could talk to herself and pretend she was talking to the cat. Even without Lucien to talk to, she stood in the center of the kitchen and asked, "Where do I start?"

And, of course, her mind went back to the woman who'd been murdered last night. "But . . ."

The death had not felt like it was connected to a vampire. She closed her eyes and tried to remember exactly what she'd perceived. An ugly death, terror laced with gloating satisfaction.

Maybe the murderer was not mortal. Vampires could and easily did kill like that. Char didn't have to approve of that sort of murder to acknowledge it was acceptable behavior under properly sanctioned circumstances. Only there were no sanctioned vampires in Seattle at the moment. She doubted any strig was brave enough to be in town, either. Or would dare to hunt on streets so recently cleaned by Istvan.

"But I have no proof Daniel wasn't involved."

Maybe the dead woman was her lead to Daniel.

Maybe she should trust her instincts and go looking for her. There might be a trace of energy around the body that she could follow.

"And then what do I do? Avenge her death?"

It was none of her business, but Char couldn't help but answer "Yes" to the question she'd asked herself.

As long as her thoughts dwelled on the murdered woman, she had trouble thinking about Daniel. Maybe the two were connected, maybe not, but somehow the woman's death preyed on her conscience more than looking for the lost kid did.

"Besides, it's a start," she told herself. "Have to start being an Enforcer sometime, somewhere. This might as well be it."

How to go about it? Char stood in the living room and took a few deep breaths to calm down. Then she walked back out on the balcony and closed her eyes in order to let all her other senses roam free. When she opened them, she found that she'd turned away from the city.

"That way." She pointed. "In the mountains."

Haven followed his instincts. He followed a trail he couldn't see and couldn't question. If he thought, he'd lose the mental scent. He focused on remembering the dream, on seeing the woman's green eyes, on hearing her scream for help. He followed the dream when he got into his Jeep Cherokee and drove.

He didn't try to make any sense out of what he was doing; he didn't think at all, not for the first few hours, anyway. He'd gotten into this kind of weird trance state a few times before, hunting vampires by somehow sensing some kind of invisible *something*. He couldn't explain it, certainly hadn't tried to. Santini and Baker wouldn't get it—or they'd suspect he'd gotten bitten and was turning into one of *them*. He hadn't and he wasn't, but he guessed the more you hunted the bastards, the more you became like them.

Or it was more likely that he was out of his mind. He decided this as he pulled off a narrow gravel road halfway up a mountain. He was deep inside a state park, and it was the middle of the night. Haven killed the headlights and switched off the Jeep's engine. He was tired, hungry, and nearly out of gas. Haven rubbed an aching spot on his forehead. He wanted to cynically ask himself what he thought he was doing and turn around and head back toward the city. Instead, he reached under the seat, pulled out his favorite sawed-off shotgun, and got out of the vehicle.

Haven had done a lot of night work in the last few years, so his vision quickly adjusted to the thick forest darkness. It was foggy under the trees, but at least it wasn't raining. It was cold this high up at this time of the year, but Haven was used to the way the high desert chilled down after the sun set. He took a black leather jacket out of the backseat and zipped it on. When he moved cautiously onto a hiking trail under the trees, he looked like no more than another shadow in the fog. He knew he wouldn't be hidden from any vampire's night vision, but he didn't think any vampires were out in the forest tonight.

•   •   •

There was a mortal in the woods. Char could smell him psychically and, frankly, she didn't think he'd bathed recently. All human senses were enhanced by the change to strigoi, and Nighthawk senses were keener still. This was not always an advantage where smell was involved. She had been able to smell the body in the clearing from a mile away, for example.

She stepped away from the body and took a few sniffs of the damp night air. Char detected leather and cotton as well as old sweat and the scent of liquor and cigarettes from the man coming toward her. The emotions she caught could best be described as concentrated curiosity, annoyance, disgust. He moved slowly and cautiously up the hiking trail. His caution gave her time to continue her investigation.

Char hadn't been around a lot of corpses. What was the point? She understood the need to hunt; it was the very core of vampire nature. There was pleasure in killing, but it wasn't something you needed to do all the time. You ate what you killed, killed only when you had to, chose the prey carefully, and treated the whole process with a modicum of respect. That was the way it was supposed to work, anyway.

She blamed modern media, the breakdown in society, and sheer childish irresponsibility for the way some vampires behaved, like undisciplined, spoiled kids who treated hunting mortals like it was a live-action role-playing game instead of sacrament and survival of the strigoi kind.

Mortals were even more irresponsible when it came to dealing out death. What had this woman done that she deserved to die? How had she been chosen? By whom? Char supposed mortals killed more of each other because there were more of them. There were only a few thousand, maybe even only a few hundred, strigoi in the world and over six billion mortals. She didn't know if it was the sheer number of people available to commit horrific crimes that made the mortals seem worse than strigoi or if most vampires were a better class of killer. Of course, Enforcers were much more effective than mortal law enforcement.

And none of that had anything to do with her standing in a cold, foggy forest next to a dead body while sensing a mortal's approach.

She was thinking again. She should stop doing that so much and focus.

Char knew the woman had been ritually slain before she saw the wounds, but was it a strigoi ritual? All she had time for now was to quickly memorize the body's position, how the victim had been mutilated, whatever details Char could discern to help determine what sort of ritual had required the woman's sacrifice. At the same time she tried to pick up any residue of the sort of energy a vampire would leave. Mostly what she discerned was a lack of energy. The woman had been mentally strong. She'd fought hard enough to psychically call for help, a call that Char had been unable to ignore even a night after the murder. But the woman's murderer left no mental scent around the corpse.

Someone was covering their tracks, and doing a very good job of it.

That was more than could be said for the approaching

mortal. He'd left the path and was nearly at the clearing. Why was a mortal on this part of the mountainside at this time of night? Criminal returning to the scene of the crime, she hoped. Some other part of the ritual yet to be performed?

Char moved away from the body but kept it in view while she waited for the man to come into the clearing. His mental signature was rather overwhelmingly strong, actually. If he was the killer, he wasn't using magic to disguise his presence at the moment. But if he wasn't the killer, how did he know where to find the body?

"Why am I here?" Haven complained as he reached the place where some weird, unwanted premonition had brought him. He tucked the shotgun under one arm and took a small flashlight out of his coat pocket. He began a slow sweep of the clearing with the light.

His intuition told him he was in the right place.

"I'm full of it," he muttered. He hoped.

He hoped he was wrong, that he was delusional. Not so much because he hated finding an innocent woman's body, even if he told himself he didn't care about the fate of innocent women. He just didn't like what it said about him if it turned out the dream was real. Or what it said about the situation. He was in town to find an FBI agent's missing kid, not to get involved with the usual supernatural crap.

As much as he hated being blackmailed into tracking down Danny Novak, he'd been thinking of the missing person job as a sort of vacation. He'd been *way* too intense in his hunt for vampires lately, and he knew it.

He was thinking too much. Analyzing. He'd even started reading books and making notes. Who needed that kind of bullshit?

If the woman was here, he thought as he quartered the ground with the thin beam of light, they had the usual sort of ball game on their hands. If she wasn't here, he was just crazy, and he could live with that.

Char kept very still in her spot on the far side of the clearing as the flashlight beam moved systematically across the ground. Light danced off the twining tendrils of fog, turning them briefly into silver ribbons, then moved on.

Either the man didn't remember where he'd dumped the body, she reasoned, or he wasn't the one who'd done the dumping. He muttered under his breath as he searched, obviously not afraid of being overheard. Interesting, she thought, and rubbed her jaw. If he wasn't the murderer, who was he? How'd he get here? Why?

Then the flashlight stopped by the spot where she'd been standing not long before, and a deep, gruff voice growled, "Shit."

He moved to stand over the corpse, shining the light directly down on the sprawled body. The light clearly showed what Char already knew: that the woman's heart was missing, as was much of her skull.

"What the fuck is this?" the rough-voiced man asked.

Good question. It finally occurred to Char that she was fully equipped to ask this intruder anything she wanted and make him answer. She was, after all, an Enforcer.

He, on the other hand, had a shotgun. And almost

superhuman reflexes. He dropped the flashlight, brought up the double-barreled weapon, and fired it the instant she moved.

It was steel shot, she noted as the blast hit her. Then the pain drove out thought, and she got angry.

He fired a second time.

A snarling wolf charged out of the darkness from under the trees while the roar of the shotgun blasts still echoed in the clearing. Upright on two feet. Wearing a raincoat.

Haven was not prepared to confront a werewolf. He had no time to reload. He turned and ran for the Jeep.

Char reached for him, claws and fangs at full extension, as he spun away from her. She would have ripped his spinal cord out of his back, too, if she hadn't forgotten about the body and tripped over it. She landed hard on her knees in the wet undergrowth and caught herself on her hands as she pitched forward. She gave a frustrated howl and dug her claws deep into the soft earth.

Her forehead hit the ground and stayed there while the healing pain burned in her middle. It rolled over and through her and kept her down long enough for her to get her temper under control. At some point she heard the sound of a car engine in the distance. Her attacker getting away. A part of her wanted to get up and chase after him, to rip off the driver's-side door of his vehicle, pull him out onto the ground, let him take a good look into the face of death, and then have him for dinner.

But such behavior was exactly the sort of thing she

most disapproved of in other strigoi, and she wouldn't let herself give in to the urge.

"Maybe he would be delicious," Char mumbled as she got to her feet. "But it wouldn't be a very nice."

He shot me! A nagging voice in the back of her head reminded her. But *I frightened him first,* she answered that voice. He probably thought she was the murderer returned to the scene of the crime. But he hurt her, and she still wanted to kill him. Char sighed.

She stood very still and looked up at clouds scudding across the moon for a while, turning herself back into human in physical as well as philosophical ways. When she was as normal as it was possible for one of her kind to be, she checked the damage. Her sweatshirt was bloody and torn, but her open raincoat hadn't suffered any damage. The numerous ragged wounds from the shotgun blast ached, but they were already raw and tender scars rather than open entry wounds. The internal damage was fixed as well, though she supposed she'd be spitting out steel shot for a few days.

"Better than lead," she muttered.

She was tired now, too tired to follow her attacker, too weak from healing her own injuries to finish psychically probing for murder clues. All in all, the evening was a bust, and Daniel was no closer to being found. And it wasn't getting any earlier. It was time to head back to Jimmy's.

She did wonder, as she started back down the mountain, what sort of person really fired first and asked questions later.

Chapter 7

"HE WON'T EAT. It's a perfectly good heart. Why won't he eat it?"

"If he won't, I will," the Demon answered the Prophet's petulant question. "I like hearts."

"You most certainly will not take the Angel's heart."

"He doesn't want it."

"Cannibal."

"Can't be a cannibal if you don't eat your own kind," the Demon countered. "Never been human . . . not like *some* people."

The Prophet, of course, rose to this insult and the pair of them kept bickering loudly over in one corner of the room. The Disciple hugged himself tightly, hunched up his thin shoulders, and tried not to listen. He knew the outcome of the argument anyway. He stared at the beautiful creature on the bed and fought to keep from reaching out and touching the marble-smooth flesh he adored.

He was worried about the Angel. Anyone who really *looked* at the beautiful, perfect angel-boy could tell there was something wrong. The Angel gave and gave of himself, sharing his blood and seed night after night. He bestowed love and immortality, but the Disciple *knew* the Angel wasn't getting what He needed. They all worshiped him, but no one loved him.

I love you. He whispered the words deep inside his mind, but the Disciple felt an answering touch in his soul. He was sure that the sleeping Angel heard.

"Your so-called magic taints the meat. That's the problem."

"So-called! Need I remind you what my magic has accomplished so far? We wouldn't have the Angel if it weren't for me. And without the Angel—"

"Your magic wears off. Someone's going to come looking for the little bastard. We have to hurry."

"Of course it won't *wear off*. Where'd you hear such nonsense?"

"Demons know about these things."

"You're just showing off. No one's looking for him. And we are proceeding the way the ritual prescribes. I can't perform the final ritual until Blessing Night. You have to wait until then."

"There should be a death every night. I know the rituals, too."

"Let me give the Angel a new death," the Vessel said. "I will bring him a heart like no other. The new heart will give him what he needs. I'll place it before him, and he'll smile upon me."

The Demon was sneering. The Prophet sounded petulant. The Disciple paid very little attention until the Vessel spoke up. He turned jealously toward the Vessel.

"This is your fault!" The Demon's claws grasped him by the shoulders before the Disciple could speak. The

Demon shook him hard. "All your fault! You brought us the wrong sacrifice, didn't you? Maybe I should eat your brain. Or let the Angel take your heart."

The Angel already had his heart, but not to eat. The Disciple knew the Angel would not take him that way. They were lovers now. He had taken nothing but the Angel's blood for months. It burned in him, purified him. He was not ready yet. There was much burning left to endure, but he was certain he would not be merely the lowly Disciple forever. The Prophet and the Demon would not control the fate of the Angel forever. The Disciple would save him.

But until then . . .

"I brought the strongest one I could find for the last sacrifice," he told them with his usual humility. "I did the best I could."

"Leave him alone. He did what we told him to do," the Prophet told the Demon. "Maybe that is the problem, she was too strong," the Prophet added. He ran thick fingers through his beard. It was his way of showing he was thinking deep thoughts. "Perhaps too strong for the link between the Vessel, the Angel, and myself."

The demon released him. The Disciple was dizzy and aching. He scurried backward, away from the Angel and toward the sanctuary door. "Shall I find another for the Vessel to kill?"

"Yes!" the Demon shouted. He waved his scaly arms excitedly. "Go. Now."

The Disciple looked to the Prophet, who continued thinking his deep thoughts but nodded eventually. "Yes," he said. "Take the Vessel with you, and find us a less toxic sacrifice this time."

There was a hole in the city. Char could see the blank spot in her memory of the landscape when she woke. Then she opened her eyes, and the details faded too quickly as her mind adjusted to being back in the solid world. The point of attempting to dream walk last day had been to find the man who'd shot her. No luck there. No mental trail or trace came to her, either from the man with the shotgun or the dissipated spirit of the murder victim. She found something when she turned her attention to the city, but now she wasn't sure what it was. All she had was the memory of being thrilled and frightened at some discovery.

The memory of having found something dire didn't do her much good. Dire was *supposed* to be SOP for a vampire cop. Or so Marguerite had assured her when she'd taken Char through the change. This was Char's first exposure to dire, and it left her more confused than energized for the hunt.

She got out of bed, frustrated and grumpy, and went to take a shower. She saw no evidence left of last night's attack when she checked her naked skin under the hot flow of water. The shower helped wake her up, but fully waking up also made the almost-memories more distant and dreamlike.

She got dressed slowly in wrinkled clothes out of her suitcase and thought about what to do with the night. She needed to find Daniel. She wanted to find her attacker. She wondered about the dead woman and whether the murder, the attacker, and the young vampire were connected. Probably. There didn't tend to be a lot of coincidences when you dealt with magic.

"Magic." There was that word again. "Psychic," she said. "I meant to say psychic." They were not the same thing, which she knew very well. Then why had she said one when she meant the other? "Because I had a bad day's sleep and I'm spitting out shotgun shot like they're hairballs and I'm staying in my old lover's place in a bed that's way too big and empty and if I don't stop talking to myself somebody is going to get the bright idea to put me away and get themselves killed for their trouble!"

Char stopped talking long enough to breathe, then put her hand over her mouth to keep from continuing to rave out her vehemence at the world in general and last twenty-four hours in particular. "Forty-eight," she corrected. She looked at herself in the dresser mirror and admitted, "Actually, it's been a bad week. Maybe I should have gone to Tucson instead of coming home for the holidays."

Holidays? That's right, it was Thanksgiving night, wasn't it? She'd formed some vague notion about going out for a meal while she was in the shower, but she doubted there would be many places open this time of night. At least anywhere she'd *want* to eat. She could have been spending a pleasant evening with Marguerite's nest, but here she was, alone as usual, and she'd probably be eating at a Denny's.

And why was she feeling sorry for herself while a woman who hadn't deserved to die was rotting up on a mountainside, with her family and friends worried sick and not having a cheerful holiday at all? And Helene Bourbon's vampire family was missing a young member and feeling the absence. Char had nothing to feel sorry about and was ashamed of herself as soon as she realized it.

She was an Enforcer. Her job was to enforce! Serve. Protect.

But she wasn't supposed to get shot at by mortals. She wasn't supposed to get shot at all. And she certainly shouldn't have let the man who'd shot her live after he'd seen her transformed into a Nighthawk. She'd seen herself in a mirror the night of her Nighthawk birth—that was part of the ritual—and it was not a pretty sight. She'd been informed there was a fierce beauty in the fanged muzzle and hideous claws that marked her as a killer of vampires, but she didn't agree. There was elegance and sensuality in the physical changes a vampire made to share blood with a mortal lover. There was a dangerous, predatory glamour about a hunting vampire. But Nighthawks were downright ugly. Fearsome, monstrous, they didn't bear any resemblance to vampires.

Jimmy Bluecorn had once told her that he didn't think Enforcers were vampires anymore at all but monsters that fed on monsters. The hypocritical part was that Jimmy, who was so honest about most things, never told her he was a carrier of the Nighthawk mutation. Char knew that she was not the only one of his children that had been reborn into a *thing* that her beloved Jimmy feared. Nor was blaming him for what she was fair to Jimmy. Not all his children were freaks.

There she was, feeling sorry for herself again. "What's the matter with me tonight?" Maybe it was the daymare still bugging her. She loved this city, and in the dream she'd searched and searched and found emptiness, streets that faded away, holes where she remembered buildings. She assumed that the violent way the area had been cleared of strigoi might account for the psychic emptiness.

"They deserved it," she added. One could encounter the aftermath and be sad, but the reasons had been sound.

Now she needed to be out on the street instead of staying home and thinking about the past. She knew full well that the older a vampire got, the harder it was to live in the present. But she hadn't been a vampire that long, and an Enforcer for hardly any time at all.

Char went out on the balcony, coughed, spat, and heard another piece of steel shot splash into a puddle below. She shook her head. "If I ever find the man who—" She closed her fist around the balcony railing and let her claws come out.

What she needed to do was find Daniel and get out of this haunted town. With no solid clues to rely on and no better way to spend Thanksgiving, she decided to follow the path taken by her dream self during the day and have a look around the heart of the city. The place would be dead on a holiday evening, she reasoned. Dead of night in a dead town: what better time for a vampire to have a look around.

"Irony, someone told me," she murmured as she went

inside for her purse and car keys. "It's your strongest weapon. Use it wisely."

He was not quite drunk. Haven never got drunk, though he sometimes let himself get close. This was one of those times. There was a bottle beside him on the seat of the Jeep, his shotgun under the seat, an arsenal in a locked case in the back and a voice in his head riding him mercilessly as he drove the streets, looking for the creature he was going to kill.

He thought that if he took a few more drinks, the voice would go away. But if he took those drinks, he'd lose his edge, and the voice that told him he was a coward would still be there when he sobered up.

You panicked. You ran. Coward.

"Did you see that thing?" Haven was looking at the reflection of his own eyes in the rearview mirror when he asked the question. He reached for the bottle, then thought better of it.

The anger inside him raged on as a stoplight changed from red to green. Haven drove the Jeep too fast as usual down the steep street. Used to driving rugged mountain roads, he didn't pay much attention to Seattle's civilized streets. He did notice the lack of traffic on a Thursday evening and put it down to good luck, for once. He'd gotten a call from Santini. He was on his way to meet him. He hoped the biker had some action lined up for them, because Haven really needed to kill something, preferably supernatural, if only to shut up his own carping inner demon.

He wasn't a coward. He'd shot the thing, and it still

kept coming. He'd never seen anything like it before. He thought it had come to the clearing to feed on the dead woman and figured him for fresh meat. There had been no use hanging around waiting to get torn to shreds when you could live to fight another day.

That made a lot of sense, but it didn't stop Haven from calling himself a coward. He was glad Santini had telephoned him. Haven needed someone to talk to. That wasn't easy for him to admit. He always firmly maintained that he didn't need human contact, but after what he'd seen in the woods . . .

"Screw it." He reached for the bottle at the next stoplight. He took a long pull and decided that maybe all he really needed was to get laid.

Chapter 8

CHAR DID NOT know where she was. She did know two things with certainty. One, that the night was colder than it ought to be on some streets, made no sense. The second was the identity of the woman standing behind her.

Char stopped hugging herself in the effort to get warm and turned to face Della. Krystalle's companion had changed a lot in the last few years. Blue eyes looked out of an unlined, dark-skinned face, but her heavy black hair was now peppered with white and cut buzz short. The mortal woman who had been slender to the point of anorexia ten years ago was now rounded and curved, gone from elegant to earthy. Her age showed in her eyes more than in the gray-streaked hair. Della wouldn't start to show mortal age for a long, long time. That was one of the benefits of being a long-time companion, even a lost and abandoned one. Della carried Krystalle's blood in her, still enhancing the psychic gifts she was born with.

Della held herself with a wary pride where Char expected haughty disdain as they looked into each other's eyes. Char had lied when she'd told Helene Bourbon that she'd only heard of Della. For a while Krystalle and Jimmy had shared a nest. Krystalle had a roving eye and hadn't tried too hard to control her companion. Della had been jealous and had made life hell for everybody in the nest. Char hadn't lived in the nest, but she'd been more than delighted when Jimmy decided to get his own place and had her come live with him.

"You're thinking about the old soap opera," Della said after a few tense moments. There was a smile on her face but not in her extraordinary eyes. She waved her hands. "Water under the bridge, Hunter." She gestured toward an open doorway. "Come in out of the cold."

How did Della know she was an Enforcer? Char wasn't exactly wearing a sign.

"I know too much of everything." Della tapped her forehead and laughed softly as Char looked around. "Street's empty of everyone but you and me. Come inside and have a hot meal." She gestured again. "You look like you need it." She laughed. It was a rich, warm sound. Warmth had been very alien to the companion Char remembered. Della wagged a finger under Char's nose. "As long as you don't eat any of my guests, that is."

Della was right about the street being deserted. There were only the two of them on the broken concrete sidewalk. This was not a good neighborhood. Subdued noise and warm light spilled out from the open door in an otherwise blank-faced brick building, but there was no one within hearing distance. Char recalled passing a bar that was open a few blocks back. Now she was in a warehouse area not far from the water, but whether she was closer to Lake Union or Elliot Bay she wasn't sure. She didn't remember where she'd parked her car. Somewhere along the line, she'd gotten completely lost, thoroughly disoriented, and ended up in the one place she hadn't intended to go.

"You're confused," Della said and took Char by the arm. "Come inside."

"This is a homeless shelter," Char said, remembering what Della did these days.

"Then you'll feel right at home, won't you?"

Char almost pulled away, but there was no barb in Della's question. Well, not much of one. Sympathy far outweighed the sting in the words. "I—we—need privacy. To talk."

"You," Della said firmly. "Need a hot meal and a bit of company. Spend too much time alone and you get weird when you're crazy like we are."

"We aren't crazy."

"Do you have a cat?"

"What?"

"Bet you have a cat you talk to just to hear the sound of your own voice."

"I have a cat," Char answered without meaning to, "because a stray jumped in my window and won't go away."

"But you still have a cat instead of a lover," Della answered with a wide grin. "And now you're blushing and I think your claws are starting to grow."

Char knew Della for a tease but had never known her to be caring with it. "You *have* changed."

"You should talk." The humor went out of Della after she spoke. She stood very still, blinked back tears, then tugged on Char's arm again. "Inside, Hunter. It's cold out here."

It was cold, all right, but not as cold as some of the places Char'd been this evening. This street was empty. Char looked up and down the blocks that stretched away under too-dim streetlamps. Empty, yes, but not devoid of—

Something.

She shook her head. "What am I missing?" She looked at Della. "What's wrong with me?"

"You're the hunter," Della said, amiable expression going suddenly sly. Her body went stiff, her voice turned familiarly cold. "You figure it out."

Char bit back the impulse to say that this was the Della she remembered. Della had been through a lot and had survived better than most. Char knew that if she'd lost Jimmy Bluecorn—

"Well, you didn't!" Della dropped her hand from Char's arm. "You've got it all. I have nothing!" She glared at Char as she wiped away angry tears.

"You're alive." Char grabbed the former companion's shoulder. She kept her voice very low as she added, "And I know why."

"But I didn't think he'd kill her!"

"You knew very well what he would do. You like to pretend now that you didn't." Char hated the coldness in her own voice. She was appalled that she could be so callous. Well, honest, actually, but honest words could hurt. She liked to think of herself as more diplomatic than this. She eased the tightness of her grip but didn't let Della go. Her demeanor was a great deal gentler when she told Della, "You did the right thing when you told the Enforcers about the child abuse ring. You didn't know so many strigoi were involved. Your help saved innocent lives."

"Like Danny's?" Della asked. Then she laughed. And when she stopped laughing, she was different again, back to the woman who invited a vampire in out of a cold night and offered her a free meal. "It's Thanksgiving," she said. "We always have food donations to spare on the holidays."

Char didn't hesitate any longer. She managed a stiff smile for the woman. "Thank you. I appreciate it."

The first thing Char noticed was the smell of lemon-scented cleanser when she stepped into the entryway of the shelter. The room held a desk with an ancient Macintosh computer, a number of battered chairs, plastic shelving, and battered filing cabinets. The furniture in this room was old and scarred and nothing matched, but there was an air of comfort to the place. Maybe it was the colorful scattering of afghans and quilts on the chairs, or the play area with buckets of used plastic toys set up in one corner, or the warm blue and yellow tint of the walls. Char didn't know what made the place seem homey. She had never been in a shelter of any sort before and hadn't known what to expect of a place that took in the addled, desperate, and addicted.

"Most of my people have jobs," Della told her as Char followed the former companion down a long hallway toward the rear of the building.

"Really?" Char heard a murmur of voices in the distance and the sound of rattling dishes. She could smell turkey, cigarette smoke, and about forty mortals.

They passed a succession of brightly painted doors along the way. Crayon and watercolor drawings decorated the walls between the rooms. Della answered, "Really. Not all homeless people are stoners and crazies. Some women who come here with their children have two jobs and still can't make ends meet, so they have to sleep here. Those aren't the regulars, though. Those are the ones who get on their feet eventually and find somewhere they can afford to live. The regulars." She stopped and turned to face Char, speaking quietly, though they were alone in the hallway. "There's some hopeless, shiftless, useless pieces of shit that wander in and out of here. Some have been leaving and not coming back lately."

But did that have anything to do with vampires? Char wondered. "Transients have a way of disappearing."

"I don't need to be reminded about the facts of my world, Char-lotte."

"Of course not. But—"

"Hush." Della's expression went from hard and not quite sane to warm and welcoming again. "Dinner first. We'll talk later." She opened the door at the end of the corridor and led Char into a large, crowded dining room.

It was late enough that most people were finished with the meal. Some lingered over pumpkin pie and coffee at a couple of long tables. Some were in the kitchen area cleaning up. A large group of women and children were gathered in front of a television on one side of the dining room. A haze of cigarette smoke curled up from the people at the tables, but no one but Char seemed disturbed by it.

She tried not to cough or glare at the smokers. Della pointed at an empty table near the entrance, and Char sat down to wait while Della went into the kitchen. Char practiced putting up a mental barrier to keep her presence inconspicuous, but no one paid her any mind anyway, so she decided she was overreacting and quit it. Maybe no one was curious about her, but she was always interested in what was going on around her. She suspected she eavesdropped on strangers in public places because she was no good at making contact with them. She hated to think she was that pathetic and told herself she was studying mortal behavior—and in this case looking for suspects or some sign of what was going on in this town that might involve the missing nestling.

And there was definitely something wrong. That she couldn't feel it or define it left her cold and frightened. It left her feeling like there were holes in her head—and who knew what might leak out if they weren't plugged with some answers. She'd gotten lost in her hometown, Char remembered with a shudder as she waited for Della. It was not possible, but it had happened.

"What's going on?" Char asked after Della set a heaping plate and glass of milk in front of her and took a seat on the opposite side of the table.

"You used to say please and thank you, Char-lotte."

"Stop calling me that! And thank you," Char added, almost automatically. She was even more hungry than she was polite, so Char the Enforcer set about eating

Thanksgiving dinner provided by charity in a homeless shelter while a mentally disturbed companion looked on with folded hands and a benign smile. Char was not used to surreal these days, even though surreal came with the territory. People who grew fangs and liked blood with their sex really should not be too freaked by anything the universe threw their way.

"You've been out of the loop, Char—"

"Don't say it."

"Almost as much as I have," Della finished. "Things don't stop being bizarre unless you live in the weird every night."

This—advice?—made a certain twisted sense to Char, even though she resented Della reading her mood and thoughts so well. "I've never lived in the weird, as you put it."

"I remember." Della gave her a look of pure hatred. "Jimmy kept you sheltered." There was nothing benign in her smile anymore. "Jimmy's gone now."

Char was tempted to taunt back that at least Jimmy Bluecorn wasn't dead, but she wasn't that unkind. And talking about their equally lost vampire lovers would only hurt them both. "Tell me about your missing people," she said. "You think they were killed?"

"Throwaways always getting killed. Drugs kill 'em. Drink. Weather and accidents and violence."

"Your people, though." Char looked around furtively. The other people in the room were giving them plenty of space for private conversation. She supposed you learned how to give and get privacy in such a communal world, but Char still settled for euphemism in this room full of mortals. "They went into the night?"

Della laughed. "I haven't heard that term in a while. Haven't heard anything from the community—until somebody decided to use me to find her lost cub."

"But did you decide to help?" Char pushed her empty plate aside and leaned across the table to grasp Della's wrists. "Why send those news clippings? What about your missing people?"

"Some of the ones who didn't come back should have."

"You think they were killed?"

Della nodded, shook her head, and shrugged.

Char almost screamed at the futility of trying to hold a conversation with this woman. She shouldn't have come to Della. Then again, she hadn't consciously come to Della. She recalled setting out to check the city on her own . . . then she was here.

"What's wrong with the city?"

Della smiled in a most disturbing fashion. "You feel it. Places you can't go." She touched her forehead. "More holes in your head than there should be."

Char considered a moment before answering. "It's what I don't feel that's . . . bothering me." She almost said *scaring* but remembered in time that Enforcers weren't scared of anything.

Della's smile turned to laughter. She said, "Magic's in the air."

Char formed a question, but someone across the room caught her attention before she could speak. Her gaze shifted from Della to the small, compactly built man who had just stepped away from one of the groups. He was dark-haired, his saturnine features enhanced by a goatee. A black T-shirt showed off muscular arms covered in colorful tattoos. He picked up a battered jacket and slipped into it while Char watched.

"I know that man," Char said. She just didn't know where she knew him from. "Who is that?" she asked Della.

Della barely glanced the man's way. "Been sniffing around. Undercover something, but he doesn't smell like a cop." She looked at him directly this time and smiled a slow, thoughtful smile. "Got the gift, though."

Interesting, Char thought. She didn't think she'd ever met the wiry, tattooed man, but she definitely knew him from somewhere. Was he the one who'd shot her? She hadn't gotten a good look at her assailant in the clearing. And she knew what Della meant about his demeanor.

Char released her hold on Della's wrists. She closed her eyes and looked around the room with more than mortal senses. The place was heavy with despondency and fear under a fragile overlay of contentment caused by a huge meal and a bit of holiday spirit. Individual sparks of consciousness blended into the overall aura in the place. The bearded man's aura stood out in this emotional mélange, a spark of awareness that was different and guarded, but he didn't feel like the man in the clearing. It was his face, not his mental signature that was familiar. Still, he was an outsider among this pack of victims.

"Wolf hiding among the sheep," Char murmured and received a slight nod from Della when she opened her eyes. "A woman died last night. Is he the murderer?"

"You are the Hunter. You tell me."

Char did not give herself the luxury of taking offense.

Nor did she take the time for more of this question-and-answer game with the lost companion. The man walked past the table where she sat and out the door. Della's gaze followed him thoughtfully, the loneliness naked in her eyes. Char gave the former companion a last glance but dared not offer sympathy. She got up and followed the familiar stranger out. She'd have a little talk with him outside.

But the man moved fast, and she moved too cautiously. He was already out of sight around the corner by the time she reached the street. Out of sight, perhaps, but Char had other senses to follow him with, even in this landscape full of blank spots and psychic craters.

Chapter 9

"I SMELL A vampire."

"Don't be ridiculous."

The Disciple watched the Demon leap in front of the Prophet and thrust his fanged snout into his face. "This nose isn't ridiculous."

The Disciple was tempted to laugh for the first time in years, but he kept quiet and backed away from where the pair faced off in the center of the room.

The Disciple was surprised when the Prophet did not rise to the perfect opportunity to insult the Demon. Instead, the Prophet put his hand on what passed for the Demon's shoulder. "Your paranoia is understandable, but we're safe. There are no vampires in Seattle. That's why we picked Seattle, if you'll recall. Everything will be all right. Everything is fine."

The Demon clearly didn't know what to make of the Prophet's mild show of concern. "There's a vampire nearby. I feel it in my bones."

The Prophet pointed toward the bed, where the Angel was occupied with two lovers. "Of course you smell a vampire. The little monster stinks up all of creation when he's in heat."

The Disciple hated to hear the Angel spoken of like that, but he held his tongue—or the Demon might hold it for him, before swallowing it. The Disciple's guts clenched painfully as a vivid image of the Demon's eating habits flashed through his head.

"Maybe you're right," the Demon said. "Maybe not. Doesn't matter to me," he added.

The Prophet rubbed his jaw, his expression sour. "No. It wouldn't." He turned the same sour expression on the Disciple. "You're not much use, are you?"

The Disciple turned his gaze humbly from the Demon and the Prophet. He caught sight of the Vessel, passed out on the floor, still holding the empty wine bottle. He'd been unconscious for a long time now. The Disciple suspected the Vessel was just avoiding facing the anger of the Demon and the Prophet because they'd come back empty-handed the night before.

"I asked you a question."

The Disciple offered no excuses for not having found a suitable victim for the sacrifice. "I'm not much use," the Disciple answered.

"Not here, you're not." The Prophet pointed to the door. "Get out there and hunt."

The Disciple didn't bother mentioning that he knew the streets would be practically deserted tonight. He didn't bother begging to spend more time in the presence of the Angel. The Angel was using the slaves tonight, anyway, oblivious to the needs of the Disciple. He had failed his task last night; he deserved to have the Angel's love turned away. He might fail tonight. He said, "I will try." He gave one last, longing glance at the Angel on the bed, then hurried from the sanctuary.

It was a feast day of gluttony. The Disciple couldn't even think the name if he didn't want his insides to twist in disgust. He knew that most of the restaurants in his best hunting place in Pioneer Square would be closed. The bars would be open, and the scent of alcohol wasn't as hard on him as the greasy, rotting stench of solid food. To get to the square he'd have to pass the Witch's homeless shelter. He dreaded the sight of her standing by the door and sneering at him. But maybe she wouldn't be there tonight. Maybe she'd be stuffing her face just like all the other swine.

He smiled at the thought of the Witch bitch being no better than other mortals, and the thought gave him strength. The Disciple squared his shoulders once he was outside and took in a few deep breaths of cold, night air, ridding his lungs of the last of the brimstone odor of the Demon. He started up the sidewalk confidently, happy to be on the hunt alone. The Vessel had his place in the great scheme of things. The Vessel's job was to make the kill, to channel some of the energy of the death back to the Prophet, to store the rest. The Prophet spread the magic. The Demon kept watch. The Angel gave life everlasting. And they all fed the Angel. But the Disciple was the hunter. His duty, skill, and privilege was to bring the Angel slaves and prey for the sacrifice.

He sent up a prayer to the Angel as he set forth. "Let me bring new blood to you tonight, for whatever purpose you see fit." He would hunt for the Angel. With that thought in mind, the Disciple was certain that fate would let one of the gifted fall into his hands.

And fate was kind when he set out with a pure heart and purpose. He skirted past the homeless shelter on the other side of the street, and no one was there to see him pass. Then, around the corner and a few blocks past the Witch's dwelling, he spotted a man standing beneath a corner streetlamp, smoking a cigarette. The buildings all around were dark. There was light traffic on the street, but a quick look around assured the Disciple that he and the smoking man had the block to themselves. Best of all, the stranger had the gift.

Even at a distance, the Disciple felt the low-level hum and crackle of energy from the stranger. He'd heard the basic gift called many things: personality, charisma, sex appeal, intelligence, focus. Sometimes it was combined with ESP of some sort. A few rare beings were born with the charismatic energy, the psychic abilities, and a fierce will to control them. The Disciple had the complete gift and knew this gift was the reason the Angel would make him immortal. The Prophet had the gift, but the Disciple sensed a weakness in him; the Demon was a mockery of the gifting, but the Disciple would be One with the Angels.

But not tonight.

Santini was much better looking in person than in his mug shots. Char hadn't recognized the bearded man until he stopped under a streetlight and lit a cigarette. She hung back in the shadows to watch him, and the connection clicked when he turned his head. It had to be Santini. She had files on the entire Tucson pest control operation. But what was one of Haven's partners doing in Seattle? Why had he been at Della's? Della's words came back to her. *"Been sniffing around."*

Implications buzzed at light speed through Char's head. For an instant, she was back in the mountainside clearing with the shotgun blast ringing in her ears and the pain in her gut. She knew exactly what sort of man shot first and didn't bother with questions: Haven. Jebel Haven, the self-proclaimed vampire hunter, was in Seattle. Looking for real vampires this time?

"Oh, shit."

Char was not given to swearing, but the circumstances seemed dire enough to warrant it. But consternation did nothing but freeze her in place and make her lurk back deeper into the shadows. She was an Enforcer. She had fantasized about her first field assignment, but no one had given her a handbook outlining what her behavior should be under the circumstances. Mortal law enforcement officers had it easier. They went to a police academy, took tests, served an apprenticeship with more experienced officers. Marguerite had not been an enthusiastic teacher, and Istvan had given her no pointers on how he'd gotten to be everyone's worst nightmare. One just picked it up as one went along, Char guessed.

"I hate being a rookie." Hating it didn't change the fact that she needed to respond rather than watch. If she wanted to find out what Santini was doing in town, she had to approach him. "I can do that."

She moved forward the several steps she'd unconsciously retreated. Santini took a look up and down the street, still calmly smoking. She was certain he was unaware of her presence. She was smiling with a sort of fierce pleasure as she took another cautious step forward, anticipating a short conversation with this mortal who thought he knew about vampires.

But the stick-figure man walked across her path and into the circle of light first. His shadow had the shape of a praying mantis, and it fell ominously across Santini. Char paused to study this development as the mortal vampire hunter turned to look at the newcomer. Santini's eyes narrowed suspiciously. Char gaped, wondering why she hadn't felt the newcomer's approach.

"Do you want to live forever?" The skinny wraith's voice was beautiful, deep and seductive.

He looked like a drunk or drugged-out derelict and sounded like the voice of God. He looked like a slight breeze would blow him over, but psychically—Char shook her head, partially to clear it. She faded into the shadows, wrapping them around her to escape detection, not that she really needed to. Psychically, this weirdo was off the scale, but all that talent was focused on seducing Santini.

Santini did not appear to be the seducable type. He flicked away his cigarette butt, and drew a knife from inside his coat with a smooth, economical gesture. "Yeah," he answered. "Do you?"

The newcomer showed no fear of the knife. He smiled and shrugged. "I'm here to help you, friend."

"Don't need my soul saved . . . friend," Santini answered.

"Eternity awaits." The smiling stranger reached out a hand, a gentle, beckoning gesture. He was unafraid of the knife. In fact, he radiated riveting confidence. His technique was mesmerizing, and Char watched with reluctant admiration.

Santini took a step closer to the curb. He lifted a gold chain from around his neck and dangled a gold cross before the other man's face. "Save it for somebody else."

A big Jeep Grand Cherokee came around the corner then. Santini let go of the cross and waved the skinny man off. The other man didn't move. The vehicle pulled up beside Santini.

The streetlight gave a clear view of the Jeep as Santini went around to the passenger's side and opened the door. It was a dark blue Jeep Grand Cherokee with Arizona plates. She wasn't surprised.

Char got a look at the driver. She would have recognized him even if she hadn't expected him to show up the minute she made Santini. The driver was a square-built man with short dark hair flecked with silver. He sat with his head tilted slightly to one side, intensely alert, thought he appeared to be paying attention to the steering wheel.

Jebel Haven, the great vampire hunter, was in town.

Vampire hunter, her butt.

"Haven wouldn't know a vampire if it bit him." *Oh, really?* she reminded herself. *Then how come he shot one last night?*

Fury snarled through her along with vivid memory of pain. Her claws began to grow with sudden, delicious anticipation. But this was no time to leap out of the shadows, rip the roof off the Jeep, and feast on the heart of her enemy. She had something more important to deal with right now. It wasn't easy, but she kept her mind on her purpose for coming to Seattle rather than on the less important assignment to rid the world of Jebel Haven.

Cold premonition crawled up Haven's spine as he stopped the Jeep. Haven didn't like the feel of the situation, even though Santini was obviously unconcerned by the skinny weirdo standing near him. Haven got the strongest feeling that he didn't want to look into the weirdo's eyes. To Haven, the area beyond the yellow circle of streetlight was too dark. The block was too empty. The closer he'd gotten to the corner where Santini told him he'd be waiting, the stranger the city seemed.

Santini slid into the passenger seat. The skinny guy said something and held his arms out wide as Santini closed the door. Santini ignored the bum and asked, "What took you so long?"

"Got lost." Haven put the Jeep in gear. He watched the side mirror as he pulled away from the curb. "You see someone back there?" Haven asked his partner. "In the shadows?"

"No."

Haven ignored Santini's answer in favor of squinting hard in the rearview mirror. The shadows had moved, he was sure of it. "There's somebody back there."

"The missionary sicko."

"Yeah." He didn't actually see her, but she was there. Her? Haven's skin prickled a warning, and his scalp stood on end. He gripped the wheel with sweating hands. The temptation was to stop the Jeep, get out, and start shooting.

Santini turned around in the seat. "Nothing back there but the loon, and he's heading the other way." Santini faced forward again. "Let's get out of here. Place makes my skin crawl."

"Yeah."

They shared a quick sideways look that spoke volumes. Spooking either of them took a lot. Haven had been spooked too much since coming to this wet, cold place. Somebody was going to pay for that. Not tonight, though. Vampire hunters worked best in the daylight. Same rules probably applied to werewolf hunters. And if there was a girl lurking back in the shadows, she was probably some out-of-luck hooker having a slow night. Haven put his foot down hard on the gas.

Chapter 10

CHAR WATCHED THE Jeep pull away and marked it down as unfinished business. She saved her concentration for the more important target. There was a vampire in town all right, one with a very powerful companion.

Char wondered if Santini had the faintest inkling of the real danger that had been presented by the skinny man. If Santini had let the companion say another word or looked him too long in the eye, he'd have been caught. And then what would have happened? Would Santini have become a slave or a victim of the skinny man's master? The former would be just desserts, she supposed, but the latter was quite unacceptable behavior.

And what vampire would that be? she wondered and stirred the shadows surrounding her to stay hidden. No way she was approaching one of her own kind's lovers until she was certain Haven was long gone from the neighborhood.

She was puzzled but also elated to have finally found some connection to the strigoi. It occurred to her that she might have found another holdover from the past, someone who'd survived on the streets the way Della had, but she didn't think so.

The companion made a rude gesture after the Jeep, then continued on up the street. Char cautiously followed. *Take me home*, she thought at him, equally cautiously. Ordering someone else's companion around was not only against the Law, it was difficult and sometimes fatal.

He wanted to go back, but he couldn't go back.

The Disciple looked around, frantic and afraid, and so frustrated he wanted to throw back his head and howl into the night. *What am I doing wrong?*

You're doing fine. Go home. Rest.

For a moment he felt almost reassured. It was as if a soft hand stroked his fevered brow. A gentle breeze pressed against the burning fear. He thought of blankets and sleep in a comfortable place. He remembered the room he used to sleep in, hidden under the streets, and all the candles he'd brought to light the place. That had been home until the Prophet found him, until the Angel took him in his arms. Sweet, sweet Angel. The Disciple closed his eyes and swayed, almost smiling.

Then he remembered that if he did not bring the Demon and the Prophet what they wanted, they would deny him the Angel's touch. If he failed them, he was also failing the Angel and didn't deserve the gift of eternity.

He would be punished. He hurried up the street, repeating the words over and over in his head.

He would go to Pioneer Square, he decided. There

would be people there even tonight. That was always the best place to hunt. He'd find someone.

Lost him, Char thought. Mind games with other people's property were not her thing, anyway. The stick-figure man was heading for Pioneer Square, Char realized after she'd trailed him for a few blocks. And Daniel had told Helene Bourbon that he wanted to return underground. She would have started her search for Daniel there if she hadn't gotten lost earlier. It was possible to access a ruined section of the oldest part of Seattle from Pioneer Square. In fact, parts of it were a major tourist attraction. The underground really wasn't a vampire hangout, it was just too obvious. During the day, tourists were led through the area, and there was a gift shop in one of the abandoned nineteenth-century buildings that had been covered over when the streets had been graded.

Char remembered going to a party down there once, a haunted house Halloween party that was put on by a tour company. It was supposed to have been spooky, but the mortal tourists had been unaware that the nests of Seattle were also at the party. The strigoi stayed on after the tourists left. Char remembered how musty and damp the place was. It smelled of garbage from nearby alleys, as well. It was certainly not an appealing place for even children-of-the-night-type vampires to call home.

That Halloween party was the only time she knew of that the local community had gathered in the Seattle underground, and that was well before Daniel's time. She supposed the strigoi that had been involved in the child sex abuse ring might have used the underground as a

gathering place, or maybe Daniel was a local boy who
played down there and that was where he had been
picked up. But why would Daniel return to a place where
he'd been abused? Maybe because he was an infant, she
supposed, and a damaged one at that. The poor kid
wasn't sane; maybe he'd gone looking for his lost innocence. Innocence, he'd discover if he lived long
enough, was highly overrated. Or so she'd been told.

There was no one in the square he could use. The Disciple knew it even before he set foot in the place. Winter
clouds were close overhead, no music spilled into the
square. Even the gulls seemed to have taken the holiday
evening off. The quiet was unnerving. The stillness, or
something in the stillness, made the Disciple's skin
prickle. A sense of being surrounded by sound-
deadening shadows crept up on him, flowed over him.

He spun around in a dizzying circle, assuring himself
all was well. There were a few derelicts asleep under the
trees or huddled on the benches. The bars that were open
were just about empty. Lights were off most places. He
stopped beneath the wrought iron bus stop pergola and
wrapped his scrawny arms around his middle. It was so
dark and lonesome here.

Go home.

The voice sounded so soft, so soothing, so kind. He
closed his eyes and he could almost make out the shape
of a black cape and hood made out of purest night.

Char hummed "*The Lady Wore Black*" under her breath
as she gave up trying to be subtle and walked up to the

companion. The poor man was shaking and hugging himself, wild-eyed with terror, and Char simply couldn't take it anymore.

"Listen," she said, putting her hand on a skeletal shoulder. "You've got to calm down before you have a heart attack. Talk to me," she crooned as eyes wide with fear and fanaticism focused on her, then slid away before she could make further contact. She sighed. "Where's Daniel?" Might as well get straight to the point. She drew the companion closer. She did not want to get any deeper into his mind, but she had to make him understand. He shook like a leaf in her grasp. "I've come for Daniel. Take me to him."

A leaf made out of spring steel, she realized a moment too late. He moved like a cat. He wasn't stronger than her, but he twisted so fast and hard he was impossible to hold on to. He got away, and left her holding his dirty denim jacket in her hands. He backed up, snarling, face so viciously transformed that for a moment Char thought she was facing a rabid rat rather than a person. Taken by surprise, she backed up a step.

Char dropped the coat and held up her hands. She spoke gently in response to his terror. Companion or not, this man was deeply mentally disturbed. "I only want to talk to you."

His breathing was harsh. "Don't touch me!"

"I won't hurt you."

He pressed up against the back wall of the bus stop and slithered sideways, shaking his head wildly. "The Prophet protects me! The Demon defends me!" He repeated the words over and over, turning them into a chant. He began to bang his fists rhythmically on the cold, echoing metal of the wrought iron pergola. The sound set Char's head ringing.

Char's temples began to throb, then ache in time with his pounding fists. Then a lance of fire exploded inside her skull.

"The Prophet protects me. The Demon defends me." His chant rose to a hoarse shout. "The Prophet. The Demon. Prophet. Demon. Prophet! Demon!"

Char clutched at her head, reeled with dizzy nausea, and fell to her knees.

"Prophet! Demon!"

It took her too long to realize that the words themselves were causing the pain. Magic. A simple spell of protection. Not so simple.

Nausea and pain twisted through her. "Oh, God . . ." She began to retch but fought to lift her head. She was so dizzy she was uncertain where she was, but she managed to turn toward the horrible voice. It took all her will to look up and up and meet the companion's eyes.

Big mistake.

His eyes were full of fire. The fire grew teeth and fangs and horrible, burning scales. Char tried to cover her face with her hands. If it didn't see her if she didn't see it—

The monster screamed, and her mind exploded.

The first mistake I made, Char thought when she realized that her cheek was resting on cold, damp concrete, *was in getting up this evening*. Everything had simply gone downhill after that. Of course, it might have helped if she'd remembered that she was the Enforcer. What was the use of being a superhero if she forgot to use the superpowers part?

"Well. . . . duh," Char said and climbed slowly to her knees.

She levered herself up just in time to be hit in the face by the lights of an oncoming truck. The truck's driver didn't even spare her a glance as he sped on by. She must not have been out long, but it had been long enough to have eaten up more of the night than she could spare.

What on earth happened? More important for the moment, where had she left her car? Too close to dawn to go looking for it now. Too close to dawn to stand here and wonder what had gone wrong with the entire night. Should she head back to Jimmy's crib on foot? Char looked at the sky and around the steep hills of the city, then across the square back the way she'd come. She was able to focus clearly on the memory of the route she'd taken. Her head was on fire and her brain had no interest in functioning beyond the essential of finding shelter for the day.

She knew how she'd gotten to Pioneer Square, but where was it she'd come from?

"Della's."

Oh, good, she remembered that much, though there were holes and blank spots about a lot of other things.

She began to walk and then to run. Her feet remembered the way back to the homeless shelter. She would spend the day there. On the way, she forced her exhausted mind to function. She had wimped out something awful tonight, and that could not be allowed to go on. Char reminded herself that she was a superhero. Despite her aching head and fear of the coming day, she had a purpose; she was here to save the night. She couldn't let a little thing like being unconscious get in her way. *Maybe* she could get a little work done while she was asleep. Then, come the night, she'd get this whole mess straightened out.

"A monster's come for the Angel! A Shadow Woman. She wore the night. And she wants the Angel. You have to protect him. You have to save him. Names have power, and she spoke his secret name!" The Disciple stood in front of the Angel's bed, putting his body between his beloved and danger. He looked imploringly at the Prophet and the Demon. "You saved me from her."

He had begun to doubt their power. He almost dropped to his knees before them to confess his sin, but groveling would have to wait. He was breathing hard from the long run back to the sanctuary. His chest hurt and his head still burned from the fire the Prophet and the Demon had sent through him. He needed to be sick, but he could not profane the sanctuary like that. Nor could he leave the Angel's side until the wise ones acted on his warning. "You must save the Angel. Now."

The Prophet and the Demon paid him no mind. They glared at each other as though danger to the Angel they all served did not exist. "The sun will be up in moments," the Disciple said to the ones who dwelled inside the windowless sanctuary. "He'll be even more vulnerable then."

The Vessel came up to the Disciple and poked him hard in the chest. This sent the Disciple back a step.

"What are you talking about?" the Vessel asked.

The Disciple stumbled another step closer to the bed. To his utter surprise, the Angel reached out and took his hand. He whirled around. The Angel looked into his eyes—into the eyes of his most unworthy servant—and smiled. The Disciple's heart filled with love, the burning in his brain evaporated into a sense of overwhelming peace. For an instant, he remembered his own secret name, and in that same instant, the Angel looked like a sleepy teenage boy. Then the Angel's eyes closed, his hand dropped, the rest of his body went limp on the bed, and all the danger and fear rushed back to fill the Disciple's heart.

"I won't let anything happen to you," he promised.

The Demon grabbed him from behind and spun the Disciple to face him. "What kind of monster? What did you see?"

"Calm down," the Prophet said. "The protective spell worked. We're safe. You felt it work, didn't you?"

"Yes. The spell wall held. This time."

"My magic is stronger than any you've encountered before."

"Magic or no magic, no one is ever completely safe. Maybe *they* sent an Enforcer." The Demon glanced past the Disciple at the Angel. "Useless brat. Sleeps and fucks and now someone is looking for their lost lamb. I told you I smelled a vampire."

"She wasn't like the Angel," the Disciple insisted. No one was like the Angel. "She was . . ." And all he could think of was a lady in black. "Dressed in shadows."

The Prophet ignored him to sneer at the Demon. "That useless lamb is the key to our immortality. Do you think it's the Bourbon woman? No," the Prophet answered his own question. "I wove that concealing spell correctly. She can't know he's missing. Shouldn't even remember he exists. I'm good," he declared, thumping himself on the chest. "The best." He walked over to the bed and stroked the Angel's hair. "I want what you have, and I don't need your Laws to get it."

"She'll kill you when she finds you, sorcerer." The Demon sneered at the Prophet and let the Disciple go.

The Disciple's arms and shoulders bled where the Demon's claws had cut into skin. He resented the loss. His blood belonged to the Angel.

"She—whoever she is—won't be able to find me. Still . . ." The Prophet stroked his beard and sighed. "I suppose it wouldn't hurt to close up shop here. You two," he said to the Disciple and the Vessel. "Organize the slaves. We're taking the Angel to a new sanctuary."

Chapter 11

"WHAT'S WRONG WITH this town?"

"Besides all the water?" Santini asked.

"I can live with water."

Haven took another sip of whiskey. He'd brought the bottle along from Tucson. Good stuff he'd been saving in one of the storage bins in the Jeep. This was the second bottle he'd opened tonight. Santini had finished off the first and tossed it out the window long before they'd gotten back to the hotel. Haven didn't recall what he'd been saving this bottle for, but the smoky, potent kick on the back of his throat was welcome now.

He was glad of the drink, glad to be back at the hotel, glad to have someone to talk to. He usually didn't care where he was or if he was with anyone. "Crazy town. Like there's holes in it. I kept getting lost trying to get to the center of it."

Santini scratched his beard. "Street layout's stupid."

No, that wasn't it. "Yeah," Haven said, reluctant to admit he'd encountered black holes in the world. It wasn't like he could describe the sensation or even get his mind around it properly. He did know that there was missing—time—from his trip into and out of Seattle. Missing time. Blank spots. It reminded him of something. "Alien abductions."

Santini was seated on a chair with his feet propped up on the room's queen-size bed. His feet hit the floor. "What?"

"Never mind." Haven didn't feel like mentioning the werewolf right now, either. He put the whiskey glass down, half-finished. "Find out anything?"

"Some. Couple of street people have disappeared. Even the cops assume this serial killer got 'em. Lot of scared folks. Some moved into the shelter I stayed at. People there think the woman who runs it is a witch. Della's strange." He took a drink. "Checked her out. Our kind of strange maybe." He shrugged. "She's got the look."

Haven knew what his partner meant. You saw enough of the weird side and it changed everything about you. "Did you talk to her?"

Santini nodded. "Della warned me away from a new cult that's recruiting on the street. Cult sucks 'em in, then puts them to work."

"Typical."

"Yeah. But the recruiter's a sicko."

"The guy you were talking to when I picked you up?"

"That's what I figured. I'm thinking maybe I should go with him after I let him talk for a while, see how much he meant it. So I played hard to get. But I didn't like the feel of it. So when you showed up, I took the ride."

"Did you connect the sicko and his cult to our Danny

boy? Anybody heard of our client's blond and blue-eyed darling?"

Santini shook his head. "I didn't exactly show a picture around. Another interesting thing. Girl showed up at the shelter tonight and got into an intense conversation with Della. Cute little chick. Big-eyed. Real dark red hair. Expensive clothes, looked smart, never seen the inside of shelter before. Got the feeling she was looking for someone."

"Our Danny boy? Girlfriend?"

Santini shrugged. "She gave me a long look when I was on my way out." He scratched his bearded jaw. "Didn't think she followed me, but you thought there was somebody back in the shadows." He shook his head. "Nah. Nobody there."

Santini grew silent, put down his whiskey glass, and got a beer out of the room's tiny fridge. Haven took this as a signal that the biker didn't have anything more to say. Haven filed away the information about the girl. He deliberately did not drink any more whiskey or get a beer. He glanced at the clock. He'd been up all night again. He was tired, frustrated, sleepy, and didn't want to go bed. He had visions of dreaming about the werewolf coming for him and had learned the hard way that nightmares could come true.

Santini opened his beer and turned back to Haven. "How was your hunting trip?"

"I found a body," he told Santini. "Looked like the pictures in Special Agent Novak's file on Danny boy. Dental impressions would show that it's the same biter that's chewed on the other bodies."

Leave it to a mom to recognize her precious darling's overbite even when the bite marks were in someone else's skin. "Danny was always a biter," she'd said, and had showed him a scar on her arm. "He gave me that when he was thirteen. We couldn't get him to wear braces." He was sixteen when he disappeared. Sixteen and already in college 'cause little Danny was some kind of flaky mathematical genius. And divorced mommy had gone off to a fancy job with the Bureau while daddy took a six-month job in Tokyo. Somewhere along the line, they lost track of their little boy, and that was nearly two years ago. All momma had left of junior were photos of his teeth. She said there were other things that led her to *know* from looking at the evidence that her baby was involved, but the teeth marks were the clincher. She seemed more than half nuts with her certainty, but Haven didn't argue with crazy people who *knew* stuff—at least not when they worked for the Bureau and had an inch-thick file on him.

The overbite evidence in Danny boy's case was accompanied by an impression that looked like fang punctures. Agent Novak assumed the fang marks were made by the fancy false teeth some dentists made for costumers and vampire wannabes, but she said it in a worried, uncertain tone.

Haven had agreed with Special Agent Novak's hope that the vampire wasn't real until the murder victim called out to him as she died miles away, until he'd been psychically led to the body, until he'd seen the monster where the body was dumped. Little Danny was in league with the devil, and it really pissed Haven off. He didn't mind that the kid was a vampire. Killing vampires was what he did. But getting the FBI involved wasn't good for business. Special Agent Novak wanted him to find her little darling and bring him home, *not* find Danny boy and drive a stake through his heart. Wasn't that just too damn bad?

He'd do what he had to do. The world was going to get saved from vampires whether the world wanted it or not, and the FBI sure as hell wasn't up to doing the job. He'd made the choice to be a hero. All he could do was keep fighting until they got him.

Haven yawned at the thought, and his mind skittered around remembering the monster in the clearing. Santini was looking at him strangely when he stopped yawning. "What?"

"You look like shit."

Haven got up and stretched. "Feel like it too." He looked at the bed, thought about having a cigarette, getting some coffee, doing anything but what he needed to do to be at his best.

"Get some rest."

He glared at Santini for a moment, then nodded. He owed it to Santini to be on top of the situation when trouble came. There were things you had to do to stay sharp, to keep the reflexes fast and accurate. He'd given up a hell of a lot to be a hero. They all had, him and Santini and Baker. All that was being asked of him now was that he get some sleep.

So he got in bed instead of having a cigarette. He was asleep instantly, and he was right about the nightmares. In his dreams, a shadowy female figure began stalking him. But instead of growing fangs and trying to kill him, the shadow girl kept shouting questions he could never quite hear. At some point during the long day of restless sleep, while he was half awake and in the act of turning over, he thought she asked him if he wanted a date.

"Yeah. Sure," he mumbled into the pillow. "See ya."

Char wasn't sure when she woke up on a mattress in Della's basement whether she'd had a productive day or not. She did know she had a headache. She suspected she'd spent the day with rats and other vermin and also suspected Della'd just been being mean when she told Char that there was nowhere else in the building she could sleep. "It's a wonder she didn't offer me a coffin," Char grumbled as she rolled off the mattress and got slowly to her feet. She stretched and went upstairs.

Della was waiting for her in the kitchen when Char opened the basement door. The smell of garlic and frying onions scented the air. The room was full of busy people preparing the evening meal to a loud radio playing hip hop. Char accepted the towel and change of clothes the shelter's director handed her and let Della show her where the communal bathroom was.

The bathroom was empty, for which Char was grateful, the thin stream of water that came out of the showerhead was tepid, for which she was not. Still, the very act of taking a shower helped her compose herself for the night. Helped her recall and assess just how she'd spent the day, as well.

She'd always been good at dream walking, at least under normal, controlled circumstances. *Yeah, well, last night wasn't exactly normal.* And her memory of what she'd done during the day was sketchy. Char gave herself points for trying; exhausted, rattled, and disconcerted as she was, she had made the effort to send her consciousness out riding the thoughts of mortals while her body stayed behind and slept.

She turned her face up to the thin stream of water, closed her eyes, and let the day's dreams rise to the surface.

Char met Della in the building's empty waiting room a few minutes later. Her hair was still damp, and the chill air in the room made her shiver, but she did feel better for being clean. She was disturbed by what she remembered, but being disturbed was becoming standard operating procedure. Della gave her a mug of weak tea. Char was both pleased and wary about the former companion's remembering her preferred choice of caffeine. Odd how she'd gotten into a habit of drinking coffee since leaving Seattle but found herself craving tea now that she was home. They sat down, facing each other, on a pair of cold plastic chairs.

"I found your car," Della said.

"Is there a demon in Seattle?" Char asked her. "Because if there is and he has Daniel, I have no business being here." Char caught a buzz from the jolt of genuine terror that went through Della, but she fought off her own predatory instincts to absorb strong emotion and kept her mind on business.

Della's mug hit the floor and rolled away after scattering a few drops on the worn linoleum. "Demon?" Her pale eyes narrowed, studying Char intently. "There's dark magic in town but . . . You mean there really are demons?"

There was a rumor that Krystalle and the other late strigoi of Seattle had made a pact with demons. Perhaps Della had heard that rumor. Char gave it no credence.

Char finished her tea, then put the cup down on a nearby table, with Della staring at her the whole time. While Della stared, Char slipped through Della's weakened psychic shielding. Eating the mortal's emotions was bad, but analyzing them was okay. What Char discerned was that the woman was resentful, compassionate, hurting, grieving, loving—but with a streak of viciousness. Della was a very confused and confusing woman, but Char was quickly convinced that Della hadn't deliberately been trying to get her into trouble.

Char gently withdrew her probing and said. "There's a very specific law pertaining to the strigoi people interacting with demons." Of course Char couldn't recall the exact wording when she needed to quote it. "It goes something like, don't mess with demons, ever."

Della looked at her with complete lack of understanding. "Why?"

Char shrugged. "There's a treaty. Probably goes back thousands of years." More likely hundreds, to the time when there were maybe a dozen vampires left in the whole world and they needed to bury traditional enmities and territorial disputes simply to survive in the mortal world. Char saw no need to tell a mortal suppositions based on her research. One of the most important survival tools the strigoi had used over the millennia was not telling anybody much of anything—oh, and downright lying worked nicely, as well. While this helped hide the existence of vampires from mortals, it also hid vampires from each other. Char was not so sure this was a good thing, but who was she to argue with policy set by the Strigoi Council?

"The point is, if Daniel is somehow involved with a demon, I doubt there's anything I can do about it."

Della went from being confused to furious. "People have been killed. People are being used. There's a missing child! Someone is using black magic to take over the city."

"At least to hide their activities. I finally figured that out. After I was hit with a spell that needed to channel a demon's psychic power to get it to work. I can't fight a true demon."

"You're an Enforcer. What do you mean there's nothing you can do?"

"Because the children of the lesser gods cut a deal with the Strigoi. The treaty was sealed with the Blood of the Goddess, making it a pact that cannot be broken."

"What goddess?"

Oh, right, Krystalle must not have mentioned religion to her companion. "Never mind. You do know what a blood promise is, right?"

Della waved a hand. "Sort of. Something to do with contracts."

Char nodded. "The most serious kind of agreement is said to be sealed in ancient blood. Very strong magic."

If truth be told, all vampire blood was, technically or at least theoretically, the blood of the goddess—if one was a religious sort of vampire. Personally, Char would rather think that vampirism was some sort of mutation or blood disease that brought about physical changes and enhanced the energy manipulation that was better known as magic. Demons, real demons, not the ones created by magical experimentation, were probably some sort of interdimensional alien. Or maybe they were exactly what they believed they were, creatures of forgotten gods whose duty it was to punish mortals. Who was she to question other beings' religious beliefs when she had enough of her own to question? She supposed it was an easier explanation than the alien theory, though she suspected that it was demons that were responsible for the recent rash of what mortal victims deemed to be alien abductions.

She was musing again, Char realized, while Della gaped at her. When Char focused on her, Della asked, "You've got an agreement with demons?"

"I didn't make the deal. I don't necessarily think it's a good idea, but I enforce the Laws."

"Oh, really?" Della snapped. "What laws have you enforced lately?"

Char winced at both Della's words and tone. But she admitted, "I know I'm a rookie."

She had a ceremonial silver knife, but no nest leader had yet to give her an owl-faced coin to acknowledge her authority to organize hunts and mediate disputes. She wanted to be of active use to the community but suspected she was more of a support-staff type than field operative material. But Istvan wouldn't have sent her out with an assignment if he didn't think she was ready. Except, he hadn't exactly set her to hunting other vampires, had he? And demons? Demons were definitely out of Enforcer jurisdiction.

"Aren't you supposed to protect people?"

"Enforcers protect mortal and immortal people from each other and settle disputes between immortals."

"Demons are immortal."

"No, they're not, just long-lived. And I can't protect mortals from them."

"I protect whoever comes under my wing."

"That's very admirable, but there's nothing I can do for Daniel if a demon has him under its power."

"Excuse me? But doesn't this treaty work both ways? If a demon's kidnapped a vampire and is using the vampire to murder people . . ."

"I don't know that Daniel was kidnapped by anyone," Char interrupted. "I don't know anything about what's happened to Daniel. What I do know is that a mortal sorcerer—for want of a better term—is killing people. I know that this sorcerer is using obscuring spells to keep anyone with psychic talent from detecting his or her presence. I know that a companion called on a spell set by a sorcerer to knock me out, and that this companion also mentioned a demon. Whether this companion belongs to Daniel, I don't know."

"But what if this wizard is in league with a demon, and they're using Daniel?"

"Then Daniel might be in deep shit with the Strigoi Council for being in league with this demon."

"But—it would be against his will."

"I would have to discover why and how he's involved

before I enforce the Laws. I might be able to let him off. I might not."

"But—"

"I know! No one says laws written thousands of years ago make any sense today, but they're still the laws I have to enforce."

"That's ridiculous." Della laughed harshly. "You're ridiculous. You're scared, Char-lotte. Scared you can't handle what's out there, so you invent a law about demons as an excuse."

That was unfair and untrue, but Char saw the woman's point. She didn't argue about it. "Whatever."

Della rose to her feet. "Something evil is going on. If you can't fix it, find somebody who can." She pointed toward the street door. "Get out of my house, and don't come back until the streets are safer for the poor souls that are under *my* protection." She tossed Char her car keys. "Hunter," she added with a hard laugh and a dismissive shrug. "Hunter, my ass."

Chapter 12

"WHAT DO YOU mean, how'd I get this number?" Char spoke into the cell phone from the exact spot in Pioneer Square where the companion's magic had attacked her the night before. She could still detect the dregs of that burst of energy and noticed that the crowds on the sidewalk were unconsciously giving the area a wide berth.

The woman on the other end of the line said nothing, and Char went on. "I knew there was something you didn't tell me when you came to my place, Bourbon. Tell me now, or forever rest in peace, all right?"

That sounded good. Sounded tough. Char gave a toss of her head as she gazed into the window of the Starbucks across the busy street. Friday night was a lot different in this neighborhood than Thanksgiving had been. Friday night was party time, with the square full of locals and tourists. Lots of noise, lots of fun. She remembered nights here years ago, Johnny and her drinking and listening to music at the clubs. She didn't want to go back in them—stirring up old memories and all that. She planned on catching the last underground tour of the evening. She didn't know if she'd find any clue to Daniel's whereabouts, but she had another purpose in mind. She looked up and down the street and saw no sign of the man she waited for. She smiled as she thought, *Maybe I spent the day sleeping, but that doesn't mean I was napping.*

She did have a plan. Despite Della's lack of confidence, Char had every intention of behaving like an Enforcer of the Law before leaving this town. While she waited, she answered the question she'd posed to Helene Bourbon herself. "You told me you were tired of playing mother to strays, but the real reason you didn't come for help sooner was because you didn't notice he was missing. Somebody put a spell on you."

The indignant answer came instantly. "Don't be ridiculous!" No strigoi, especially a nest leader, would easily admit to that. Char didn't bother replying, and after a long silence, Helene Bourbon said, almost whispered, very contritely, "That's what must have happened."

"And why didn't you mention this to me?"

"I . . . forgot?"

"Oh, puh-lease. I wasn't reborn yesterday."

Of course that was exactly what everyone thought, that Char's being a hunter was some sort of joke, a mistake, that she was naive and gullible, and maybe part of that was true. Time to change that perception.

"Was Daniel kidnapped by a sorcerer? Did he go off with a demon?" Char batted away the mental image of Huck Finn as a vampire being taken in by a pair of mortal con artists.

"A demon? I don't know anything about demons," Helene said hastily.

"What about the mortal magician?"

"I don't know anything. Daniel ran off. I did go looking for him, but I got . . . lost. I ended up sleeping in the woods near my house. When I woke up, I went home and didn't even think about Daniel for weeks. Neither did anyone else in my nest. When the spell wore off, I did what I could to find him."

Char knew she should still be annoyed at Helene's not adding this salient point about spells during their initial conversation, but she smiled. The spell had worn off. So this sorcerer wasn't as good as he thought he was. She could work with that. "Thanks," she said as she spotted her quarry crossing the square. "Gotta go. Have a date."

She shut off the phone and put it back in her coat pocket. Maybe she couldn't do anything about the demon if he was working with the sorcerer, but there was a chance she could take out the sorcerer. Then whatever magic he was using on the young vampire would fade. That might do Daniel some good. But this sorcerer was good at weaving protective spells, and she'd have to find him first. She'd work on that after taking care of some other business.

The problem with magic, Char thought as she walked toward where the tour group gathered beside one of the old buildings, was that some idiots thought they could rule the world with it. Magic, as any sensible being who was affected by it could tell you, was more of a pain in the posterior than it was a power tool. For one thing, it

turned around and bit you on the butt if you gave it half
a chance. It was dangerous to use, hard to control, and
there were always consequences for using it. Also, only
a tiny percentage of the population could even be affected by it. Just because you put a spell on someone
didn't mean it was going to work. Magic was like rag-
weed or cat fur, some people had an allergic reaction;
most didn't.

She had the most serious form of the allergy or she
wouldn't have ended up not only a vampire, but a vampire's vampire. The tall, stoop-shouldered man in the
worn leather coat standing near the tour group was also
sorely afflicted with the allergy, or he wouldn't have
responded to her dreamriding suggestion that he check
out the underground tonight.

She regretted that he'd answered her call, because she
was going to kill Jebel Haven this evening. She was
going to have to have a talk with him first, and that
would make it harder for her, but she was definitely going to kill him.

Her immediate problem was how to introduce herself.
She always thanked her luck for meeting Johnny Bluecorn, because she'd never been any good on the dating
scene. All that "Hi, what's your sign? Come here often?"
stuff was simply beyond her comprehension. *Oh, well,*
she thought as Haven's glance flicked her way and she
was caught by the intensity in his dark brown eyes, *I'm
sure something will come up.*

He'd woken up with an urge, and not just the usual one
to take a piss. A voice in his head called to him to look

for vampires in the ruins under the square in his dreams and he'd given in to it. This wasn't the first time this week Haven had let a gut feeling lead him around Washington state, but he was getting tired of it. He trusted his instincts, but right now he didn't feel in control of them, and that bothered him. It made a spot between his shoulder blades itch, kind of like it was warning him that he was about to be stabbed in the back. He gave a sour sneer as he looked around.

He wasn't sure what had called to him, whether it was his own sixth sense or the influence of some psychic evil fucking with his mind, but he wasn't fool enough to come without backup. Santini was around somewhere. If this was some sort of trap set by the werewolf, they could handle it. Besides, Santini had wanted to see if he could get any information about the nut cult from the regular drunks and druggies who called Pioneer Square home.

Haven was going to do what the dreams suggested, look underground for the lair of any local bloodsuckers. He didn't have much hope for finding vampires in a place that was basically a local tourist trap, but he knew from experience that the brain-damaged ones frequently sought out the obvious hiding places. There had been fang marks on the corpse in the woods and on the bodies in Special Agent Novak's files. So there were vampires involved as well as the monster that had sniffed out the dumped body. Haven figured he'd take out the fiends he knew how to handle first, then he'd concentrate on the werewolf and whatever else was haunting this dark, dreary city.

Probably all working together, he thought as he lit a cigarette. His gaze was caught briefly by the sight of a large fake owl on a second-floor window ledge. Some-one had attached it to the building to scare off pigeons. Then he turned his head and looked directly at the girl with the dark red hair who had been inching her way toward him for the last five minutes.

Their eyes met as she came out from under the shadow of the trees at one end of the square. She lifted her head slightly and smiled, and Jebel Haven got hit by lightning. The sensation faded after a moment, but for that moment, he couldn't remember why he was here in the first place. Or even where here was. He knew it wasn't to pick up a girl. Of course, it had been awhile . . .

He ran a finger down his jaw and tilted his head side-ways to look at her some more. Not bad. Not spectac-ular, but she had something. Enough of something that Haven gave himself a moment to wonder about the shape hidden by her baggy blue raincoat. Enough of something to keep him staring and to start his blood racing. Correction: She had spectacular legs, even wear-ing what he supposed were called sensible shoes. He hoped that the skirt beneath the raincoat was a short one, because his best guess was that those legs went on for about a week. A man needed a good long view to ap-preciate them properly.

He stepped away from the crowd, closer to her. It was a hesitant movement on his part, not his usual style at all. He tossed away the cigarette and crushed it under his heel. She smiled ever so slightly at this. She was shy, vulnerable, not his type.

He said, "You know I'm trouble, right?"

"Undoubtedly you are," she answered in a deep, husky, bedroom voice that didn't match her looks at all.

She came a few steps closer, or maybe he did. His plan to explore the underground was shelved in favor of asking her what her sign was and did she come here often. "You going underground?"

"Been there, done that."

"Yeah," he answered. "Me, too." He had the feeling neither of them was talking about walking around the subterranean streets of Seattle.

They were all alone in a big, noisy Friday night party crowd. Music spilled out from bars, but there was a little island of silence around them. He felt as if he should pour bright, clever conversation into the silence, making a gift of words to impress her. He knew she liked words, and pleasing her was important. He wished he'd shaved closer and had better clothes.

The tour group was led off by a cheerful guide, but Haven and the girl stayed behind. He didn't want to do anything but be with her. He did not believe in meeting the girl of his dreams. Why not? He hadn't believed in vampires five years ago. If they were real, why not go with the idea of love at first sight? Not that love was exactly in his game plan, but why not take the night off with a little female company? Haven chuckled, a low, wicked sound, and that broke the spell.

"Who are you?" He narrowed his eyes suspiciously. "What do you want?"

"You don't have to be rude," she responded with a sharp lift of her head that almost made him laugh.

"I'm always rude."

"So I see."

She took a step back, toward the shadows. He followed.

She'd had him! For a few seconds there, Char knew she'd drawn Haven to her in the good, old-fashioned, tried-and-true, put-a-vampire-glamour-on-the-object-of-desire way. Okay, Jimmy had always said that nobody but a loser vampire nerd would pick up chicks by hypnotizing them in this day and age. Well, she *was* a chick, and a nerd as well as being a vampire, and doing the fatal attraction thing had seemed like the simplest way to distract someone as dangerous as Jebel Haven. Problem was, when she *looked* at him, he *looked* back. The results were disturbing and distracting. Took her mind right off seducing him, and put it on . . . well, seducing him, but for all the wrong reasons.

Maybe she should have gone about this differently, or rather, traditionally. The easy way would be to unleash the urge to hunt, stalk the man, absorb his fear like a dark drug, consume his emotions, feast on his flesh, and dump the remains. Looked at objectively, that was a fairly disgusting scenario and one she wanted no part of. Whatever danger he posed to the strigoi, Haven did not deserve a death that should be reserved for only for the deepest and most irredeemably evil of mortal kind.

"And members of grunge bands," Jimmy had added when he'd taught her the basics of vampire killing. But

she was pretty sure he'd been joking, even if he had left town right after Kurt Cobain's body was found.

The point was, she'd been attempting to attract Haven to find out what he was doing in Seattle, not to initiate a hunt. When it came time for her to murder Jebel Haven, she would do it in a humane way, which would give her inner beast no physical, emotional, or sexual gratification. Damn it.

Well, whatever she'd done and however he'd responded didn't matter now. He was still looking at her intently, but his manner was now wary.

Char was not sure what to do next, but she was distracted by bumping into someone as she took another step back. When she turned around to apologize, there was Santini. *I used to be smarter than this,* she thought as she noticed the two men exchange looks. *I really was.* Of course Haven brought Santini with him. The two men were partners, there for each other, watching each other's backs while they defended the world from vampires. She almost growled at them that they'd just met their first real vampire, but she already knew that they didn't think vampires were particularly intelligent and saw no reason to prove them correct just now.

"Hi," Santini said, with a smile that was curiously charming. "We've met before." He said this to Haven rather than to her.

"We weren't introduced," she answered. She'd recognized Santini, and he remembered seeing her with Della. How charming.

Haven's hand landed on her shoulder. "The girl from the shelter." Not a question.

Nor was it a problem, Char decided. She looked into Haven's very suspicious face. Might as well get this over with and confront the situation head-on. "Are you looking for Daniel, too?" she asked.

Haven looked around and scratched his jaw. She heard the rough scrape of his finger against dark stubble. "Come on," he said, and directed her toward the nearest coffee bar with his hand still tightly grasping her shoulder. Santini didn't come with them.

Chapter 13

CHAR COULD HAVE broken his hold on her easily enough, but since he was doing exactly what she wanted, this was no time to oppose any macho high-handedness. They reached the front of the line quickly, and he ordered two black coffees. Char translated this for the confused counterperson, and they ended up taking a pair of regular double-shot talls to a booth in the back. She let Haven pay.

"Where are you from?" Haven didn't know why the hell he cared, but he asked anyway.

"Portland." Char supposed that if she was going to get information from him, she might as well give some in turn. She took a sip of coffee, grimaced, and reached for a packet of sugar.

"How do you know Danny Novak?"

"I don't, but I am trying to trace him. He's missing from a—youth home—in Oregon. The director asked me to look into it."

"Why you?"

"Why not? How do you know Daniel?" she asked in turn. "Why are you hunting him? You're a long way from home and your usual pursuits, Haven."

Haven leaned back in the booth and studied the girl through the rising steam as she took delicate sips of coffee. She somehow managed to look fragile, ladylike, and tough as steel at the same time. She'd taken off her raincoat, and he thought it a pity that her long legs were tucked out of view under the tabletop. Under the coffee shop lights her tousled hair looked like wet autumn leaves. She had big gray eyes, flat cheekbones, a pointed chin and wide mouth, porcelain skin, and a general glow of curious enthusiasm. *Perky*, he thought, *pretty rather than beautiful*. She had nice tits, though, round and full and nicely outlined by the lightweight blue sweater she was wearing.

She also knew his name and that he was looking for the Novak kid. "What do you mean, *'usual pursuits'*?" He took a sip of coffee and tried to ignore the scalding heat that spread from his mouth and all the way down his throat when he swallowed. It took him a second to get his breath back, and she watched him with big gray eyes the whole time. "What's your name, sweetheart?"

Char considered her answer. The longer a strigoi was around, the more likely it was for him or her to go by a single name or attribute. She'd certainly been working on developing her persona, the vampire identity of Char the Hunter. Well, she hadn't done anything yet to earn the persona, but she'd been thinking about it a lot. Sitting across the table from a man as bone-deep dangerous as Jebel Haven, she felt rather silly proclaiming her *Charness*. She knew very well that in theory she could kill him in a blink, but she owed this character who had done a good many bad and brave things a bit of respect.

"Charlotte McCairn," she answered his question. "My friends call me Char. I mention this in passing," she added, "not as an offer of friendship." Then, because she was far too curious and couldn't help but ask since she had the man in front of her, "Is your name *really* Jebel Haven?" She assumed the name to be an alias but hadn't tried to trace the man's identity beyond the incident that had changed him from a criminal to a hero.

"Yes." Haven didn't know why he answered. Maybe it was because the intense, focused interest she turned on *him* was almost impossible to resist. Kind of cute, too. "My dad worked for an oil company in the Middle East. He heard that Jebel means mountain, or something like that, in Arabic. Thought it was cool. And I don't like being called Jeb," he added. Sometimes Baker or Santini called him Jeb, but they were friends, so he let them live. He put the cup to one side of the table and leaned closer. "And how do you know who I am?"

Char stirred another packet of raw sugar into her coffee and considered how to answer him. She flicked a few of the brown sugar crystals into her hand and licked them off her fingers. She was surprised at the intense way Jebel Haven focused on this simple action. It occurred to her that some of her clumsy effort at seducing him had carried over into this meeting. When she glanced at him, he looked as coolly self-possessed as ever. She assumed an equally poker-faced countenance for a few seconds.

Finally she smiled and answered quietly, "That's

easy, Mr. Haven. I know who you are, because I, too, am a vampire hunter."

His surprise registered against several of her senses, but his expression didn't change one bit. "Really?" was his sarcastic response.

He glanced around. He had amazingly dark brown eyes and quite long lashes. No one was close enough to where they sat to overhear. She wondered if he wondered about the absence of anyone at nearby booths and tables on a busy Friday night.

Once he was sure they weren't overheard, Haven said equally quietly, "You kill vampires."

She was surprised that it wasn't a question. She gazed at him steadily. "I notice you have not yet denied the existence of such creatures."

"I've met a few fiends from hell," he answered.

"So you have." She drank more coffee, enjoying the combination of caffeine, sugar, and delicious irony without disrespecting the man's skills.

In a manner of speaking, he had faced fiends from one religion's version of hell. Faced them and fought them quite bravely, but until a few minutes ago, he'd never met any vampires. Strictly speaking, Char supposed that he still hadn't met any regulation strigoi, as she was something of an *ubervampire* these days.

"How many vampires have you killed?"

"One," she answered honestly.

"What was it like?"

Delicious. Char barely caught herself from saying this. She gave him a slightly confused look. "What do you mean?"

Dark brows came down over dark eyes. "What *kind* of vampire did you kill?"

She wondered if she should innocently ask what he meant. "You don't believe me," she said instead. He didn't deny it. Char held her hands above the table. They were long-fingered and slender, delicate-looking to this big man, she supposed, though the shape at the base of the cuticle might appear a bit thicker than normal to someone who looked closely. She kept her nails short and wore no rings. Her hands didn't grow any larger when she changed, but the claws of a Nighthawk were quite impressive. "You don't have to appear dangerous all the time to kill vampires," she said.

Haven looked her over in a way that would have been deeply insulting if it hadn't also been so warming. Char blushed from the inside out in a way that left her very nearly light-headed. Meanwhile, Haven laughed softly and said, "I believe that you killed a vampire, sweetheart." He shrugged. "I've seen a fifteen-year-old girl kill vampires." His face lost all expression again, except for a flash of pain deep in his dark eyes. When he went on, his voice was flat and hard. "I asked you what kind of vampire you killed."

Char supposed this was where she ought to deviate from telling the truth for the good of the secret world Jebel Haven was on the edge of discovering. It was not lost on her that she had approached him to learn what he was doing in Seattle but that he was the one acquiring all the information for the price of a cup of coffee. "One of the smarter ones," she told him. "An urban one. I know the blood-drinking creatures you've dealt with

hide in the countryside and—How shall I put this?—
that they've spent too many generations marrying their
cousins."

He laughed. "If that was how the bastards reproduced,
I'd agree with that. They've got some cunning, but
mostly they're stupid little shits. With big teeth," he
added.

"The creatures you kill spread an infection. Death really is the best thing for them."

The infection was the result of a spell gone wrong
and had nothing to do with the Strigoi way of becoming
a vampire. Haven's creatures had been created when a
priest prayed over some Native American slaves he was
trying to convert so he could better exploit them. The
prayer was from an ancient book the Church had banned
and ordered burned (along with the alchemist sorcerer
who'd written it) hundreds of years before this
seventeenth-century colonial joker decided to set up the
spell to help his search through the Southwest for gold.
Who knew how the priest had gotten his hands on the
forbidden grimoire? What was known was that he
thought a spirit of meekness would enter the people he
was trying to control. What he got was a total mess. Yes,
the people the spell transformed ate flesh, feared the
light, thirsted for blood, and were afraid of crosses in
the manner of movie vampires. That was because of the
priest's melding Catholic dogma with an ancient magical
spell.

"You sound like you feel sorry for the bastards."

"Sorry for all the centuries' worth of victims, yes. But
let's talk about urban monsters, shall we? And Daniel?"

She put her arm on the table and leaned forward. "Why are *you* interested in Daniel?"

"Why are you?" was Haven's grudging, suspicious answer.

She wanted to hit him. No, she wanted to spit a piece of shotgun ammunition in his face, and *then* hit him, with her claws extended. But Char was very good at controlling herself. She said, "You are a pain in the posterior, Mr. Haven."

He ducked his head and smiled up at her through long lashes. "Posterior. That's a dainty word." He straightened up. "What does an amateur vampire hunter—"

"Amateur!"

"—have to do with the Novak kid's being missing from a shelter in Oregon? And how'd he end up at a shelter in Oregon?"

"He was kidnapped and sexually assaulted." She answered his second question first and tried to be more amused than annoyed at his granting her amateur status.

"This was when he first disappeared? From college?"

"He was in college?" She held up a hand. "I know very little about Daniel's past. I only know that he washed up at the home of a woman who takes in damaged adolescents, then disappeared again. She suspected Daniel of being involved in a . . . human-sacrificing satanic cult for want of a better term. She knows I look into that sort of thing. I looked into it. I think he's involved with something a great deal more serious."

He stroked his jaw thoughtfully. "Most people would think that kind of cult was pretty serious."

"We're not most people, Mr. Haven."

He gave a slight shrug.

"You still haven't told me how you came to be looking for Daniel."

"His mom hired me to find him."

She tilted an eyebrow at him. "You aren't a private investigator."

"His mom's with the Bureau. A profiler. She thinks he's involved with a human-sacrificing satanic cult, too."

Char sat up straight. "The Bureau? FBI?" He nodded. She bit off a swear word as she fought down a flash of panic and an urge to look around suspiciously. "The last thing we need is any involvement with the feds."

"Especially if there's been permanent changes in Danny boy's overbite."

Char couldn't think of any response to this. She was too taken aback by the news of FBI involvement with the strigoi to do much more than stare at the mortal slouched in the seat opposite her. What had Daniel gotten the strigoi into?

She was almost frazzled enough to look the mortal in the eye and ask this question out loud. As if the man she'd been ordered to kill because he was likely to stumble onto the truth about real vampires was suddenly some sort of ally. Fortunately, she was able to keep her tongue in her head, though she gripped the table so hard she left finger marks in the laminated wood.

Also fortunately, Jebel Haven didn't have time to notice her wrecking the furniture, because his partner shoved through the crowd to reach them. Santini's face split into a wide grin as she and Haven turned their heads to look at him.

Santini pointed at Char. "One of us, right?"

"Yes," Char answered, giving Santini an intense, convincing look. Strong-minded as he was, he also had a touch of psychic gifting. She could influence him. She smiled at him and thought good thoughts.

"She made claims," Haven told his partner.

"Night's not getting any younger," Santini said, rocking back and forth on his heels. He jerked a thumb toward the exit. "Let's take a walk, Jebel, miss."

"Char."

"Welcome to the club, Char."

Haven slipped out of the booth without another look her way. The two men walked away, Haven elaborately ignoring her. Santini was excited. He obviously had news, information. Char didn't hesitate a moment before grabbing her raincoat and following them.

Chapter 14

OF COURSE CHARLOTTE McCairn followed them into the night. Haven gave her a warning look as she came up behind him and was answered by a quizzically tilted eyebrow.

"We're both looking for the same thing," she reminded him. "What have you got, Santini?" she called to the biker leading the way across the square.

"A guy with an address," Santini called back to her. "His sister's been living with the Angel's Children." He laughed. "That's what they call themselves. He's pissed cause she's turning tricks for them instead of him."

"Charming," Charlotte said. Haven *almost* smiled at her sarcasm.

Santini looked back, his glance going to the girl instead of Haven. "You're packing, right, Char?"

"Definitely." She moved up to walk beside Haven. "We're just going to check this group out, right? Not get into a firefight?"

"We?" Haven asked.

Santini gave his manic grin. "Well, if the kid's there, maybe we can shake, bake, and stake."

Haven silently cursed Santini's in-your-face, what-the-fuck attitude. Discretion was too large a word for the biker's limited vocabulary. Hell, usually it was too much for his. What Haven was good at was killing. Only lately he'd gotten a stupid idea that there were things going on beneath the surface of even the underground world that needed more than good reflexes, stubbornness, and cunning to deal with.

The way the woman called out as she died, and the werewolf encounter were proof that there was more evil than he'd realized in the world. All he'd had to do was leave his usual territory to hunt for Danny Novak, and he'd landed smack in the middle of a situation that was deeper and darker than he was prepared for. Prepared or not, he'd handle it. He'd been handling it, even before the appearance of a new girl in town.

He'd planned on finding out what the girl knew, then dumping her and getting on with his business. It was not his problem if the kid wanted to call herself a vampire hunter and get herself torn to shreds or worse for her trouble. She wasn't going to be dying because of him. But he didn't want her dying in front of him, either.

Sara had said that it wasn't his fault, had forgiven him, had tried to smile at him just as he put the wooden bullets into her brain and her heart. Sara had been eighteen and a veteran of the vampire wars. A partner. A friend. A victim. She was dead because of him.

"Screw it," he muttered and firmly shut off thoughts about the past. "Where's this new friend of yours?" he asked Santini as they reached a spot under a streetlight a few blocks closer to Elliot Bay.

"Guy said he'd wait here," Santini answered. "Looks like he didn't." He gave a casual shrug. "Doesn't matter. He gave me an address. Native guide would have been nice."

"You've got one." Char told the men from Tucson. "Seattle's my hometown." She pulled her car keys out of her raincoat pocket. "My car's near here." She looked at Haven. "Just how close is your car? Time's fleeing, Mr. Haven."

"Yeah, yeah," he growled. "Fine. You win. You drive. Let's go."

"Not much farther," Char said, though no one had actually asked her about an ETA. Friday night traffic in the downtown area had been bad. Then, once they were in quieter streets, she'd made a few false turns and had to backtrack a few times. The magic was making navigating hard but not impossible. What did bother her was that the digital clock in the dashboard read 2:05.

When she hadn't been psychically suggesting that Jebel Haven meet her this evening, Char had spent her dream time really *looking* at the city. Now that she was aware of the obscuring spells, she was much less confused by them. She did not have to use her complete concentration to drive, which was good, because she had a lot to think about regarding the man sitting so closely beside her. He was large, her car was small, he couldn't help but fill the front while Santini sat in the backseat.

Jebel Haven had a guilty conscience. He radiated anguish while he stared expressionlessly through the windshield. Char knew all about Sara Breslow, the young woman who'd died while working with Haven, Baker, and Santini. Haven was probably comparing her to Sara. She was sure he blamed himself for the girl's death. Then there was the guilt over all the things he must have done before an attack by a band of blood-drinking parasites on a desert hideout converted the survivors into a band of God-fearing crusaders. Jebel Haven had done a good deal to make up for his past, but he still didn't have a lot of reasons to like himself very much. He'd probably be grateful to be put out of his misery when she finally got around to killing him.

Much to her annoyance, she had to change her plan to whack him tonight. Killing Haven before dawn was no longer an option. She had a lot more to find out from him than she'd originally thought. Char recognized this fact and was furious for having been so honest with him. It was all very well and good to tell him the truth when she thought he only had a few minutes to live, but then he'd dropped the bombshell that he was working for the FBI or someone in the FBI. Her plans had had to change.

She wondered if that was why Istvan had ordered the hit on Haven. Not only was the mortal looking to turn his formidable destructive talents on different types of supernatural beings, but the Council was aware that he was now working with the feds. No government anywhere in the world could be allowed to know of the existence of the strigoi. It was a Law. But how could the Strigoi Council know that and not tell her? After all, she was the one whose research had uncovered Haven's existence in the first place. If he could feel guilty about

Breslow's death, she could feel guilty about his. On many levels. When it happened.

In the meantime, there was Daniel, the sorcerer, and the demon connection to untangle. Soon, she hoped, as she pulled into a parking space half a block away from a building she couldn't see but knew was there. She couldn't see it because of the deep concentration of protective spells. Something had to be hidden in the heart of all that magic.

"We're here," she announced to her passengers.

"Where?" Haven got out of the car and slammed the door behind him. Char and Santini followed him onto the sidewalk. He gestured. "There's a hole . . . in . . ."

"Let's go," Santini said, and started forward.

Char followed the biker. "There's a building here," she said. "Santini can see it. Can't you, Mr. Santini?"

"Sort of," Santini answered.

Char noticed that Santini was now holding a very large gun. She wondered where upon his short, wiry frame he had concealed the weapon. She looked back at Haven. "You coming?"

"I don't miss parties." Haven shook his head as if to clear it, then slapped a palm against his temple. "What do you see, Santini?" he asked as he brought up the rear.

"Here's the door," Santini said.

Char chose to believe him rather than her eyes. Her confused senses showed her—nothing—a black slab of nothing edged in between two run-down warehouses. Seattle was one of the largest ports in the country. It was also a town with limited space due to its location between mountains and water. Economics and logic told her that Santini stood in front of the main door of a warehouse building. The metallic sound that came out of the darkness when he rattled the doorknob was a reassuring one.

She and Haven exchanged a quick glance. "Magic," she told the monster hunter. "He isn't as affected by it as we are."

"Magic." Haven gave her a long, hard look. His dark brown eyes appeared obsidian black to her. He put a hand on her shoulder. "Sweetheart, you and I are going to have a long talk when we're out of here."

"Definitely. But first—"

The roar of Santini firing his gun against the lock mechanism effectively drowned out Char's voice. The unexpected, explosive sound also almost made her vamp out. She whirled away from Haven to hide any slight change in her appearance, but Haven's attention was on his impetuous partner.

"That ought to set off a few alarm systems!"

"Then we better hurry," was Santini's buoyant response. He took a step back and kicked open the door Char couldn't see. "Bless me, Father!" he shouted and moved inside the dark, his pistol held steadily before him in both hands.

"I think he must be blessed," Char murmured quietly to Haven as they followed.

"He's nuts."

"Holy fool, then. Deep breath." She grabbed his hand. "Let's go." What they stepped into was an utter void, blackness darker and colder than any arctic night.

"What the hell?"

"Just keep walking, even though you don't feel your legs," she advised Haven. She couldn't feel his presence, even though she was sure he was beside her. She knew that his warm fingers were clasped around her cooler ones. She followed her own instruction to keep moving, though she wasn't absolutely sure where her legs were, or the ground. Reminding herself that to her night did not in any way resemble this black emptiness helped. "Once we're inside, we'll be able to see."

"You sound like you're miles away."

"Right beside you, Jebel."

"Make sure you stay there."

"Found a light switch," Santini said from not two feet away.

Even as she jumped in surprise at Santini's voice, Char went from being shrouded in absolute dark to having her senses flooded by bright, white light. She caught her breath, blind from the sudden dazzle, and stumbled forward. Haven grunted and lurched into her, and they caught each other and held on while the blinding light faded down to a bearable level.

Char noticed after they regained their balance that her hand was on his shoulder, his was on her waist. She scanned the room behind him. He looked past her shoulder. Several rows of overhead fluorescent lights gave off harsh light, but the room was still full of skittering shadows. Shadows she knew very well were her imagination.

"No one here," she said.

"Don't see anything," Santini agreed. "Feels deserted."

"You okay?" Haven asked. His hand was still on her waist.

"Fine. You?" Her hand moved down his arm.

"Fine."

"You coming?" Santini asked them.

Char took a deliberate step away from Haven. "The magic's on the outside," she explained as the disorientation finally subsided completely. "Our senses, regular *and* extra crispy, work fine in here."

"Makes sense. What do you think?" Haven asked his partner.

Santini pointed toward a metal staircase. "Place is only two stories. Offices upstairs. Nothing down here. Let's have a look up there."

"You stay here," Haven told his partner. "Watch our backs."

Santini grinned. "Fine. Have fun, kids." He stepped back toward the center of the room. "See if I can find where the culties have scuttled off to." His grin widened. "And maybe there'll be some vampires in the basement."

"Call for help if there are." Haven jerked a thumb. He drew a pistol from inside his jacket. "Let's go upstairs, sweetheart."

Char bit her tongue and followed one step behind him up the stairs. Calling her sweetheart wasn't the worst thing Haven could do, but it still set her teeth on edge. Setting a vampire's teeth on edge was not a wise move. Oh, well, he could certainly be behaving worse, and he was a dead man anyway, so being offended was pointless.

The building was eerily quiet, the air still, smelling of old blood. Blood and remnants of sexual energy.

Please, please, please, she thought. *Don't let there be any bodies up here.*

Char tried to temper the excitement and dread that lit her. Haven didn't sense it, but she knew they were about to enter a vampire nursery.

She took a deep breath to calm herself as they reached the hall at the top of the stairs. The musty reek that filled her senses drove out awareness of her own kind. In fact, it very nearly made her choke. She fought down a cough. She didn't know why she hadn't gagged the instant she stepped through the warehouse entrance. She made some noise, and the mortal whirled to face her.

"What have you got?" Haven asked.

"Demon," she answered automatically. Only after she spoke did Char wonder at his easy acceptance of her extra senses and her easy response to that acceptance.

He pulled her into an empty office and closed the door. She could see him clearly in the darkness and figured he must have extremely good night vision for a mortal.

"What about werewolves?" Haven asked.

"What about them?"

"Can you sense them?"

Char shrugged. "Don't know. I've never met one."

"And you've *met* demons?"

"I'm not on a first-name basis with any, no." Char chuckled. "I've never met any demons, but I know the scent," she explained in case he didn't realize she was joking. "I do a lot of research on the supernatural. I've handled demon artifacts. Demons leave a very distinct psychic signature. They stink," she elaborated.

"And our boy Danny's involved with a demon?"

There was a stern note of finality in his rough voice. This man was already prepared to execute Daniel at the first opportunity. Now she'd just given him another reason to kill the kid she was trying to help.

"We don't know anything about Daniel's involvement. However, if you want to kill the demon, feel free to . . . to . . ."

"Charlotte?" He passed his hand in front of her face. "You in there, sweetheart?"

She blinked. "Feel free to kill the demon." She spoke slowly and flatly, almost tasting each word as it came out of her mouth. "Feel free to kill the demon," she repeated, and a ripple of delight went through her. She focused on Haven, smiling at him, thinking, *I could kiss you!* She said, "You can kill demons."

He was looking at her suspiciously. "It's been known to happen."

"Good." She patted him on the shoulder. "Good."

Of course! Haven would kill the demon for her. That wasn't against the Law. And then she'd kill Haven before he had a chance to do any harm to Daniel. It was an elegant solution; it solved both her problems. It was a nasty, disgusting, cynical way to use the mortal, but her job was to protect Strigoi interests.

She turned her back and opened the office door. "I think we should continue, Mr. Haven."

Her sudden change of mood wasn't lost on Haven. It was like a cold wind had blown through the room. She'd been calling him Jebel. Suddenly it was back to being formal, to putting mental distance between them. It'd been a wild night with this girl so far. One second he thought she wanted to seduce him, the next help him, the next pump him for information. The next, he wanted to seduce her, but that was his mood swings not hers. It wasn't like he trusted her or thought her part of his team, but . . .

"Shit," he muttered. She was right. Besides, anyone in their line of work was crazy, anyway. Mood swings were normal. He followed her back into the hall. He didn't ask the demon-sniffing Charlotte McCairn where the enemy was.

He began to feel it as he led the way cautiously from one empty room to the next. There were signs that people had come and gone and left their refuse behind. There was a litter of empty fast-food containers, lots of other human junk, but there was plenty of other litter as well. An emotional mess had been left behind, too. He wasn't sure how he was picking it up, but the residue of what people who'd been here had experienced was very real to him. It was like there was this part of his brain that had always been tuned in to a radio station, and the volume control had recently been cranked up to the max. This wasn't the time to ask his new witchy friend if she knew what was happening to him.

Then the very real stench hit him strong enough to make him gag, and that stopped him from worrying about invisible magic crap. "Oh, God!"

"Yes. Moloch, I believe. Stand back, please, Mr. Haven, and let a professional work."

Her voice was cool and crisp and full of confidence. Haven responded, even though he didn't have any idea what she meant. He stood back, prepared to cover her, and let Charlotte McCairn open the door.

He was pissed as hell about his reaction by the time the door was open. He pushed her aside on an angry rush of adrenaline.

"No!"

He heard her shout. Then the room went up in a ball of blue fire. She screamed. And the blue fire turned into pure hell.

Chapter 15

"IDIOT," CHAR COMPLAINED. For a moment, she wasn't sure if she was referring to herself or Jebel Haven. Then she muttered, "Protective idiot," and decided that she must be referring to the mortal. He'd pushed her aside and taken the full blast of the booby trap himself. *She'd* been aware that there was a spell waiting to be triggered when the door was opened. *She'd* been about to attempt a counterspell. Haven got in the way.

"Idiot." Kind of sweet, though, his being chivalrous and all. "Idiot," she repeated once more, and this time she was referring to herself.

She was lying on something lumpy in the cold, dark room. It was warm and had a heartbeat. "Haven." She touched him on the throat. Pulse was normal. She considered breaking his neck while she had the chance, then rolled off him and got to her feet.

She left Haven where he lay and cautiously approached the inner sanctum once more. Better to have a proper look around without the mortal. She paused at the threshold, closed her eyes, and made sure the malevolent magic had all dissipated in one single blast. She wondered if the spell would have killed Haven if she hadn't been there to deflect the shock. Or maybe he was too tough and mean to be killed by a someone else's evil thoughts.

She put Haven out of her mind for the moment, nodded in acknowledgment that the spell was dissipated, and reached around the door frame to find the light switch. She braced herself for what she would see and stepped inside. Only to breathe a sigh of relief to discover that there was no physical evidence to accompany the psychic residue that haunted the room. The residue was bad enough, and her head was already muzzy from the magical booby trap. Still, it was good not to see bloodstained walls and rotting corpses littering this cave of decadence and dark magic.

The room was large and bare, empty but for some chairs and a queen-size bed pushed into the farthest corner. She moved forward reluctantly to examine the bed. The sheets were stained and filthy—and bloodstained. Only a few rusty spots, though, telltale evidence of vampire sexual activity. No one had been murdered in this bed. Daniel was not guilty of that. She hoped and prayed.

She wasn't sure of the young vampire's exact age, but his hunting instinct shouldn't have kicked in yet. Its first need would be for love, always, to touch, caress, hold, connect. Blood was for mating. The taste for flesh and fear came later.

"And it can be controlled," she murmured aloud. She felt like she was apologizing to a million casualties in this room where death had taken place. But the deaths here could not be laid at Daniel's door. There was a demon, a sorcerer, and possibly mortal accomplices committing multiple murders. She was pretty sure she knew why.

She also hoped they'd left a psychic trail when they took Daniel and vacated this warehouse. But if there was one, there was no way she could sense it tonight.

Not with this headache.

Char wasn't only feeling halfway to psychically burned out, she hurt physically as well. She needed a good day's sleep, a very large meal, and lots and lots of caffeine before she was ready to take up the trail again. Okay, so she was a superhero, but she was new on the job. If she thought Daniel's life was in any danger from the jokers holding him, she might not let herself consider resting, but she figured the last thing they were going to do was harm their ticket to eternal life.

"Idiots." She rubbed the back of her neck. Idiots or not, they'd slowed her down tonight and escaped for the moment. Her fault for having approached Daniel's companion the night before. She wondered if the scrawny weirdo even knew he *was* a companion. But wondering didn't do her any good right now. She checked her watch. Time to pack it in before she keeled over and spent the day passed out in this den of iniquity.

Speaking of people who had no doubt spent time in dens of iniquity . . .

She turned around and marched out of the room. She squatted beside the unconscious man and shook his shoulder. "Mr. Haven?"

Nothing.

She checked his pulse again. Somewhat to her disappointment, he was very much alive. Maybe she could leave him here. But who knew how long he'd be out? The Angel's Children or whatever they called themselves might come back to finish moving the furniture before he woke up. Haven could end up their next human sacrifice. That would solve one of Char's problems, but it wouldn't help her dispose of the demon or find out how much the FBI knew about Haven's vampire-killing crusade. She was going to have to take him with her, wasn't she?

She stood, picked Haven up, and slung him over her shoulder. His weight didn't bother her, but he was a big man and she was a medium-sized woman. Carrying him through the second-floor offices and down the metal stairs wasn't hard, but it was awkward.

She didn't remember Santini until she was in the main area of the warehouse. Not that remembering him did any good, because when she left Haven on the cold concrete floor and went in search of his partner, the man was nowhere to be found. She finally came back to retrieve Haven and headed for the door. She was going to assume Santini was safe, and if he wasn't safe, it was his own fault.

She wished he was there to help her through the dark barrier before the doorway, but she'd negotiated it once before, she did it again. It wasn't quite so terrifying the second time.

Haven finally started to come around by the time she had him stuffed into the passenger seat of her car. She was getting ready to start the car engine. He grunted.

She checked her watch again. She wondered if he'd be able to drive if she took him back to his Jeep. Doubtful. Would it be her fault if he was mugged if she simply dumped him by his vehicle? Which might not happen. *He* could wake up in the daylight, which was not an option for her.

Maybe she could get him back to his hotel. He moaned. She shook him and asked him where he was staying. He mumbled an answer that had airport in it. She swore and put the car in gear.

It looked like she was going to have to take him home with her.

"Where am I?"

"Go back to sleep, Mr. Haven."

Haven's head hit the couch arm again—this was the second time he'd almost come awake—and his mouth opened slightly. His body went slack, and his arm slid down toward the floor. He hadn't opened his eyes this time. Char took that as a good sign.

Char stood in the doorway between the bedroom and living room and shook her head at the sight of Jebel Haven, vampire hunter. Getting him into the condo had been relatively easy, but keeping him neutralized while she slept the day away . . .

"I'm an idiot." She shook her head again. "This time, stay asleep," she told him, whispering into his mind as persuasively as she knew how. " 'Cause I have to go to bed now. We need our sleep."

"Bed," he said, and rolled over. It was a wonder he didn't fall off the couch. He tucked his hands beneath his cheek and smiled. She would have expected him to look innocent in his sleep, or perhaps a bit foolish. He was smirking, and he didn't look any less dangerous.

She shook her head again and left him where he was so she could get ready for bed.

This was possibly the stupidest thing she'd ever done, she told the image in the bathroom mirror as she brushed her teeth. Char knew she was too softhearted when she ought to be stern, commanding, and ruthless. Bringing even an unconscious vampire hunter home was probably against some official rule. It certainly bore no relation to common sense. It was enough to make her wish that she at least owned a pair of handcuffs. He was a victim of a nasty psychic bombing, she reminded herself. He wasn't likely to regain coherence for many hours, even if he did wake up. And he wasn't likely to wake up. Really.

Char repeated this to herself several times while she hurriedly washed up, got undressed, and pulled on the T-shirt she used as a nightgown. She almost believed it by the time she opened the bathroom door.

To find Jebel Haven sprawled on his back across the queen-size sleigh bed.

"What do you think you're doing?" she shouted as she stepped into the bedroom.

"Bed," he said. He was still smirking. "We sleep." He turned his head on the pillows but didn't open his eyes. "You said bed."

She'd brought this on herself. She realized this even as she fought off the panic reaction. She'd suggested bed to him, and his filthy male subconscious had responded in a typical libidinous way.

"Men," Char muttered. And now she was going to have to lug this lummox back to the living room couch. "Like I have time for this."

Unfortunately, sunrise caught up with her just as she reached the bed. She was hit with a flash of amazement that worrying about the fool man had actually screwed up the excellent sense of time that was standard issue along with her fangs and claws. A rare wave of dizziness hit her, and she fell forward, just barely able to catch herself and settle onto the unoccupied side of the bed before the dizziness turned to a wave of enveloping darkness. She couldn't keep her eyes from closing or her muscles from going slack. All she could do now, no matter who shared her bed, was go to sleep.

That was a daymare, right? A ludicrous, farcical daymare. Had to be. Char would have breathed a sigh of relief if she had any control of her body at the moment. Her mind was the only part of her that was free during the daylight, though her awareness was limited, and perception was weird when she was in the waking dream state at all. Most days she spent in sweet, sleeping darkness, and her dreams were real ones.

And the daymare about Haven in her bed was a doozy.

Must have been what roused her. Just as well. She needed to get her mental act together and try dream walking again today. The combination of telepathy and astral projection and elements that were unique to the

strigoi was wearing yet, but if she was going to find the
sorcerer and demon holding Daniel, then she needed to
make the effort. Besides, practice made perfect and all
that.

The first thing to do was make herself remember what
she'd done last night, separate what had really happened
from the weird daymare about her and Haven and Santini at the abandoned hideout and the magical trap and
bringing Haven home and checking out with him sleeping in her—

Bed.

Oh, good lord.

She had, hadn't she? Brought him home. Where was
he now? How long had she been out? Was he awake?
Had he noticed her lowered body temperature? That she
was still as death and that her pulse was slowed to the
point of being undetectable? It wasn't like she was dead
or anything, but she understood how her daylight condition might appear a little odd to, say, a stake-wielding
vampire killer. The older a vampire was, the more the
narcolepsy resembled a deep, sound sleep. Well, she
wasn't all that old in vampire terms, and what she looked
was dead. She would most likely be dead if he noticed.
Unpleasant images of being staked, beheaded, and
burned flashed through Char's mind. Haven was the
thorough type.

It took a great deal of concentration—it took a hellish
amount of concentration—but Char went looking for the
man lying in bed beside her.

Please let him still be lying beside her.

She floated, hovered, searched without sight or hearing. She became aware of the heat of familiar blood, scent of warm skin, the scrape of the rough edges of a mind in turmoil, blunted, thoughts disassociated but still rasping on her awareness. Haven. She'd found him.

Having found him, she touched him.

He was sleeping.

Char's awareness resonated with relief, but she couldn't relax, couldn't do anything but will him to remain blissfully, deservedly, deep, deep asleep.

This ploy lasted for about three hours, until he grunted, shifted, muttered, "Gotta take a leak" and heaved himself up out of the bed.

Char couldn't have moved if she'd tried, but even if she could have, she might have curled up on her side, frozen with the mortification of sharing a bed with a strange man.

"Sound sleeper, aren't you?" he said when he slipped in beside her.

Had he just slapped her butt? Yes, he had; she was certain of it. And he chuckled in her ear, as well. He was lying on his side, long body stretched out close to hers, spoon fashion. She was aware of his warmth all along her back and against her thighs. Sweet, mortal warmth. Jimmy always said that one of the best parts of having a companion was to be in that hovering state, body in a trance, mind weirdly aware, and to *know* in a half-dozen almost impossible-to-define ways that your lover was there, warm and waiting beside you. That it made a strigoi feel protective and protecting at once, safe, but with a hint of unpredictability, because complete control was gone and only trust remained.

Well, Jimmy was gone, Haven was no one's companion, she was totally out of control, and it was three or four hours yet before the sun released her from the paralysis of daylight. And Haven wasn't exactly asleep. She worked through her terror to realize that much. He wasn't awake, exactly, but hovering in between, halfway in both worlds, as she was, but in the less restrictive, mortal fashion. Dozing. That's right, that's what it was called. She'd all but forgotten the mortal terms for sleep. He was as aware of her on some level as she was of him. Her senses were tuned to thought and emotion, his were tactile.

His hand was on her thigh. And moving higher. She didn't think he was aware of it, but nonetheless, the man was taking the opportunity to feel her up. Was that an erection that had worked its way between them?

She wasn't sure whether she was mortified or amused. She knew that if she were able to, she'd push the hand away, shift her hips, say something sarcastic, and maybe smile a little to herself at his unconscious interest. After all, just because she was a vampire, she wasn't dead, and having a man touch her was rather pleasant under certain circumstances. She didn't have room right now in her emotional spectrum for any reaction other than a survival response.

Any moment now Haven was going to wake up and notice he was aroused. He wouldn't do anything about it other than be relieved that she was asleep and didn't know that he couldn't control his body. But he'd be awake. He'd rest beside her for a while, maybe staring at the ceiling with his hands tucked behind his head, his subconscious would take notes. He'd take a closer look. Good-bye Char the Enforcer.

Rookie Enforcer.

Not a rookie strigoi, though, are you, girl? Or rookie female of any branch of the species? She would have smiled smugly if she could smile at all at memories of what she'd gotten up to in a similar bed in this very bedroom not too many years before. And she'd been a baby strigoi herself once, as sexually insatiable as young Daniel. She'd hunted, mortal and strigoi. She ought to be ashamed of herself if she couldn't distract an already-aroused male for a couple of hours. All it should take was a lot of suggestion and a little imagination.

Char chuckled, in a virtual way, and got to work.

Chapter 16

"You don't have to look so smug."

Haven smirked, leaned back against the headboard, and put his hand over his heart. "You did the seducing, sweetheart."

Pleased to be alive, Char supposed that letting him revel in his prowess wasn't too much of a price to pay. His chest was bare and fuzzy. Scarred in places, as well. Then there was the tattoo, a sharp, angular black design that stretched from his shoulder all the way down his left arm. The overall effect of his appearance was barbaric, to say the least. He looked every inch the ex-con, and there were a great many square inches of him visible all the way up from where the sheet barely covered his hips.

"Nice place," he said, looking around the bedroom while she looked at him. "Thought you said you're based in Portland."

"Not my place," Char told him. "Belongs to an old boyfriend. He's out of town. I've still got a key."

"Old boyfriend, eh?" He finally looked at her. "You

don't seem like the old-boyfriend type. You seem like a keeper type."

Haven's assessing expression made Char wonder what he'd heard in her oh-so-neutral voice when she mentioned Jimmy Bluecorn. What was with him, anyway? Haven didn't seem like the getting personal type. He seemed like the sex-as-recreation, leave-the-money-on-the-table-on-the-way-out type. Talking about Jimmy wasn't easy, especially not to another man—one who was under the misapprehension that they'd spent the afternoon having sex.

"He was special," she admitted. "We're still friends—from a distance."

"Generous of him to let you crash."

Jimmy's condo was, technically, what Haven would call a lair. There was no use giving up a place if you weren't using it; you might need a secure place to sleep someday—or a good friend might need it. Keys got passed around, connections got made, all with a minimum of fuss and communication. You didn't let just anyone crash, not in a place you'd called home. Or maybe Haven would think of it as a tomb with a view?

"What are you smiling about?" Haven asked.

"Nothing." She ran her hands through her hair and checked the clock. "I need a shower."

"Yeah," he agreed, sliding out of bed. "I'll join you."

Char didn't make any objections, and she could tell by the tilt of Haven's eyebrow and the slight smile he gave her that he expected a protest. Why did she always give the impression of being the fainting maiden type?

'Cause it was true most of the time? "Planning to check me for bite marks, Haven?"

"Should've checked already." He ducked his head and scratched his stubbly chin. "I didn't pay much attention this afternoon."

"Neither did I." She waved him toward the bathroom. "Come on. We can soap each other down."

"When'd you get to be so sexy?" he asked when the hot water was rushing over them.

She squeezed shower gel into her hand and slapped his chest. "I'm off duty until I've had caffeine. I'm not being sexy," she added as she spread white foam all over his chest. "This is efficient. I'll be all business in half an hour."

He followed her example and began to rub the slick pink shower gel over her front, paying close attention to make sure her breasts had enough soap. The scent of strawberry rose with the steam. His thoroughness produced a pleasant tingle and buzz of sensation. Char arched into his palms when he cupped her breasts.

Then she remembered that she was going to kill Haven, and she slid away to face the falling water instead. She wished now that she hadn't deliberately tried to attract him last night or had to seduce him in his dreams today. Or that he'd unselfishly acted to take her out of harm's way when the psychic bomb went off. He was a hero in his own badass way, and she was the villain of this piece. She hated using sex as a weapon, because it had a tendency to backfire and leave the person who used it as damaged as the target.

They fit together into the large shower stall, but it

was a tight fit. Haven was a big guy. A big, hairy, hard-muscled guy with big, quick hands. He cupped her bottom with them and ran them down her thighs, and she found herself leaning back against him because real contact felt too damn good to deny for the sake of a little thing like ethics. The man's touch felt so good it made her fangs tingle.

"Found any bite marks yet?" Char asked around faintly protruding teeth.

"Got to be thorough." His fingers slipped between her legs as he spoke and began a soft, sweet stroking.

She bit her lower lip and tasted a drop of her own blood before it was washed away. She pressed her palms against the blue tiled front of the shower. A quick check of her fingertips assured her that her claws were safely sheathed. Of course, she was turned on, not hungry. She didn't get hungry for mortals anymore. Yes she did—in the typical way a woman grew hungry for a man. She closed her eyes and let him touch her for a long time, absorbing the pleasure it gave him as much as responding to the stimulation he gave.

Eventually, she shifted against him, turned, and closed her hand around his erection. She rested her head on his shoulder, breathed in the warm scent of him, stroked him as he stroked her and made that be enough. After a time, the water that poured over them was cold as ice, and that served as good a signal as any to bring this joining to an end.

He wasn't getting involved. He looked at Charlotte, who was very much not his type, and reminded himself that he didn't get involved. They'd only been passing the time. Usually Haven never put thoughts of sex and involvement together. He approved of one, avoided the other. "I'm not likely to live long," he said to the woman seated across the kitchen counter from him. He rubbed his freshly shaved chin.

She gave him an odd look but said, "I'm well aware of that, Mr. Haven," as cool and calm as you please. "Do you want the last piece of toast?"

He could use some fresh clothes, but he was clean, and he felt pretty good. "Too bad the boyfriend didn't leave any of his stuff behind."

"He's a lot smaller than you," she said. She ate her toast, drank some tea, and then went on. "Here's how you think it will be, one of the revenants you hunt will finally get its teeth into you. You'll fight the infection, try to kill yourself before you lose your mind and change into one of the creatures. If you don't manage to commit suicide, Baker and Santini have promised to do you, as you've promised to do them. If they don't manage to kill you immediately, the hope is that they'll hunt you down and get you before you get them."

He nodded. "You have somebody to take you out when they get you?"

Charlotte ignored his question. "We're talking about your survival strategy right now. The danger in Seattle isn't from the blood-drinking monsters you're used to dealing with. You know nothing about demons or sorcerers, and that might have gotten you killed last night."

He took a sip of coffee, then lit a cigarette. Charlotte frowned as the smoke curled up to fill the kitchen, which only amused him. "At least tobacco won't get the chance to kill me," he told her.

"It might be a contributing factor," she said as she drummed her fingers on the countertop.

For a moment Charlotte McCairn looked very dangerous. It was kind of sexy. Then her big eyes widened and she began to cough. A choking fit took her, and her pale face went red. Haven figured the smoke bothered her, or toast crumbs must have caught in her throat. She grabbed a napkin and pushed away from the counter. She turned her back on him as she spit up into the napkin, but dropped it as she started coughing again. Haven heard a ping of something metal hitting the floor, but Charlotte scooped up whatever she'd dropped before he had the chance to look over the counter.

She straightened, took a deep breath. "This is your fault."

She turned a glower on him as she tossed the napkin into a wastebasket under the sink. The venom in her eyes was almost enough to make him crush out his cigarette. Almost. Then she turned around with the coffeepot in her hand, poured him another cup, and sat back in the chair across from him. "Where were we?"

"Talking about dying."

"Been there, done that. Let's move on."

"Demons," he reminded her. "Sorcerers." He finished the cigarette and put out the butt in a saucer she passed to him. "And what the hell happened last night?"

She nodded. "First, though, do you have any idea where Mr. Santini might have disappeared to? The spell we encountered left you too incoherent to be of much help, and he was simply gone."

"He'll be in touch," Haven said after he thought for a moment. "He always is." Santini wouldn't have abandoned them unless he'd come across something that needed to be followed. He was a hell of a tracker, and he did things his own way. Haven thought about another smoke but intercepted Charlotte's look as he reached for the pack resting beside his coffee cup and changed his mind. The young woman across from him was full of information he desperately wanted. They'd had sex, they'd had breakfast. It was time to talk.

Char was aware of Haven's sudden surge of hunger with an intimate flash of recognition. Looking at him was like gazing into a flyspecked, warped mirror. They were a lot alike, she and Jebel Haven, only he'd come to the hunger for knowledge later than she had. She was a scholar, a researcher. He was . . . scum. Would probably be proud to acknowledge it. The scum scholar was also a man of action with barely any education, but he was smart, in a native cunning sort of way. He'd discovered a small piece of the hidden world beneath the ordinary, and it had lit more than a sacred fire to defend the world from monsters in him. One small peek behind the curtain had sparked a latent need to *know*. He was looking at her right now like he could eat her up, and she was rather flattered that his lust was for knowledge rather than another roll in the sack.

"Demons aren't immortal," she told him, beginning with what she needed him to know. "Long-lived, yes, but not immortal."

"How do you kill 'em?"

"I'll get to that. They come in different shapes, sizes, and colors, all of them ugly. They run the gamut of horns, fangs, claws, scales, and leathery skins. Typical modus operandi is to hide out somewhere isolated, gather a group of mortal followers, and send the minions out to do their bidding. Control of the minions is usually achieved through the worship of some old god and/or the help of a practitioner of ritual magic. The demon helps to enhance and focus the mortal sorcerer's natural talent. So you frequently get the demon/sorcerer pairing. In some cases, the demon attaches itself as a familiar to several generations of a family of magic users. There's some evidence of mortal and demon matings and off-spring, but the demon seed B-movie 'having my monster baby who'll grow up to rule the world' scenario is not what we're dealing with here."

"Then why'd you bring it up?"

"Because once I get started on a subject, I have trouble shutting up."

"Focus, Charlotte." He did that head tilted look up through the long eyelashes disarming smile thing that was so appealing she almost forgot she was scheduled to kill him. Then he reached across the table and poured her a cup of tea from the blue Fiesta ware pot, waited for her to take a sip of orange and spicy Constant Comment, before prompting, "Go on. What's Danny boy have to do with demon boy?"

"This is supposition," she said, sipped, and put her cup down. "But my theory is that the sorcerer and the demon are on a quest for immortality. If you want immortality, you need a vampire. At least in every recipe for the stuff I've ever encountered."

His eyes narrowed with more than their usual suspicion, and his curiosity emissions went up by several thousand. Char could anticipate all his questions. She would even like to answer them. She so rarely had anyone to talk shop with. Never, actually. Istvan asked her for research, she hunted up the data for him, but all he wanted was extracted answers, not discussion. Istvan wasn't much of a talker. Probably too many teeth.

"You're going to explain about immortality recipes, right?"

She'd gone off on one of her mental digressions, hadn't she? That's what came of being a fount of knowledge with no one to spout off to. Well, here was the perfect audience, a captive one, so to speak.

"Okay." She rubbed her hands together. "Stop me if this gets boring."

"I doubt you could ever be boring."

She wondered what he meant by that and knew he did, too. They let it go, and she went on. "What I think we're dealing with here is black magic."

"Satanists?"

"More than likely they're pulling an angel of light scam, using the young vampire they've captured to make slaves that serve their bidding. You think that vampires are bad enough on their own, but believe me, when you bring unscrupulous mortals into the picture, things can get much worse."

He nodded. "Add human greed to unnatural evil.

That's an easy complication to imagine. How does this scam work?"

"The cult members get to have sex with the 'angel,' who drinks a bit of their blood, they drink a drop of his." And she knew that there was at least one of the cult members who'd had enough of Daniel's blood to develop a companion bond with the youngster. This was very bad for both Daniel and the companion, though she was sure neither of them knew this. She almost shuddered at the memory of the intense insanity of the thin creature that attacked her in Pioneer Square.

Haven made a gagging noise. "Sex with a vampire?"

Char refused to indulge in any indication of irony. "The blood connection ensures that the followers do their master's bidding. Only in this case, it's the sorcerer who tells the cult members what the master wants them to do. So we'll probably have to go through the usual mob of rabid fanatics to get to the inner sanctum of this nut cult. Your shotgun will come in very handy, I'm afraid."

"How do you know I use a shotgun?"

"I do very thorough research," she said, countering his sudden suspicion. She glanced at the digital clock on the microwave. "And I really should explain what the bad guys are up to so we can hit the streets and continue looking for them."

"Good point. Go on."

"The spell the sorcerer is preparing is ancient and dangerous—"

"Aren't they always?"

"Yes. It sounds melodramatic, but the world you and

I inhabit is. It's fraught with dark and dire Gothic non-sense—that can get you killed and damned and cursed."

"Fraught." He tapped a cigarette out of the pack, but rolled it between his fingers instead of lighting it. "That's a good word. Fraught. That makes us the Fraught Squad."

She gave a low and throaty laugh. "Perhaps the reason the vast majority of the world remains oblivious of the supernatural is because it's just too bloody embarrassing to pay attention to. Pretend paranormal stuff isn't happening on the bus seat next to you, and you won't have to cringe in response."

"I'd rather die with my eyes open."

"I'm sure you will, Mr. Haven." She wished she hadn't said that. She couldn't look him in the face, but she found herself studying his large, capable hands as she went on. "The murders have a lot to do with what the sorcerer's brewing. It's not the vampire that's committing the murders, by the way."

She heard his snort of disbelief. "Wrong. I've seen one of the bodies. Covered in fang marks. The kid's mom has a collection of crime scene photos, too. That's a vampire."

"I didn't say he wasn't having sex with the victims, but he isn't the murderer. He can't be if this spell is going to work. Magic is a form of energy. The sorcerer is trying to achieve immortality without going through the usual channels—"

"Usual?"

She wasn't about to explain the process of becoming a strigoi to Haven. "Vampires are the only immortal beings I know of, and I'm not even sure vampires are really immortal. They can certainly be killed."

"No shit."

"Language, Mr. Haven." She was smiling despite her prim attitude.

"Fuck that." When he picked up his coffee mug, he held his pinky out delicately. "Dainty enough, sweetheart?" She gave a gracious nod. "I can see where this sorcerer bastard's coming from. Who wants to be a vampire?"

Takes commitment and discipline. Also too many rules and regulations for this magic chanting loser and his pet demon, she thought. Char said, "Not this sorcerer or sorceress. He or she is planning to steal the vampire's immortality by means of a spell—ritual black magic. The bad guy might be a woman, you know. Point is, he or she is ritually murdering psi-gifted people, using magic to drain the psychic energy from them and storing it to use in a ceremony that will transform him—"

"Or her."

"—and the demon into immortal beings. At least that's the theory. It's almost impossible to make a spell like that work. Look what happened at Sodom and Gomorrah, for example."

Haven considered this comment for a pregnant moment, with his coffee mug half raised to his lips, then he put the mug down very slowly and said, "Let's worry about Seattle right now."

Char got up, gathered empty dishes, rinsed them, and put them in the dishwasher. He stood as she turned back from the sink, wiping her hands on a towel. "Shall we hit the streets, Mr. Haven?"

"Since when did we get to be a team?" he asked.

"Since I still know more about how to counter the magic that's being thrown at us than you do. I'll get our coats," she said without waiting for any more macho protests. "And we can be on our way."

Chapter 17

VAMPIRES, HAVEN THOUGHT, slouched down in the passenger seat of Charlotte's car. *Ritual murders. Demons. Sorcerers. Cults. Ritual magic. Sodom and Gomorrah.* No, he didn't want to go there. "What about the werewolf?" he asked as Charlotte turned a sharp corner.

Her gaze slid sideways to give him a quick look as she negotiated heavy traffic. Her eyes took on a bright glitter with the reflection from oncoming headlights. That was a reflection, right?

"You've mentioned werewolves before, Mr. Haven, but I don't know what you're talking about."

He knew she was lying but let it go for now. He was always suspicious. Of everyone. No need to telegraph it to Charlotte McCairn. He was getting what he wanted out of her, in more ways than he'd thought he would. As long as she remained useful, he'd back off on some of her secrets. Everybody had secrets, maybe even more in their line of work than in his original profession.

There was silence for a while as she negotiated narrow streets and sharply angled hills. The intermittent slap of the windshield wipers made the only sound. He found himself unprofessionally thinking about her great legs.

Then she said, "Werewolves have fur, Mr. Haven. And are prisoners of the moon."

She was using her lecture tone, but he heard something else under the coolly spoken words. Like maybe he'd said something to offend her. She was a funny girl. Great legs, though. And ass.

Thinking back to the night in the forest, he couldn't remember if the creature's muzzle had been covered in fur or not. His attention had been on that mouth full of hideous fangs. Maybe it hadn't been a werewolf. Maybe he'd gotten a glimpse of that demon she'd been talking about.

"Demons wear raincoats?" he asked her.

After a considerable silence she replied, "Not that I'm aware of."

"Hmmm."

Char didn't like Haven's silence. It was too considering, too much like there was intelligent thought going on inside his pretty head. She liked to think of him as being more cunning than bright, but that wasn't particularly realistic of her, especially since she'd been tracking his progress as he moved out of pest control into areas that might make him a threat.

She knew about his orders from some very specialized bookstores, the Internet searches, the interlibrary loans, and his growing correspondence with other psychic investigators. Most people who investigated the outer fringes of the underneath world were harmless cranks, some ended up tax-paying members of strigoi society. Haven—well, Haven wasn't harmless, and she doubted he'd ever paid taxes in his life.

He thought he'd seen a werewolf in the woods, and she knew she shouldn't take it so personally. It was certainly better for the strigoi to let him believe in werewolves. And what was her problem? Did she expect him to compliment her on all her lovely fangs and the elegant length of her muzzle when she transformed into a Nighthawk? He wasn't her lover. Besides, even a real mortal lover would most likely be terrified of a Nighthawk's game face. She thought she might have been repulsed by her darling Jimmy if he had ever made that final step in the transformation of his bloodline. If Jimmy saw her as Char the Enforcer, would he be repulsed? Frightened for his life?

She shrugged slightly as her hands gripped the steering wheel. Her gaze slid to Haven's intent profile. At least Jimmy wouldn't empty a shotgun into her. Mortals were more dangerous to her kind than her kind were to mortals, she reminded herself—if one took the long-term view. *Homo sapiens sapiens* was a species with a well-deserved reputation for jealously guarding its place on the food chain. Haven was very much a hairy ape, my species right or wrong kind of guy. It would be very hard to make him understand that strigoi and mortals weren't all that different. They wouldn't be able to mate and have offspring if they were. Strigoi wouldn't crave the love of mortals if they weren't the same; that would just be too sick and weird. Jimmy had been fascinating and maybe a little kinky, but he was certainly a nicer person than Jebel "Mr. Shotgun" Haven.

She deliberately took her mind off Jimmy and focused her attention on the mortal seated silently beside her. Silence implied thought, and it was her job to make sure his thoughts were squarely on eliminating the demon they were driving around Seattle trying to sniff out. She wasn't sure where to look, but all her extra senses were alert. Something would turn up.

"Why did you change?" she asked him, when she should have explained more about demon history and physiology in order to expedite the demon's execution and Haven's own.

Haven remained silent for several minutes. When he did speak, his answer wasn't what she expected. "I robbed a convenience store. It went bad. I took a hostage, a teenage girl." His words were terse, tight, acid with bitterness. "Sara Breslow. Sara was just fifteen. Scared I was going to rape and kill her. Might have killed her. Wouldn't have raped her. Not my style."

"Well, thank goodness for that."

Char hadn't meant to speak, to encourage this confession. He already knew she'd researched how he'd become a vampire hunter, but he was sharing the why at her request. Maybe it was because he believed they'd slept together and thought she wanted to get closer. He wouldn't want that, and the truth was certainly enough to disgust most people. He didn't mind her sarcasm. In fact, he chuckled. The sound of his laughter was painful to hear. She could tell that he expected—hoped—to shock and repulse her.

"Go on," she urged, when she should have changed the subject. Her intent had been to find out why he'd taken it into his head to seek out creatures far more dangerous than the ones he'd been killing in the Southwest. Instead, he thought she was asking about *his* superhero origins.

"I took my hostage and ran from the cops. We stopped along the way at a very remote spot out in the desert. Wide place in the road—not very wide. A bar, a few houses. Doubt if there were twenty-five people that lived in this town. The night we blew into the bar, there was a trio of bikers passing through. Then Baker and his partner wandered in. Made 'em as undercover cops right away. Things got tense. Then the vampires showed up. Everybody in town ended up in the bar that night, fighting and dying together. Sara held her own. She and Baker, Santini and me. It changed us." He gave his low, painful chuckle again. "Saved us. Killed us—killed Sara a couple years later. She'd turned into quite a monster hunter, but they got her. No going home for her. Or Baker. Ruined Baker's marriage and career. Gave Santini religion. Gave me—"

"Purpose?"

He lit a cigarette. She hated the stench in the close confines of the car, but this was no time to protest.

"They were my partners from that night on," he said. "Friends. Family. And yeah," he agreed reluctantly. "Better to save the world than help it go to hell."

"Like you were doing the rest of your life."

"Yeah," he said, grim and tense and quite thoroughly loathing himself.

Guilt, she thought. *Guilt, remorse, and an attempt at redemption. Not bad emotions and goals. Still . . .* "It's easier to fight evil when it wears such obvious faces, isn't it?"

He turned in the narrow passenger seat to face her. "What?"

"Because something doesn't look human doesn't necessarily make it a monster," Char answered.

"You on their side, sweetheart?"

"I'm playing devil's advocate for the moment."

"The devil doesn't need advocates."

Char braked for a stoplight. "Demons certainly don't."

Haven could tell that she'd decided not to get into an argument with him. Too bad, he'd like to hear her defense of, say, werewolves. He wanted to ask her how she'd become a vampire hunter, but getting to know people was dangerous. Fucking this woman had been bad enough—in that it had felt too good.

Haven peered out through the beaded raindrops on the windshield. "We're driving around in circles. You got a plan for tonight, sweetheart?"

"Yes." The light changed, and she put her foot on the gas.

"Going to tell me about it?"

"I'm looking for something I can't see. A place I can't feel."

"I've been looking for that place a long time." He didn't know what made him say that. It didn't sound cynical, it sounded like the truth. Sharing the truth with someone was more dangerous than having sex with them. With Charlotte McCairn, he was making every mistake in the book. He might even invent a few more mistakes to pull on her before the hunt for Danny boy was over.

Char chose to explain what she meant rather than pursue Haven's comment. She wasn't here to analyze him or hear his confession. "Remember the building we were in last night? How it didn't appear to be there but was?"

Haven caught on fast. "Magical camo. Holes in the city."

"Precisely."

"Look for something that isn't there." He leaned his head back and closed his eyes. "I can do that."

"You sure this is the way?"

Haven grinned at her. "No." He gestured toward the entrance of the alley. "You want to take point or should I?"

"Chivalry, I see, is dead."

"Better chivalry than me, sweetheart."

"Good point. Follow me." Char ignored the stench of rotting garbage and human waste and went in.

The alley was clogged with overflowing Dumpsters on this end. Farther in she could make out rubble, piles of pipes and bricks and shards of broken glass from the caved-in back wall of a burned-out building. She ignored the ruin and concentrated on the black emptiness at the far end of the narrow alley. Magic was thick all around them, muffling the sound of their steps, muffling their senses as well.

This is a dangerous place, Char thought and reached out to touch a damp brick wall to reassure herself that she was not imagining reality. She encountered cold slime and jerked her hand back to stare at it. Her palm glowed sickly green for a moment, then faded as she fought off the warping of reality.

"You with me, Charlotte?"

"I'm here."

"Get moving, sweetheart."

Not only was this dangerous territory, full of barely structured magic and possible trap spells, but the annoying part was that Jebel Haven had been the one to find it. While she'd driven, with her senses tuned to the rhythm and pulse of her city, Haven had slouched in his seat with his eyes closed and his emotions tuned down to nothing. She'd decided he was napping when he suddenly announced he had something, and they'd followed his internal radar to this area near the docks.

He had his uses, did this mortal covering her back. He *was* behind her, right?

Something was behind her.

Paranoia blossomed as Char turned to see and cursed herself because she thoughtlessly moved faster than was mortally possible.

Haven was not behind her. She had a moment's relief before the worry set in. "Haven?"

No answer.

"Jebel?"

Char put her hands on her hips. Where had the man gone? A noise from inside the burned ruin gave her a clue. A tingle of recognition deep inside her mind sounded a warning. Daniel? She moved toward the blackened hole. She had to step over a pile of rubble to get to the opening. A sharp piece of metal caught the hem of her jeans, slowing her for a moment as she bent down to tug her pant leg free. A foot-long piece of torn and twisted metal came away from the pile and she grabbed it to keep it from falling noisily to the ground.

With the pipe in one hand, she gazed into the skeleton of the building. The darkness inside the ruin was not as complete as the complete absence of light at the end of the alley, but it was still pretty damn dark. Black soot on every surface added to the interior darkness. Despite the dampness, the smell of old smoke permeated the air.

Char peered up toward the roof. The place looked like a stiff breeze would finish pushing it over. It would not be safe to enter the ruin, even if there weren't all sorts of supernatural creatures and evil minions that could be lurking about. So, of course, for some reason unknown to god, goddess, or strigoi, Jebel Haven had decided— without bothering to mention his intentions to her—to have a look inside.

Something had moved in here, and it hadn't moved like a human. Haven spared a glance for Charlotte through the broken stretch of wall. Her attention remained intently centered on the darkness ahead. He wasn't going to let anything distract her. He'd take out whatever lurked in here, waiting to ambush her from behind. He didn't hear anything or catch any other movement, but he was aware of a shape deep in the shadows, watching him. He didn't move directly toward it or look its way. He took another step away from Charlotte, putting himself between her and the lurker. He wished he had his flamethrower with him. Too bad his shotgun was back in the Jeep. What he did have in his hands was a semi-automatic pistol with a cross carved on each bullet cartridge. Too bad there was no silver in the bullets, but he didn't think it was the werewolf inside the ruins.

"Yo, motherfucker," he said quietly, not wanting to draw Charlotte's attention to the situation. "Let's have a look at you."

"Watch your mouth, snack food," a deep, masculine voice replied from the darkness.

Haven smiled.

Something moved, faster than Haven's eyes could track it. Haven's reflexes responded; he fired at the blur, saw that the blur had fangs, and kept firing. A yowl of pain filled the night in front of Haven. A banshee screech sounded behind him.

Charlotte shouted, "Jebel, look out!"

Then the wall fell down on him.

Char pushed Haven aside as she rushed past. He fell toward the weakened wall she'd pushed down in her hurry to get inside. He went down under a pile of bricks. She slammed the vampire into the back wall of the ruin with deliberate violence.

Then she started hitting him.

He struck back, kicked at her. She darted backward, danced forward, ducked under his guard. He snarled and snapped. Char laughed.

She didn't know when her claws came out, but she'd ripped long slashes on his face and chest before she noticed the enticing smell of vampire blood in the air. Fury fueled sudden hunger. It made her want to taste him, to rip his heart out and swallow it whole. He continued to flail at her, but it did him no good. He was no match for her, and it was time to make an end. She'd punished him for daring to attack what was hers; now he'd die.

The realization that she wanted to kill this strigoi was what kept her from following the impulse. It didn't lessen the craving for the kill, but reason helped put a leash on her impulses. She might be the judge, jury, and executioner of her kind, but she firmly believed everyone deserved a trial.

Let's make it a short one.

She stopped playing with her food and pushed him back against the wall, holding him there with one hand on his chest. He was a lot taller than she was. This could not be Daniel. He was strong—and sane. Not young. "Who are you?" The words came out slurred, but she spoke in a language that minimized the difficulty of talking around a lot of teeth. She shook him and made him look her in the muzzle. "Strig or nest? Tell me about the demon. What were you doing with my mortal?" She glanced over her shoulder. Haven was stirring, but not fully conscious yet. "Good thing Haven isn't dead."

"He's supposed to be dead," the vampire answered. "There's a bounty on Haven."

She realized that the vampire had a bullet hole just below his left eye. Haven had fired several times. She'd bet that the mortal had hit his attacker more than once. "Good." She dug a claw into the vampire's chest. "Haven is mine."

The vampire looked past her to the man on the

ground. He licked his lips. "What good is he to you, Hunter?"

Her stomach twisted in disgust. "He's not prey. You don't have permission to hunt."

"I'm no strig," he answered indignantly. "Word came that Haven was in Washington. I came looking for him. From Carnation. Thought Haven might be on the trail of the sorcerer that blew into town a few months ago."

"Haven's with me."

"I can see that."

Istvan, she thought. Istvan didn't know she was using Haven to track a demon. He must think that Haven had gotten away from her. Or, more likely, he thought she'd fallen down on the job he'd given her. So he'd put a contract out on the street. Made Haven lawful prey. *Bastard.*

But if Istvan had declared a hunt, she couldn't very well kill a vampire that was simply looking for a kosher meal.

"Haven's mine," she said again. "I don't care who declared a hunt; I'm the Enforcer of Seattle right now, and I rescind it."

"But—!" She dug a claw into his chest. "Yes, Hunter!"

Haven groaned behind her. He was definitely coming around this time. She heard him pushing bricks aside.

"Wha—?" He groaned again. "Vampire!" She heard him hunting for his dropped gun.

Char wasn't finished with the Carnation vampire, but this was no time to continue their conversation. "I've got him!" she called back to the mortal. Her back was to Haven, her Nighthawk form hidden in the pitch-dark corner beneath a stairwell where she'd pushed Haven's attacker.

She'd dropped the pipe when she'd jumped the strigoi but remembered almost tripping over the jagged piece of metal during the fight. It was still near her foot. She snatched it off the ground and plunged it into the vampire's heart with one swift, hard thrust.

He screamed and clutched at the pipe as he slid to the ground. Char knelt beside him and spoke low and swift, "Play dead, or I'll rip your heart out." She twisted the steel shard for emphasis. Blood spurted over her hands. A trickle of blood flowed from the vampire's mouth. He instantly stiffened and rolled his eyes back in his head, holding his breath when she knew he really needed to scream. He looked quite convincingly dead, at least here in the darkest corner of the burned-out building in the middle of the night.

Then, on a flash of inspiration, Char whispered, "Tell your nest leader I'll be on my way to Bainbridge tomorrow."

Haven was beside her in the next instant. "You okay?" they asked each other at the same time.

Char got to her feet and backed away from the body. She wanted Haven to follow her, but he stared down at the still form instead. "You wounded it," she told him. "Enough so that he wasn't too hard to finish off. Is that Daniel?" she added for verisimilitude.

"Not our boy." He nudged the body with his foot. "Too bad."

Haven swayed on his feet, and Char rushed to take

his arm. He tried to shake her off, but she wasn't having any of it. "You look terrible," she told him.

"How can you tell? It's dark."

"There's blood on your face." She touched his temple and her fingers came away sticky with fresh mortal blood. They were already covered in the vampire's blood. Messy night. Haven didn't protest when she ran her hands over his chest and sides, he just groaned. "Cracked ribs, too, I think." She pulled him toward the alley. "At least bruised. I'm getting you out of here."

She very much wanted to find out what was behind the black veil of magic at the end of the alley, but getting Haven away so the Carnation vampire could crawl off to safety was her top priority. Besides, Haven needed some first aid.

She wasn't taking him back to her place, though. Not this time. "Let's get you back to your hotel, Jebel." She put as much psychic command in her words as she dared with someone like Haven.

The blow to his head muddled his thought processes enough to let her get away with it. "My hotel." He blinked at her. "Yeah. Sure." A stupid smile lifted his lips. "We'll go back to my hotel."

"Oh, brother," she muttered, and led him out of the alley.

Chapter 18

"GOOD MORNING."

Good. Morning. Jebel Haven considered these two words, and that it was Santini who had spoken them. He did not feel good. He'd felt worse, but good was not how he'd describe his condition. Morning. Okay, he could deal with morning. He hadn't seen the world in the daylight for a while.

"Where the hell have you been?" was his response to Santini's cheerful greeting. He did not open his eyes yet. He knew the blazing headache would only get worse when he opened his eyes. He wanted coffee. He wanted a cigarette. He didn't want to have to move from the bed to get them. "Where's Charlotte?"

"Chick split. Said she was going demon hunting."

Haven didn't remember being dropped off. He remembered—a wall falling on him. A body with a stake sticking out of its heart. And Charlotte McCairn covered in blood and not particularly concerned about it. Cute little Charlotte had done the monster—fast, efficient, no nonsense about it.

"That's my girl," he murmured.

Or werewolf, possibly.

Sitting only increased the blazing ache in his head and side, but Haven was used to ignoring his injuries. He made himself think around the pain and went looking for memories of the previous night.

He opened his eyes and noticed that Charlotte had thoughtfully left a bottle of aspirin and a glass of water on the nightstand. She'd brought him here and cleaned him up. Yeah, right, he remembered that. Her hands had been gentle. More memory returned as he got up and downed four tablets. Pity she'd had to push the wall over on him to get to her prey, or he wouldn't have this head-ache she'd been so concerned about.

He didn't think she'd hit him on the head with a wall on purpose. Charlotte was—nice. You know, for a monster. Girl said she was a monster slayer. And she'd undoubtedly saved his life last night. But . . . He took the piece of shotgun ammo he'd fished from her kitchen garbage can from his pocket and he rolled this evidence between his fingers. He'd filled her full of steel shot, and the worst damage it had done was to make her spit up. He'd actually recognized the baggy raincoat first but told himself he had to be nuts.

She hadn't finished him on the mountain. She'd slept with him. She'd saved him last night. What was she up to?

What was he going to do about her?

He didn't want to think about it. He didn't want to think at all. "Coffee?"

"Right here."

Santini handed Haven a cup from the room's little pot. It tasted awful, possibly the worst cup of coffee in

Seattle. It was scalding hot, and Haven finished it in three gulps. Charlotte made great coffee. He remembered sitting in the kitchen at her friend's place, drinking coffee and talking shop. It was all domestic and cozy— and warped. The thought almost made him smile.

"Screw it," he said and squinted around the headache to look at Santini. "Why'd you take off the other night?"

"Spotted the skinny asshole that tried to pick me up. Think he came back to the abandoned headquarters to get something. Had something in his arms when I chased after him." Santini sat on the room's other bed and tossed Haven a pack of cigarettes.

"Thanks."

Santini gave one of his manic grins while Haven lit up.

"Charlotte's been teaching me manners." He dragged smoke into his lungs. "I don't suppose you caught the bastard and made him take you to Danny boy?"

"Didn't let him know I was following him, did I? Think I found the new hideout. Been staking it out waiting for you to show up."

"You *think?*" *Santini waited?* The biker wasn't the patient type. "How many of these fuckers are there?"

"Two, three dozen. They've got guards posted now. And there's . . ." He shrugged. "Whole area around their new place feels wrong. Must be magic," Santini concluded. " 'Cause I get scared and confused when I go near it, and I don't get scared and confused. Della says the dark magic's growing."

"Della?"

"The lady at the shelter. I've been sleeping there," Santini answered.

"Sleeping with her."

Santini raised an eyebrow and gave a knowing wink. "Woman's hot. Into things I only seen in porn movies."

"Bites and scratches, does she?"

"Better her than what usually wants to bite me. You have a problem? You haven't been sleeping at home. I've checked. You're doing pretty Miss Charlotte. Della says so."

"How would Della—"

"She says it's inevitable—and a lot of stuff I don't understand. Della sees things."

Haven kept his response to himself. Della's hallucinations and Santini's getting laid were none of his business. Killing Danny and the demons were. And Charlotte.

He'd had sex with a werewolf. Jesus.

He scrubbed his hands over his face. He needed a shave. He needed a plan.

He didn't need the loud knock that sounded on the door just as he turned to go into the bathroom. Haven had a gun in his hand even as Santini moved to take a cautious look through the small window next to the door. They were not expecting company. Of course, the company they usually got wasn't polite enough to knock.

"Charlotte?"

Santini shook his head. The biker looked disgusted, but he didn't hesitate to unlock the door. Haven cautiously lowered the gun, but he didn't put it down.

Haven almost wished he was being attacked by vampires when he saw who Santini let into the room. "I'm tired of waiting for a report, Haven," the woman said.

It was Special Agent Brenda Novak, the mother of the vampire he was going to track down and kill.

"Isn't this fucking great?" he greeted the woman, and sat back on the bed, wishing he could pass out again.

"Not good enough! Pitiful creature! How am I supposed to work with the dregs of the streets? The sacrifice is barely worth killing."

"I want to kill," the Vessel said. "I like it when the magic flows into me. The way it's building in me—I need the rush."

"It's not about you," the Prophet snapped at the Vessel. "You serve a higher purpose."

"Yeah, yeah," the Vessel said. "You're going to make us all immortal."

"The one that idiot brought in last night is hardly worth the trouble of performing the ceremony. The Angel barely bled him. What was that fool thinking?"

"He doesn't think," the Demon said. "He obeys. All the kiddies are in off the street. Might as well light the candles and sharpen the knife."

The Disciple listened, but only to make sure all the shouting, pacing, and raging in the other room didn't disturb the Angel. He hadn't dared close the door all the way, but he'd pushed it closed far enough to give a semblance of privacy with the Angel. Everyone was gathered, preparing, waiting. He'd have to join in the ceremony soon. They'd notice his absence in a minute.

The Prophet, the Demon, and the Vessel would call

him out, or worse, march in and disturb the Angel's sleep with their complaints. They didn't think the Angel could hear them in his holy sleep, but the Disciple knew better. He knew because the Angel spoke inside his head. Not often, and he had to listen very hard. It had to be utterly still, and they needed to be alone. It was best if he touched the Angel; then the Angel spoke to him skin to skin—no words or images when they touched, but the Disciple would *know*.

The Disciple knew the Angel was unhappy, deeply troubled. Giving and taking the blessing of blood was growing less important. The Disciple was worried about the heretics that searched the city even though the Prophet and Demon were smugly certain that nothing could happen to them.

All they thought about were themselves. They didn't give a damn about the Angel.

But he did.

"I have to go." He stroked the Angel's strong white hand. He knelt and cupped the Angel's beautiful face in his hands. "We're going to have another sacrifice," he told his lover, his master, his Angel. "To help you."

Some of it would. The ceremony would grab the sacrifice's soul and transform it. Some of the magic would go into the Vessel, stored for the Great Transformation. But some of that magical energy, far less than the Disciple liked, would serve to protect the Angel. They needed something, someone, stronger. It was up to the Disciple to find a truly powerful sacrifice.

"Tonight," he promised his sleeping lover. "Tonight I'll bring you what you need."

•   •   •

"I kicked major butt. Me. Char. Nighthawk. Enforcer. Hunter. Me," she addressed a passing gull. "That's me." Char giggled, glad to be alone on the top section of the observation deck. The water below was smooth and beautiful, black and deep out here between the island and the city. She pressed a closed fist to her chest, then punched the air a couple of times. Her eyes glittered in the dark that was not dark to her. She wanted to crow. "Superhero. With my secret identity intact. I've got what it takes. Really. How 'bout that?"

Char turned her face to the wind, lifted her cup of Starbucks in a salute to herself, and looked back on the city skyline as it receded in the distance. She took in a deep breath of sea air and smiled. This was her third ferry trip between Seattle and Bainbridge Island tonight, and she wasn't bored yet. She doubted if she would be, even if she rode all night. It was about a half-hour trip each way on the big commuter ferry. It had still been rush hour when she'd come aboard soon after sunset among a huge crowd of pedestrian traffic. She'd stayed on after her fellow passengers disembarked. She was enjoying the privacy, and the water was soothing.

She chuckled, remembering that one of the legends about her kind was that they couldn't cross running water. Terribly inconvenient, as well as ridiculous. She'd always loved the Washington State Ferries, even when she'd had to use them in the winter and had no aspirations of becoming a vampire. Okay, they made commuting hell and you had to live your life by the ferry schedule to get to and from the islands in the Sound.

But she still loved the big white boats that tied together the islands and peninsulas of Puget Sound.

On board the ferries, she could be part of the crowd and anonymous all at once. In the world but not of it. Besides, they had Ivar's clam chowder in the cafeteria tonight. She'd had a celebratory bowlful for dinner, then brought her coffee up to the top deck where it was too windy and cold for even the tourists to go. Up here she could gloat a little without anyone being any the wiser.

I really am an Enforcer. When I had to act, it just came to me. I've been so scared it was some kind of mistake. Well, hot damn! As Mr. Haven would say.

"Jebel, baby, I owe you." Not that he was anybody's baby, of course.

Last night she'd been too busy to savor her victory. In fact, she'd been too angry at first at the vampire's presumption at attacking Haven, then too concerned with seeing to Jebel's injuries to even realize what she'd done. Then during the day, the daymare had been too vivid to let in any echoes of last night's events.

Char shook her head, sobered by the knowledge that another mortal had been ritually murdered while she was frozen in her bed today. She finished the coffee and studied the lights of the city. Somewhere down near the water, a man had died horribly. She couldn't pinpoint exactly where, but she'd felt it happen. She studied the docks, gantries, and warehouses down by the shoreline. Somewhere in there was a sorcerer, a demon, and a dangerous buildup of energy that was likely to blow the city apart if she didn't stop the fools soon. Laws or no Laws, she couldn't just find Daniel and walk away. Fortunately, she had a plan.

Char checked her watch. She had a plan, but a big part of it had better show up soon. She didn't have all night.

She tapped her foot impatiently and concentrated on the city once more. It seemed to her that she should somehow be able to see the stored magic, that all that power should set off a huge, pulsing, hot glow. So far, the sorcerer had been able to hide a lot from her, and she didn't like that one little bit.

Char gripped the railing and kept up her solitary watch for a few minutes longer. Then she decided that the combination of elation and trepidation had made her hungry. Maybe she'd get a hamburger from the cafeteria.

A woman rose with serene grace from a seat on one of the outside benches when Char came down the stairs to the next deck. There was no one near her. Char met the strigoi's gaze, nodded slightly, and came to join her. "Hi, Connie," Char greeted the nest leader of Carnation breezily.

She almost apologized for her tone when the nest leader frowned. Char knew very well that the reserved Constance ran a tight, old-fashioned household and didn't go in for informality. In fact, Constance politely waited for Char to invite her to take a seat on the bench.

Char sat down and graciously gestured for Constance to join her. Then she held out her hand. Constance placed a heavy gold coin in Char's palm.

Char looked at the incised image of a stooping owl on the coin, and her light mood sobered with the seriousness of the moment. She clutched the coin in her fist. It was still warm from Constance's hand. This was treasure indeed, the first acknowledgment that she was indeed Nighthawk, Enforcer of the Laws. Enforcer of the City. She gazed out once again on the skyline of Seattle, shaken with the wonder and rightness of it all. She'd been born here, twice. It was right that she would come into her own in the place that was her home.

In the meantime, it was time to put ceremony and sentimentality aside. She slipped the coin into a velvet pouch she'd brought for the occasion and tucked the pouch into her pocket. Char folded her hands in her lap, looked at the waiting Constance, and said, "Thank you for coming."

Constance gave a slight nod. "I am at your disposal, Hunter." She added, "Pascal sends his apologies for interfering in your affairs. He thanks you for his life."

"He lives to hunt again." Char smiled. "Soon."

Constance tilted her elegant head to one side. She had high cheekbones and uptilted eyes. Char would have killed for the nest leader's makeup secrets. Constance lifted one beautifully shaped eyebrow in question. Her serene expression hadn't changed one bit, but Char was well aware of the woman's intense interest. "You're declaring a hunt?"

"Pascal mentioned that your nest is aware of a mortal sorcerer practicing in Seattle. How?"

"We don't live that far from the city, Hunter. We come into Seattle sometimes. It's hard not to be aware of the . . . dark spots. Not very pleasant. We've been avoiding Seattle for the last two months because of it."

"You know about the serial killings?"

"Only what's been mentioned on the local news." Constance made a slight gesture. "None of our affair."

It is now, sister. Char said, "Do you know anything about a missing nestling? Or a demon?" Constance shook her head. "Didn't think so. Never mind them. What I need from your nest is a hunt."

Constance favored Char with a wide smile. "In time for the holiday. Happy to oblige, Hunter. Who do we hit?"

Char didn't know exactly how many members belonged to the sorcerer's cult, but there would be a great many fewer loyal minions for her and Haven to have to deal with after the Carnation vampires got in on the act. She'd had a few qualms about the deaths of so many mortals when she'd come up with the plan last night. That was before she'd felt today's ritual. The minions had all been there. They'd participated. Maybe they were slaves to a vampire, but they were also helping a mortal commit vicious, dangerous crimes. Besides, Daniel was too young to have slaves.

"There's a nut cult called the Angel's Children. I want them all dead."

Hunger flared in Constance's eyes. "We're a small nest, Hunter, but we'll do our best. When do we hunt?"

The ferry was coming into the Seattle dock. Char stood up. "You have a place in town?" Constance nodded and told her a phone number. Char memorized it. "I'll get back to you soon," she told the nest leader and walked away. She thought she did a credible job of disappearing mysteriously in the crowd heading for the pedestrian exits.

Chapter 19

"THERE'S A SPLATTER pattern on the back wall, Haven." Novak swept the tight beam of the small flashlight she'd taken from her purse from the wall to the ground. "Bloodstains here. But nothing in the crime scene bears any resemblance to the serial killer's signature. Local homicide isn't my problem . . . even if you're the perp. What happened to the body? I suppose the cult members took it," she answered her own question. "More importantly, what did the attack have to do with Danny?" A hint of excitement entered her voice. "You must be onto something after all."

"After all?" Haven asked.

"Don't see any scorch marks," Santini said, drawing Haven away from confronting the woman. Santini squatted and ran his fingers over the ground. "No ashes." He sniffed, shrugged, and bounced to his feet again. Haven knew that his partner wasn't going to say anything more in front of Special Agent Novak. Santini stepped back into the alley and walked into the darkness at the end of it instead. He came back in a few seconds. "Nothing in there."

"How can you tell?" Novak asked.

"He can tell."

"Walked in and had a look around," Santini said.

Novak rubbed her upper arms, chilled from the inside out, Haven knew. "I can barely look in that direction. It's like there's a hole in my vision."

"You'll get used to it."

"It's spooky."

After the seriously sick shit he'd heard FBI profilers got involved with, the last thing he expected was one to be spooked. He guessed the magic worked on Agent Novak as much as it did on him.

"Safe house, maybe," Santini suggested. "Or a decoy." He gestured to the blood-streaked wall. "Trap."

"Sprung and survived." Haven took a drag of his cigarette and tossed the butt away. It sizzled out in the nearest puddle. This town had plenty of puddles. With all the rain in this part of the world, it made him wonder how the ruins he stood in could have burned down.

"Arson," Novak said.

He knew he hadn't spoken aloud, but she didn't seem to notice. He'd gotten to expect any kind of weirdness since blowing into Seattle, even an FBI agent reading his mind didn't faze him at the moment. It was too dark in the ruined building. He stepped out into the alley, closer to streetlights and car headlights. Novak followed him.

Her angry glare as she stepped over a pile of bricks to stand in front of him didn't disturb him, either. "Don't tell me, Novak, you don't care about missing bodies or empty buildings you can't quite see."

"I don't care about where Danny *isn't*. I want to find out where my son *is*."

Fine with him. He hadn't wanted her to tag along when he brought Santini back to the scene. *She* insisted when he mentioned being attacked near what he thought was the cult's new headquarters. After all, *she* was the expert at forensic analysis. She'd grown impatient waiting for them to deliver sonny boy and had come to help. Novak wanted a look at the crime scene. He hadn't mentioned anything about vampires—or Charlotte—to the FBI agent.

"You've come up with some leads," she said. "I'm grateful for what you've done. But it's time I followed up on those leads myself." Santini came up to stand beside them, and she turned to him. "I want to talk to this woman you said put you onto the cult."

"Della."

She nodded. "I'd like to meet her this evening, Santini."

Santini looked at Haven.

"Take her." Haven very much wanted Novak away from the alley and burned-out building. He glanced back into the deep darkness by the broken wall. "Go on," he told Santini. "I've got other plans."

Once Santini and Novak were out of earshot, he turned back to the deep darkness a few feet inside the alley mouth. "You can come out now, Charlotte."

Char unwrapped herself from the shadows and took a step toward Haven.

"How do you do that?"

She couldn't help but notice he'd slipped a small cross out of his pocket. "Is that silver?"

"Yes."

She held out her hand. "May I?" He frowned as he handed her the cross. He flinched, as if he expected her to go up in flames when her fingers closed on the metal. She balanced it on her palm "Heavy. Solid silver, I think. Beautiful workmanship." She held it up before her eyes. "Spanish, isn't it? And very old. Silver doesn't bother me," she added, handing the cross back. "Why would you think it would?"

"You're not human." He didn't sound happy.

"I most certainly am human."

Haven's wide shoulders blocked the alley entrance. Char stepped forward, then moved with immortal's speed to duck past him.

He whirled, still holding the cross, but no other weapons that she could see. He showed no surprise at her maneuver, nor did she feel any surprise from him. He was, indeed, a very cool customer. He asked, "What are you? A werewolf?"

"I'm a vampire hunter, Mr. Haven."

"Why'd you attack me?"

She didn't try to deny she knew what he was talking about. "Because you shot me."

"I thought you were the killer."

"I thought the same about you at the time. We were both drawn to the body. The dead woman called us there. I attacked you, Jebel, because you hurt me, but I managed to calm down before I caught you. If I hadn't gotten myself under control, I would have killed you.

But I gave *you* the benefit of the doubt. I realized that you assumed I was a bad guy when you fired. It was a reasonable assumption."

His expression remained hard, uncompromising. He gestured behind them. "What happened to the vampire?"

"Burned up by the sunlight?" she suggested.

"In this town?"

"There is daylight in Seattle at this time of year."

"That wasn't wood you stabbed it with."

"But it was effective."

"He didn't burn up when the sun came up."

She smiled. "Perhaps the rain washed his ashes away."

"His blood should have burned, too. That's how it works when vampires are staked. Everything goes up in smoke. No evidence left."

"Convenient. But I told you urban vampires are different." She thrust her hands in her raincoat pockets. "Let it drop, Jebel. We're on the same side."

"You're not human."

"I'm not mortal." She tried hard to hide her exasperation; it tended to make her fangs come out. "But I am human."

"If you're not mortal, you're a monster."

She gave a sarcastic laugh. "Excuse, me, Mr. Haven, but *I've* never done time for multiple felonies. Nor have I escaped from prison, kidnapped anyone, or even so much as jaywalked." She discovered that her hands were on her hips. She definitely sounded self-righteous. How hypocritical for someone who'd just arranged for a mass murder talking to a man she planned to kill! "I do not fire shotguns at strangers, either," she finished. "Unlike some people I know."

"We aren't strangers now."

And that was a problem, especially where the killing him after she used him part came in. "Are you planning on using something more personal than a shotgun now that we're on a first-name basis?"

He shrugged. "What kills a werewolf?"

Char shrugged back. "Rabies?"

Haven didn't want ambiguities in his life. It bothered him a little that he even knew what the word meant. Made him wish he hadn't started taking college classes before he broke out of prison the last time. She was a monster—of some sort. His life had been nice, simple, laid out for him until he met Charlotte McCairn. If it grew fangs, he killed it. Nice girls didn't grow fangs. He protected the nice girls of the world. That was how he paid the world back. It was his redemption, his purpose, his quest for goodness and honor and all that other crap.

"You've screwed up my life, girl," he told her. "Big time."

"I've broadened your perspective. You could look at it that way."

"What am I going to do with you?" *What would Baker say? What would Santini do?* He could almost hear Sara laughing at him from beyond the grave. Charlotte was like no one he'd ever met. Oh, yeah, this was complicated, all right. He rubbed the back of his neck. "What happened to you? You got bit and now you're out to get even?"

Char considered for a moment and tapped a finger against her lips. "Something like that," she said at last. "It's not catching, if that's what you're worried about." *Unless I bite you,* she added to herself.

"Unless you bite me."

She didn't think he'd picked up the thought. Just a good guess. "You're not my type," she told him. "Now, will you relax so we can get to work?"

"I'm not going to relax."

He smiled at her: that shoulders hunched, head tilted, looking up through those thick eyelashes, boyish, disarming, charming smile thing he did. She didn't understand why he smiled at her like that, but the tension that stretched out between them shifted dramatically without lessening one little bit.

Then he was kissing her, turning them back into the dark alley and pressing her against a wall. Char didn't know how *he* had moved that fast. His mouth was hard on hers, smothering her gasp of surprise and using it. His tongue thrust deep inside her open lips. His body was hard and heavy, pinning her, and Char molded herself against him, caught in a chaotic rush of pleasure. This was the last way she'd expected this confrontation to go. That he ran his tongue over her teeth did not surprise her, but it felt very nice indeed. She wanted to let it go on until their heartbeats matched and her mating fangs erupted, but she shifted her head just a fraction, and her tongue danced with his, refocusing the pleasure. His temperature rose and his scent deepened, intense enough to make her giddy. Char clutched Haven's back. If she tasted the warm blood rushing beneath his skin—

Big if. Big fat not-going-to-happen if.

It wasn't easy to stop kissing him, but Char was nothing if not stubborn once she'd made up her mind. There would be no vampire sex with Jebel Haven. Not tonight.

But that wasn't to say there wouldn't be sex.

She didn't stop him from moving his mouth down to kiss her throat. If Haven bit her on the neck, she would have laughed and enjoyed it, but he sent aching pleasure through her without having to take a nip. His hands moved over her, frantically pushing aside clothing, and she helped him. They were uneasy allies, playing with fire by coupling against a wet wall in a filthy back alley. It was sleazy, disgusting, and a complete rush.

Her one concession to propriety as Char reached for Haven's zipper was to draw the darkest, deepest shadows she could conjure around them for a few wild minutes.

Think. He had to think. The Disciple pressed his fists to his temples while he paced the hallway outside the Angel's room. There were two girls in the Angel's bed. The Disciple could hear them panting and groaning, hear the creak of the bedsprings. He could smell their musky sweat and the sweet scent of blood. The Angel's pleasure thrummed on the edge of his senses, just beyond his reach, as thrilling as it was taunting.

They'd locked him out of the room, the Demon and the Prophet, to punish him, but he didn't mind. He had to think. The Vessel was drunk, full of the magic they stored in him, sated from taking another life. Poor, stupid Vessel. He didn't understand that he was going to die. That was his purpose, to be another, grander sacrifice.

The Disciple was beginning to make out the pattern of how the Prophet and Demon were going to bring about life eternal. They were planning a great work of magic. He must bring them more sacrifices. They had to drain all the magic in the city to do their work, steal it for themselves.

They needed magic to protect the Angel. That was all that mattered to the Disciple. He had to think. Where could he find more magic? There was someone . . . someone . . . somewhere . . . he knew . . . What was the image he was trying to catch? He paced and beat his fists against his head and prayed to the fucking Angel.

And then the image burned like acid in his mind. A caustic voice burned his ears. The Witch's disdainful face snarled in his memory. It hurt to think of her. He didn't want to think of her. He hated her. Feared her. He wanted her dead. Always had. But . . .

The Witch was powerful. Stronger than him. Her death would free all the power the Prophet needed. He should have thought of it before. Her power would strengthen the spells that hid them from the hunters.

He couldn't take the Witch. His voice could not snare her to follow him. But the Angel needed her.

He had to do it. But he couldn't do it alone. "What to do? What to do?"

Not alone. The Disciple stopped pacing and cackled. He hadn't laughed in so long the sound hurt his throat. Not alone. He was not alone. There were slaves. Many slaves. More slaves than the Witch could handle. They could take her. Silence her. Hurt her. Bring her to the Prophet.

He laughed again. Yes. They'd do it tonight.

Chapter 20

Sex without blood was so cheap and tawdry.

That wasn't to say it wasn't fun, but there was no emotional commitment other than swift, fantastic, physical gratification. Char was an emotional commitment sort of woman.

Right now what she wanted to commit to was a hot shower as her breathing calmed and her heartbeat slowed to normal.

She didn't know when the cold rain had started. It was a wonder her skin didn't sizzle as the rain hit it, but instead it only served to turn the sooty muck covering her to smelly mud.

Char turned her face up to the slow, icy rain and said, "I'm filthy." When Haven chuckled in her ear, she slapped him on the shoulder. "Not like that."

"Yes, you are."

It was her turn to chuckle. She wasn't sure who was holding who up at the moment, but the wall behind her was wet and rough, and she had strained muscles as well as dirty hair and clothing. "This is so romantic I think I'm going to puke."

"That'll add to the ambiance, won't it?"

"You're not supposed to know words like ambiance," she reminded him, and pushed against him.

"Sorry."

"Say it again," she surprised herself by saying. "It sounded sexy."

"Smart's sexy, huh?"

"For me it is."

"You're weird—in a nice way."

He turned his head to look at her, and there was a smile in his bittersweet chocolate eyes. Ghiradelli had never tasted like him, she thought, and noticed a pinhead spot of blood at the end of a thin scratch on his cheek. She was tempted to kiss away the owwie and leave him to speculate what she meant by it. But she had him confused enough already, and tasting him would make a sleazy incident of hot, hard sex seem too much like an emotional encounter. So she fished a tissue out of her raincoat pocket and wiped his cheek.

"Not a good time to be playing mother, Charlotte," he said and kissed the tip of her nose.

No. That was too cute. She couldn't deal with him being adorable or acting as if she were cute and adorable. "Get off me, you weigh a ton."

She looked up and down the alley after he took a few steps away from her. She missed his warmth instantly. "I hope Santini was right about this area being abandoned by the cult people."

"If not, we just put on a show for them. But I'm betting Santini was right. There's nobody around here but you and me, and I don't think we can blame some kind of lust spell."

"That anyone cast on us," she conceded. She put her hands behind her back. "Well, we didn't solve anything. But that was nice—in a sick, perverted, disgusting way."

He ran a hand through his short hair. "About what happened—us." Haven gestured vaguely toward the wall, and walked forward, herding her onto the sidewalk beyond the alley. When they were under the nearest streetlight he said, "I'll kill you if I have to, Charlotte. If I think you're dangerous to humans, I'll kill you."

"Fair enough." She answered quite calmly, despite the ache that gripped her heart in the oddest way. Fair enough, indeed. She shook water out of her hair. "I'm freezing. I need a shower, and I need to change clothes." She checked her watch. "You, Santini, and I already know everything Della knows about the cult. I doubt the FBI woman will find out anything new."

"Keeps her out of our hair for a while."

"I'm glad you see it that way. I don't like having someone from the government knowing anything about— our profession."

There was an Enforcer who lived in Washington, D.C. Her name was Olympias, and her only function was to make sure that no government agent or official ever found out about the strigoi in America. Olympias was a vampire lobbyist, so to speak, and she would be very annoyed if all her hard work was screwed up by a rookie Enforcer thousands of miles outside the Beltway.

"I won't have the FBI finding out about vampires, Jebel."

"You giving me orders, Charlotte?" he snapped back. "You think I like having any kind of cop involved in my life? She's blackmailing us into looking for her little boy. When I have to kill her vampire baby, she's not going to be happy. I don't want Novak around any more than you do, sweetheart."

"Good. My car's just down the street," she added. "Want to come back to my place and take a shower?"

"I want to go back to your place and use the bed."

"Fine." What was she saying? They needed to be hunting Daniel and the demon! "But not until after we clean up."

"I see Jimmy left you a key."

Helene Bourbon stood up as Char crossed from the kitchen into the living room. Haven followed her in through the condo's kitchen entrance. He held a small-caliber gun in his hand.

Other than a brief, disdainful glance, Helene Bourbon ignored the mortal and the weapon centered on her. "Jimmy is a good man," she said to Char. "He likes to make people comfortable. He and Geoff issued an open invite when they left town."

Char was surprised at her lack of jealous reaction to hearing about the companion who'd followed her into Jimmy's life. She'd never met Geoff Sterling, but she hated him. Or had when he'd been Jimmy's lover after her. She shouldn't have, it was the strigoi way. Vampires took companions, who they made into vampires, and vampires could not remain lovers with the children they'd made. Incest taboo. Very big deal. She got to kill and eat people who violated it. Jimmy and Geoff had parted ways years ago. Jimmy was in Alaska now. Geoff had gone his own way. She was currently standing between a nervous nest leader and a vampire hunter with a gun. This was no time for a stroll down memory lane.

Helene wore no makeup and obviously didn't follow the current vampire fashion for tanning beds. She looked drawn and worried and not particularly mortal.

Char gestured her back into the living room. It had the softer lighting commonly used in a strigoi home. Char expected Haven to start shooting if he got a good look at the woman. Or even if he didn't. She knew well how Haven liked shooting things. That he stood warily back to find out what was going on said a lot about his overwhelming curiosity.

Having Haven with her like this, knowing what they looked like, gave Char a wincing sense of having just been busted making out with a boyfriend from the wrong side of the tracks. Mentioning Jimmy only added to the feeling. Char dismissed this reaction by reminding herself that Helene Bourbon specialized in taming teenage vampires, and she was no teenager.

"I'll join you in a moment," she told Helene. Char put her hand on Haven's arm as Helene backed into the living room. Her touch was light, the gesture seemed somewhat reassuring, somewhat pleading, but the intention was to knock the weapon away should Jebel Haven do anything rash. She glanced at the gun and said, "Why didn't I notice that earlier?" It wasn't as if she hadn't had her hands all over him.

"You were paying more attention to a larger—"

"Never mind."

"You're blushing, Charlotte." He slipped the gun into an inside pocket of his jacket and stroked her cheek. With Jebel Haven, the tender gesture and his hard expression meshed perfectly. Interesting man. "Who's your friend?"

"She's not well," Char told him, "so don't do anything else to frighten her."

"She didn't look frightened. Who is she?"

"I've told you about her. She's the woman who has me looking for Daniel."

"What's she doing here?"

"What's Special Agent Novak doing in town? Same thing as Helene. Looking for Daniel. Maternal types worry about their kids." She moved her hand up his arm to his shoulder, urging him toward the bedroom. "I need to speak with Helene. Get the shower started." She looked him in the eye and put all her power of suggestion in her next words. "Please give me a few minutes with Helene." She added a huge dose of sensual promise when she said, "I'll join you soon."

He wasn't happy about it, but he said, "Fine."

Char moved quickly as he went toward the bedroom. She didn't for a moment believe her whammy was going to last too long on Haven, if it had worked at all. The instant the bedroom door closed, she was in front of Helene Bourbon. She didn't take the time to ask what the woman was doing in Seattle. "Daniel's birth mother is with the FBI," she informed Helene. "She's in town looking for her son." Char waited until she heard the sound of the shower going on. "You take responsibility for Daniel now, therefore you should deal with his mother."

The nest leader considered Char's meaning for the length of a heartbeat. "I'll see to her, Hunter."

Char hated the Enforcer's choice she'd just made and that Helene so quickly agreed to murder a stranger. Helene understood her duty to protect the strigoi's secrets. The mortal woman who only wanted to find her child would die in an unsuspicious way, and Char would let her conscience bedevil her after she had the city and the strigoi safe.

"What about Daniel?" Helene asked. "Have you found him?"

"His exact location, no, but I know what's being planned for him. He has to be found very soon—or the official investigation will probably decide that a massive eruption of Mount Rainier is what caused all the destruction."

The release of enough magical energy had strong effects on the same parts of the physical world—fault lines and volcanoes, for example. The Northwest was a very active ecological area.

"What are you talking about?"

"A sorcerer and demon are planning a transformation. Old-fashioned, unstable, volatile, almost impossible to control, soul-stealing black magic."

"You're joking."

"You wish."

"But—this is a mortal magician?"

Char nodded. "With a demon sidekick." She gestured vaguely toward the bathroom. "I have someone to deal with the demon."

Helene put her hand on her forehead. "Oh, my goddess. Thousands of people could be killed. Hundreds of thousands. We have to stop them."

Another vampire might have pointed out that since there were no strigoi living in Seattle what happened to the city wasn't the vampire community's problem. Helene Bourbon was good people, humanity in all its variations mattered to her. "You one of Jimmy's kids?"

The nest leader gave the slightest of wistful smiles. "We knew each other, long ago."

Jimmy made a point of picking good ones, though Char had heard that Geoff Sterling had been heavy into the silly blood-drinking Goth scene when Jimmy picked him up. Well, as long as it was all voluntary, good dirty fun, she supposed what adults did—

Char fought off her tendency to think too much. She was the chief action hero in this crisis and had to act quickly. "Daniel's mother went to have a talk with Della," she told Helene. "I think you should meet her there." She gave Helene her cell phone number and showed her to the front door. "Let me know how your meeting turns out."

Helene nodded and was gone. Char walked out of the living room. "You don't look very clean," she said, and moved past Haven, who'd been eavesdropping just out of sight. He followed her toward the bathroom. "That better be only cold water you've got running," she told him.

Chapter 21

"TELL ME I'M mistaken."

Charlotte stood in front of the steamed-up mirror; he was looking at her naked reflection. He wanted to reach around her, cup her breasts, and watch her expression as he stroked them, but he settled on being satisfied with her having a reflection.

She gave him a wary look over her shoulder as she finished brushing her hair. "Mistaken about what?"

"Tell me you didn't order a hit on someone." The women had chosen their words very carefully and spoken low enough so that he could barely hear, but there was something in the air.

She gazed at him with those big, innocent eyes of hers and said, "Do I look like someone with the authority to order other people around?"

"Maybe you showed her your fangs."

She put down the brush and tossed her hair. "I'm not that kind of girl."

She tucked her hair behind her ears, then walked out of the bathroom. Silence drew out between them while they got dressed. He knew she was waiting for him to ask a question, but he put it off while he zipped up his jeans and put his shirt back on. He thought about himself, wondered why he had the hots for her. Some kind of spell she'd put on him? She didn't deny knowing magic. Animal magnetism? He almost laughed at the thought. He was used to being the one who was the animal.

"You like talking to me," she said. "That's the attraction."

"Stop reading my mind."

"It's your body language."

Haven finished buttoning his shirt and faced her. "All right." It surprised him that he had to pause and take a shaky breath before he spoke. Maybe he really didn't want to know. "What are you?"

He watched her pick up a slender silver dagger and slip it into an arm sheath. "A Virgo?"

"I'm not laughing, Charlotte."

"Char. Please call me Char."

She took out a black leather jacket from a suitcase and put it on over a black turtleneck and black jeans. Her dark red hair was pulled back from her face. The overall effect did not make her look tougher or more dangerous than the young woman in the loose blue raincoat he'd been spending time with, but she did look sexier.

"Why Char?"

"Because it suits what I do, who I am."

He gestured toward her. "Which is?"

"An Enforcer of the Law. A kind of cop. I don't think I should tell you more than that."

"But you're going to, right?"

"Jebel! I can't!"

He smiled at the exasperated whine in her voice. "Chaaar," he whined back. Then the humor left him. He looked around this bedroom that had belonged to her old lover and remembered her conversation with the other woman. "This is a safe house, isn't it? And you ordered a hit, didn't you? Who are you?"

He should reach for a weapon, but he didn't want to. The world was bigger, deeper, darker than he'd ever suspected. He was used to being an executioner, but he was new at discerning shades of gray in the evil he fought. Ambiguity sucked.

Char sat down on the bed to put on her shoes. She looked up at him as she answered. "Up until now, I've been an archivist, a researcher, a supernatural librarian. I've hidden in books and behind a computer—I'm really good at hacking, by the way. I keep track of things and provide information. These are useful and necessary tasks for a loosely organized bunch like the Enforcers. But there are so few Enforcers that no one of us has the right to hide and refuse to do the job we're reborn for."

"Reborn?"

"You heard me. I think you know what I mean."

"I think I want you to tell me."

"You've seen me in my working outfit." She drew her lips back in a snarl, but didn't sprout any new teeth. "I'm not a werewolf. I'm a Nighthawk."

"You can fly?"

She gave an exasperated sigh. "No, but I can run pretty darn fast."

"An Enforcer of the Law. What law? Whose law?"

She stood. "You don't want to go there, Jebel. Not if you want to live until morning."

"Why, Charlotte McCairn, I do believe you're threatening me."

He thought about drawing the gun in his jacket but figured shooting her would just annoy her. She was physically tougher than he was, wasn't she? He actually found that kind of attractive. Mentally, though, he figured he had the edge.

"Jebel Haven," she said as she rubbed a spot on the middle of her forehead. She shook her head. "I can't do this; I just can't." She got up from the bed. He stood back and let her pace the width of the room a few times. She finally stopped in front of him. "My people are different," she said. "Human groups fear other groups that are different than they are. My people are more vulnerable to this innate prejudice than any other ethnic group. My job is to protect my people. I believe in trying to do it without harming . . . any other ethnic group. I'm as much of a good guy as I can be—and still protect my people. I don't want Agent Novak to die. I really don't. But she can't find Daniel and take him home. He belongs to my people now."

"He's a vampire."

"Yeah. How about that?"

"You said you're a vampire hunter."

"I am."

He couldn't take it any further. He should. He looked at her. He remembered making love to her. A vivid image of the half-rotting, almost mindless monsters he fought out in the desert flashed through his mind. One of them wore Charlotte's face. The vampire that attacked him in the alley had talked to him. She'd talked about smart urban ones. Her *people*? He couldn't ask.

"What have you done to me?" he asked her.

"Typical male. Always blaming the woman. Let's go." She walked out of the bedroom.

He could do nothing but follow. "Where we going?" he asked when they were in the car.

"To Della's." She backed out too fast and put the car in gear with an angry, jerking motion. She looked straight ahead through the windshield as she added angrily, "I can't let Helene go through with murder. I just can't do it."

Haven relaxed in the passenger seat. "Wimp."

Charlotte's faint laughter told him she accepted it as the compliment he intended.

"What the fuck is going on?"

"Nothing to do with us," Char said as they waited for the police to clear the angry crowd from the middle of the street. "For once. But I do wish they'd get out of the way." Char refused to move her hand to the middle of the steering wheel and add her horn to the raucous chorus coming from all the disgruntled motorists caught in the traffic jam. She looked at the dashboard clock and shook her head. "What are these idiots doing out here at this time of night? Getting plenty of media attention." She answered her own question. The noise and lights of a news helicopter circling overhead confirmed her cynical remark. There was a lot of shouting nearby, and the sound of shattering glass. Windshield? Windows? Beer bottles? Hard to say. It wasn't her concern. "Honestly. I'm all in favor of free assembly and protest rallies, but why now?"

They were stuck in traffic on the edge of the downtown area, somewhere near the hotels where delegates were staying, she surmised. They'd been stopped still for some time, and Jebel Haven was not a patient man.

The delay was making her nervous. She'd tried calling Helene's cell phone but had gotten no answer. An attempt at mental contact with the nest leader hadn't been any more successful since they might share a bloodline but certainly didn't know each other. The night wasn't getting any younger, either. That could work for or against them, depending on what Helene planned for Daniel's birth mother.

"So, I repeat, What the f—"

"Language, Jebel."

"—hell is going on?"

"You don't listen to public radio, do you?"

"I don't even listen to country radio. And CNN isn't my thing, either," he added.

"ESPN?"

He flashed her a grin. "Guilty as charged." He gestured at the chaos outside the car. "Explain, please?"

Char had read about it all in a newspaper she'd picked up on the ferry. "Some sort of huge trade organization meeting in town. Lots of protesters protesting." Char thought there might be more police officers on the street than actual protesters.

"What?"

"Globalization of markets, I guess."

"Sorry I asked." He shook his head.

She smiled. "Wouldn't you rather find out how to kill a demon?"

"Definitely."

A cop directing traffic motioned them forward, and Char followed other cars as they inched through the congested intersection. She was grateful that the traffic cleared within a couple blocks. Driving in Seattle was bad enough. Clots of angry humanity adding to the traffic snarls didn't help. The last time Char recalled anyone taking to the streets had been . . . 1992, wasn't it? Some small-scale rioting after the Rodney King thing in Los Angeles?

Rodney King. Riots. Los Angeles. That reminded Char of some strigoi history she'd researched, and her smile had a slight amount of fang in it. She recalled that in Los Angeles, rioting had been used several times to cover the activities of hunts, and she had a hunt to cover. "This could be useful."

"What could?"

"Ever heard of the zoot suit riots?"

"No."

"In Los Angeles, in the forties. Never mind, they had nothing to do with killing demons. Do you own a sword, Jebel?" He gave her a sardonic look. "I guess not. You might want to get one, because the only way to be sure to kill a demon is to behead it. I should have mentioned that sooner, shouldn't I?" she asked after a few moments of annoyed silence from Haven.

"Lots of things you should have mentioned sooner, Char."

"Possibly." Her cell phone rang before he could react to her equivocal answer. "Hello? Helene! I'm glad you called. Listen—What?"

"What?" Haven repeated her question.

Char banged a fist on the steering wheel, then tightened one hand around the wheel while she clutched the phone to her ear with the other. She pressed her foot down on the accelerator while Helene Bourbon talked. "My fault," she answered. "I should have expected something like this. How many? Della? What about Novak? Right, you've never met her. I'd completely forgotten about Blessing Day. The eighth this year? That could be."

"What could be?" Haven said.

"What about Santini?" she asked Helene.

Haven grabbed her arm, she shook him off. "What about Santini?"

Char drove like she was immortal, ignoring all the honking and crunching of metal she left in her wake. "Little guy with a beard," she told Helene. "Tell me he isn't dead." She listened for a few tense seconds. "Thanks. I know where it is. No time. Meet me there." She turned at the next corner and headed uphill.

"The shelter's the other way! Where are you going?" She noted that Haven was holding his gun, but he hadn't threatened her with it.

"Hospital," she said to Haven. "Santini was alive when he was put in the ambulance."

"Ambulance. What happened?"

Char tossed the small phone on the dashboard and concentrated on driving very fast. She deliberately didn't look at the car clock. "Della's shelter was invaded. Helene arrived about the same time as the police. She waited to find out details before calling. The police are blaming everything in this town on demonstrators tonight. That gives us a break. A lot of people are injured. Della's missing. I'm betting Novak was taken as well. The police have no idea who took them. Or even *if* anyone's missing."

"We can guess."

"Magic is confusing the police. The cult took them, of course. Alive," she added significantly. "Della's very psychic. So's Novak. I noticed how she felt when she studied where the vampire was staked. The sorcerer will want her, too."

She and Haven exchanged a grim glance. "Human sacrifice," they said together.

Haven leaned back against the headrest. "Holy shit. You're right," he added. "You should have thought of this before."

"They may not be sacrificed right away. Helene reminded me of something just now." She held out a faint hope to him. "If this sorcerer's done his homework, he'll think that the new moon before the winter solstice is the perfect day for casting his transformation spell." Assuming this idiot knew more about the strigoi than he should. Assuming he wanted to fill his human Vessel up with all the magic he could just before he sacrificed the man. That's why she hadn't been able to detect more of the stolen psychic energy, wasn't it? It was stored in human form. Why hadn't she remembered that part of the ritual slayings sooner?

"How long do we have?" Haven's practical question interrupted her analyzing.

"The eighth. We have a few days until the eighth."

She braked sharply for an emergency vehicle, then swung into the long drive that led to the huge hilltop hospital complex. She dropped Haven off at the emergency entrance and told him to find Santini while she found a parking place.

Then she drove back to the corner where she'd seen Helene jump off the flat roof of the emergency vehicle and paused long enough for Helene to get into the car.

The woman's hair and clothes were disheveled, her eyes were bright with excitement. "I haven't done this for a while. What next, Hunter?"

"We can spare a couple hours looking for Della," Char said as she pulled back out into traffic. "Then we better find somewhere to stay for the day. Della knows where I live."

Helene nodded at Char's explanation. The truth was, that while Della *might* be compelled to reveal strigoi secrets, the real reason Char didn't plan to go home was that she didn't trust Jebel Haven not to go vampire hunting come morning. And he might pick a real vampire to hunt this time.

Chapter 22

"You came back." The Angel looked at him. Recognized him. Spoke to him.

The Disciple knelt before where the Angel sat on the bed and dared to rest his cheek against the Angel's knee. "I brought you women," he said, fighting the jealousy that raged in him. "For your bed."

The Angel stroked his hair. "I missed you." The Angel drew him up onto the bed and they stretched out side by side. The Disciple rested his head over the Angel's heart and could barely breathe for the happiness. "Don't leave me," the Angel pleaded. "Take me with you when you go again. I don't want to be here," the Angel whispered in his ear.

I love you," the Disciple told him. "I came back as soon as I could. I want you to be safe."

"Safe with you. We can go down into the dark together. I remember the dark . . . under the ground."

The Disciple longed desperately to give the Angel everything he wanted. He lived to serve. Once he'd wanted to live forever and had wanted the Angel only for that gift. But the more the Angel gave him, the more the Disciple needed to give back. The Demon and the Prophet were fools. He'd thought them so wise and powerful. They were nothing. Except—

"The Prophet's sacrifices protect you."

"Sacrifices?"

The Disciple hated the confusion and worry in the Angel's voice. Everything should be perfect for the Angel. Evil creatures were hunting the Angel. The Woman in Black wanted to take the Angel away. She knew his name. He'd felt her power. "She won't have you."

"She?"

"The Witch's death will protect you."

"My head hurts," the Angel said. "I'm sleepy."

"Then sleep," the Disciple urged, glad no one was in the Angel's bed but him. He forgot the pain in his arm and leg, in his jaw, and the burn along his ribs where the man who had been sleeping with the Witch had shot him. They'd overpowered the bastard, taken the gun away. Stupid slaves hadn't had the sense to turn the gun on the man, but they'd beaten him senseless. The Disciple hoped they'd beaten him to death. The other woman had had a gun, too, but she hadn't gotten a chance to fire it. She was beautiful, the woman with the gun, her soul full of the magic fire. He was delighted to find her with the Witch. They'd brought her back to the houseboat with them. They would both be sacrifices, but they were not in the Angel's bed. He was.

He sighed with contentment. His blood hummed with joy. But the Demon roared from the doorway, destroying his peace within moments.

"Get away, you!" the Prophet shouted over the De-mon's bellow.

The Angel held him tight, but the Demon's claws bit into the Disciple's back, grabbed, hauled him away. The next thing he knew, he slammed into the wall on the other side of the room. He passed out for a moment and woke up on the floor. By the time he'd regained his senses, the Vessel and two slaves were pushing the na-ked prisoners toward the bed. The women's hands were tied behind their backs, sacred signs were painted on their skin with blood. The Angel was on his feet.

The Disciple began to crawl toward the Angel, but the Angel didn't look his way. He had eyes only for one of the beautiful women. He paid no attention to the Witch.

The Vessel laughed.

The Prophet said, "They're all yours for the next two days."

The Demon said, "It's dawn."

The Angel took a step away from the bed. He shook all over. He stumbled back, his body going slack. He fell on the mattress. As he did, he pointed at the prisoner. "Mother?"

"Where have you been, sweetheart?"

"How's Santini?"

"In a coma. Where you been?"

Char tried not to take in the ruin of the condo. Think-ing about the wreckage might get her pissed off. Haven was seated on the counter that divided the kitchen from the dining area. His shotgun rested beside him. All the chairs were broken. So was the table. The dishes had been pulled from the cabinets and smashed. It wasn't her place. It wasn't her stuff. She took a deep, calming breath. Jimmy Bluecorn wouldn't know or care that a mortal had had a tantrum in his old home.

She looked at the large black nylon bag on the floor at Haven's feet. It was longer than it was wide and had a shoulder strap. "What's that?"

"Been shopping."

She nudged the bag with her foot. Definitely something metal in there. "Doesn't feel like a sword."

"Where have you been?"

Char gestured, taking in the shattered contents of the condo. "Avoiding a confrontation." She put her hands on her hips. "I assume you did this and that it wasn't the demon's minions that broke in."

He shrugged. "I got a little frustrated when I didn't find you at home."

She could picture exactly how it had happened, though she'd spent a day dream-riding in a different part of town. Haven would have sat by Santini's hospital bed, thinking over everything that had been said and done between him and her. He'd weigh the experience against his mission to rid the world of monsters. And he'd choose to make a vigilante raid on her place.

"Stopped by to bring me a present, did you? Something for our *wooden* anniversary."

"Thought you might like a stake," he admitted. "Didn't want to wake you up, since you work nights. Was just going to plant it and go."

"Sorry I wasn't here."

She almost was sorry; he would have found the results surprising. Most likely a wooden stake would bounce right off her tough Enforcer's hide. Then again, knowing Jebel, she figured he'd have sawed off her head and filled it with garlic for good measure and probably burned her body. A simple stake through the heart wouldn't be good enough for Jebel Haven. They'd slept together, they'd worked together and laughed and eaten and talked. But she was a monster. Accepting her as a person was wrong if he wanted to keep his narrow, focused point of view. He had a score to settle and a conscience to assuage for almost letting her get to him. More than almost—or he wouldn't have made a mess of the place where they'd spent so much time together. She'd been right to think that trusting him through the day would have been mistake.

Char picked up a piece of broken chair leg and held it out to him. "I'm home now."

He batted the impromptu stake out of her hand. "Bitch."

"Ambivalence sucks, doesn't it?"

"You'd know about sucking, sweetheart."

"Bitch," she snarled back. "Listen, Jebel. If one of those desert monsters you hunt bit you, it would be over. Death is sweet release from what those creatures do to people. But if I were to bite you, it would be a whole different ball game."

He looked at her with narrow-eyed fury. "What would it be, sweetheart?"

"Heaven."

They looked into each other's eyes for awhile. He

looked away first. He jumped off the counter and shoul-
dered the black bag. It looked heavy, even heavier after
he put the shotgun in it. "Sleep well, sweetheart?"

"Not particularly. We didn't find Della last night.
Couldn't feel her today." Char took a step back. "Are
we allies again for the evening?"

Haven spat. She bit her lip rather than complain.
"Yeah. Why not?" She was surprised when he put his
hand on her shoulder. "The first time we had sex," he
said.

"Was in the middle of the afternoon."

"Did we really have sex, or did you—?"

"Make you dream it?"

"Yes."

"Define reality." Char fought the smile but lost. "We
both came, didn't we?"

He backed away from her. "Stop confusing me."

"Too late. Let's get to work. While you've been trashing my ex's place, I have been rousing the rabble." She
decided it was best that Haven not know about the Carnation nest's role in the rescue. Both she and Helene
Bourbon had spent their sleeping hours at Helene's safe
house monitoring and attempting to increase the tension
growing in Seattle. Not that it had taken much work.
There was a dark anger already present in the city.

It affected the outsiders who'd come to protest the
trade organization meeting even more than the citizens
who'd lived with the magical radiation from the ritual
murders for weeks. Tempers were ready to blow at any
excuse. With the arrival of both the trade delegates and
the protesters with many agendas, the mob exploded.

The nest members were out among the rioters tonight, working. Constance and Helene were supposed to call her with periodic updates. She was willing to bet they wouldn't remember; a hunt without the gnawing drive of blood fever would be too much fun.

"What rabble?" Haven asked.

"I keep a radio on when I'm asleep," she equivocated. "I've been monitoring the local riots. The city isn't exactly going up in flames, but the protesters are keeping the authorities busy. No one will notice our activities."

"Good thought," he had to agree. "Baker's not here to cover my usual trail of violence and destruction. And there's a lot more cops per square inch in Seattle than my usual territory."

"So nice to work with someone with your lack of scruples. Because I have a simple, if somewhat brutal, plan," she said. When he gave her a questioning look, Char explained, "So far, we've had more luck finding where the demon and sorcerer *aren't* hidden than where they are. We need to catch and question one of their minions. Then we'll know where to look."

"Sounds good," he said. "In theory."

"You have a better idea?"

"I'm working on it. Why'd you come back here?" he asked as he followed her toward the door. "Looking for me? Or did you just want to take a shower?"

"I enjoy your company, Jebel."

"I'm bad-tempered, violent, and wanted to drive a stake through your heart."

"Fine qualities in a monster hunter. My heart is definitely not safe with you." She sighed. "That doesn't mean we don't make a good team."

He put his hand over hers as she reached for the door-knob.

She turned back to face him. "Yes?"

He kissed her, swift and hard. It was quite unexpected and wonderful and lasted only a few seconds.

"We're quite ridiculous," she told him.

"Have you put a spell on me?"

"I could ask you the same thing, Mr. Haven." She put her hands on his shoulders. "You're not my type. And no jokes about blood types, please." A few nights ago, she would have felt like a hypocrite, completely guilt-ridden and mortified to be kissing him, talking to him like this. A few nights ago, he was her lawful, chosen prey. He still was, but all the polite, civilized constraints she'd lived by before meeting Haven didn't matter right now. She needed him.

To kill a demon, she reminded herself. She stopped looking into his deep brown eyes and finally managed to open the door. "We had better concentrate on saving lives."

"Killing demons and vampires—"

"And sorcerers, oh my."

"We'll take my Jeep," he said and led the way down the back stairs. "For once I want to drive."

"Have a destination in mind?" she asked when they were in his vehicle.

"You'll know when we get there," he answered and pulled into the street. "Tell me about this sacred magical vampire holy day," he said as he drove. "What happens that makes it so special? The mouth of hell open or something?"

Char stared at him in confusion. "What sacred vampire—oh, you mean Blessing Day." She laughed.

"What's so funny? I thought the world was going to end on this Blessing Day."

"Vampires don't want to end the world—especially before they get the chance to exchange all the gifts they don't want. One of the Laws is to always keep your Blessing Day present receipts."

"But—"

"The new moon before the winter solstice is just—Blessing Day."

"But what is it?"

She pressed the bridge of her nose between two fingers and made a decision. "What the hell, I've already told you too much. Vampires have a religion, and all religions have festival days. Blessing of the Knives is the holiday's full name."

"Charming."

"But no one calls it that anymore. It's sort of the opposite of the winter solstice celebrations. Mortals have ancient fire festivals in the middle of winter to reassure themselves that the sun will return soon. Vampires have a festival that revels in the long nights of winter, but sadly commemorates the fact that the days are destined to get longer. These days it's more like what Christmas or Hanukkah have become to most Americans—a chance to party and give presents." She made a dismissive gesture. "Blessing Day's no big deal."

"But last night you said—"

"That the sorcerer would assume it has significance. His research is going to be ninety percent bogus. Has to be."

"Why?"

" 'Cause the Enforcers have spent hundreds, maybe thousands, of years keeping information about our people away from mortals."

"This guy knows enough."

"To be dangerous. If he's planning to kill a vampire to steal his immortality—"

"And why should I mind his doing this?"

"Because of all the other people he's killed and is going to kill."

"Right."

She peered at a figure standing under a corner streetlight as Haven slowed to a stop. "Is that Santini?"

"Yes."

"You said he was in a coma."

Haven ducked his head and smiled. "I lied."

Chapter 23

SANTINI WAS COVERED in bruises, wore a bandage on his head, and a manic grin on his saturnine face. He was also carrying a huge crossbow and had something Char suspected was a flamethrower. He said, "Hi," stowed his gear, and climbed in the backseat of the Jeep.

"I feel underdressed going to this party," Char commented. "All I've got is a knife." Haven tilted an eyebrow sarcastically at her. "And big teeth and claws," she added. "But I don't use them on mortals. Generally."

"Wanna borrow a gun?"

"Yeah," she said after a moment. "I'd like that." Haven reached over and opened the glove compartment. She took her pick of several firearms inside and tucked the .22 into her waistband. "Thanks."

"You know how to use that, right?"

"Yes." In theory. She'd had lessons. It seemed the sort of thing an Enforcer should do. Teeth and claws weren't everything. Though the karate lessons had been a mistake. She never could fake being slower and weaker than her instructor.

Santini reached from the backseat and patted her on

the shoulder. "Della says you're wussy but have a good heart. I promised her I wouldn't open you up and take a look for myself just yet."

"I'm happy to hear it," Char said.

"Glad you didn't do her today," Santini said to Haven. "We need her to get Della back." He touched his forehead. "Della talks a lot."

She certainly does, Char thought, curious to find out what the former companion had told Santini about the strigoi. People get lonely, then they talk too much to anyone willing to listen. Look at her and Haven, for example.

"Where are we going?" she asked Haven.

"A lake," Santini answered. "We need to find a lake."

Haven ignored his partner for the moment. He still had some questions for Charlotte. "The guy who's got the spell—the sorcerer dude. You said his information was ninety percent bogus. How'd he get these spells he's using in the first place?"

"Internet, maybe. Maybe the ritual's been in his family for generations. And the Vatican library was broken into a couple years ago. You'd be amazed at what's in there. He might have got his hands on some black market grimoires from that theft." She smiled at his snort of disbelief. She told him, "When people go looking for information about vampires, they're likely to find trouble."

"And when they get close to some truth?" he wondered. "What happens then?"

She gave him a sideways look, but her cell phone started buzzing before she answered him. She listened to the caller, then announced, "Got one." She flashed him a smile. Then, "Dead? I said to . . . oh. Suicide," she told Haven. "Helene says the slave she caught chose death over dishonor." She spoke back into the phone. "Keep hunting."

Santini spoke up behind them. "Too much water in this town."

The phone rang again. Char listened for a second, then grinned at Haven. "Spotted another one."

"That was fast."

"Helene has help. From the people at the homeless shelter," she added after a pause. "Besides, anyone who's shared blood with a vampire is easy to spot if you know what to look for. Helene knows what to look for."

Haven was too paranoid not to be suspicious about how many vampires were out tonight, but he let it go. "Where?"

"Seattle Center."

"Where?"

"Head toward the Space Needle. Take Denny Way until you get to Fifth. Keep going. I'll tell you when to turn."

He drove.

She took another call, then told him, "There seems to be a concentration of cult members in the Seattle Center area and over by Westlake Mall. I think they must have been sent out to take advantage of the rioting."

"Do some looting for the cause?"

"Even evil sorcerers have overhead," she agreed.

"We need to go looking for a house on the water," Santini said. "That's where Della is."

• • •

Dark water slapped against the flat-bottomed hull. The
skyline showed bright beyond the glass door that led
from the bedroom to a small deck that stuck out like a
back porch from the houseboat. It was never meant to
sail anywhere. The door was warped, letting in a cold
stream of wet air and the tainted smell of the water.

The Disciple ignored where he was. They'd moved a
lot since the Lady in Black came to town. The Disciple
disliked this place least of all. He studied the ceremonial
implements laid out on the long table, trying to decide.
The sacrificial altar wasn't usually kept in the same room
as the Angel's holy bed, but there wasn't enough room
on the boat to keep the holy spaces separate. He usually
kept his hands behind him when he was near the sacred
objects, lest his touch defile them, but this time he
reached out to touch the ivory hilt of one of the silver
daggers. The blade was about ten inches long and very
sharp. His hand closed around the hilt.

His back was to the bed and the women tied to the
brass headboard. All the slaves were gone for the night.
When the Angel woke this evening, he had left the bed
by himself for the first time the Disciple could remember. He'd broken the Disciple's heart when he told him
he wanted to be alone, to get away from the women.
The Angel was in the bathroom. The Disciple could hear
the Prophet and the Demon bickering in the other room.

"What are you doing?" the Disciple heard the mother
say, but her question wasn't for him.

"Thinking," the Witch answered. "Thinking very
loudly."

"I don't understand." The mother's voice shook.

She'd spent the day crying. She thought the Angel belonged to her. It had made the Disciple jealous. The mother was more dangerous to his love for the Angel than the Witch. The Witch just sneered at the Angel and declared him unworthy. The Prophet had let him hit her for her blasphemy. The Disciple would be glad when the women were silenced forever.

Then he remembered that the women would not be dying tonight, as they should. The women should die by magic to strengthen the dark shields that hid the Angel from harm. But the Prophet had declared he needed them for his own purposes—for the Great Becoming. The Prophet no longer cared that the Angel needed to be protected. The Angel was being hunted, but the Angel was no longer important to the Prophet and the Demon. Perhaps he never had been, not for himself. The Disciple could barely stand the pain of knowing how his beautiful Angel had been used.

He took the dagger and hid it inside his shirt. Just in time, he stepped back as the Vessel came into the bedroom. He hated the Vessel, but the Vessel was just the person he wanted to see right now. He almost smiled at the Vessel. But the Disciple had never been good at smiling.

"The Angel isn't safe," he told the Vessel. "We're going to make him safe."

The Vessel was only interested in the women. He began to stroke the mother's breasts. "He hasn't touched them, has he?"

"He doesn't want them."

"Lucky me." The Vessel unzipped his fly.

The Disciple came closer to the bed. "I know the protection spell. The one that wraps the dark around the Angel. It needs to be stronger. You're going to help."

The Vessel ignored him. He pulled off his shirt and pants. He was naked when he got on the bed. The Vessel was full of magic. He glowed with it from within, like a translucent chalice filled to the brim with power. He pushed the woman's legs apart and stretched out on top of the mother.

The Disciple began to mumble the spell beneath his breath. He concentrated on a precise spot on the Vessel's back as the Vessel penetrated the woman.

The mother screamed, and the sound masked any noise the Disciple made as he moved closer still to the bed. Only the Witch saw him pull out the long, silver dagger, but she laughed rather than shouting out a warning. All the Disciple had to do now was watch carefully and wait until the moment the Vessel came.

Char turned around to look in the backseat. Santini looked dazed. She wondered if it was from the head injury. But a strange suspicion gnawed at her. Della had only been Krystalle's companion. But ... maybe ... How close had Della been to rebirth when Krystalle was executed? Della survived her lover's death, so the cord between them must have been close to breaking. Santini certainly had an odd form of psychic gifting. And he'd healed awfully fast. Maybe they had . . .

"Mr. Santini?" Char wasn't quite sure how to phrase this. "Have you and Della been engaging in—uh—"

"You bit each other, right?" Jebel asked for her.

Santini gave his manic smile. "Beats being bit by a vampire."

Not by much. Char sighed. "Congratulations, Santini, you're engaged. Jebel," she said, turning to Haven. "He and Della have a psychic bond. If she's broadcasting for help, he's picking it up."

"Water," Santini said. "A house on the water."

"What's he mean by that?"

"Houseboat," Char answered. "But where? Lake Union? Portage Bay? Any clue on specific location, Santini?"

He shook his head wildly. "Don't think she knows. All I have is—a house on water."

Char muttered under her breath and punched numbers into her cell phone. "Helene? Look for a houseboat. We're closer to Lake Union, so we're heading that way." Char took a moment away from her call to give Haven driving instructions. He ran the next red light and turned left as she waved and pointed. Honking and crushing metal followed in their wake. She got back to her call. "Fairview North. Meet us. Tell the others to keep hunting."

Blocks sped by. Haven saw the glitter of water in the distance. "Close," he said. "Feels—"

Black fire burst in his brain. The pain shot through his blood and nerves, muscle and bone, consumed him in a wave of dark flame. His skin turned to ash. He screamed, and Char screamed, and Santini screamed— but their joined anguish only blended into the horrible cry that filled the night.

*All the light in the world went out. The stars died.
The temperature dropped to absolute zero.*

*Hands reached for him—grasping, horrible, blood-
stained. He fell into the gaping, screaming mouth and
fell and fell through a sea of burning blood. A huge
snake reared up out of the burning red gore, its scales
made of jagged shards of mirrors. A screaming face
looked out from each facet of those mirrors. The snake
convulsed and writhed, shaken from within. The mirror
monster shattered, scattering a deadly blast of glass
blades. All of them penetrated his heart at light speed.*

*The roar of escaping souls filled Haven. And then they
were on him, in him, through him, showing him their
deaths and blessing their release—blessing him. Leaving
him. He was tortured, shaken, smashed, trampled.
Freed.*

Crying.

Breathing.

He could breathe.

He didn't know how he'd stopped the car, but the
Jeep was pulled to the side of the street, engine off.
Haven blinked and slowly turned his head. The passen-
ger door was open. Char was not in the car.

He found her on her hands and knees on the cold
sidewalk. He held her while she barfed her guts out.
Then he held her close while she cried, rocking them
both back and forth like a mother with a child instead
of the meanest badass on the planet and his vampire
girlfriend.

But in less than a minute, Santini came up and said,
"Let's *go*, man!"

It was Char who helped him to his feet. She wiped tears away from her eyes and looked past him toward the lake in the distance. "I think it's safe to say that we can follow that—energy burst—to its source."

Somebody had died, and called out as they died—like the woman who'd been murdered and dumped in the forest. Only this time he was happy about the death. "Evil. That bastard was evil."

"More than evil," she said.

"Let's go!" Santini shouted.

They ran back to the car. Haven started the engine and drove. Char got on the phone again. "No, that wasn't the transformation spell." Haven assumed she was talking to Helene. "That was one of the most important ingredients for it going to hell. I have no idea. Maybe Daniel woke up and killed him. Meet you there in five." She flipped the phone closed and said, "We still have to get through the demon and the sorcerer. It isn't going to be easy."

Chapter 24

"WHAT'S THE PLAN, Hunter?"

"I'll think of something," Char answered the bright-eyed vampire matron. Helene needed to get out more often. Char looked back at the Jeep, where the men were hauling out an impressive array of weaponry. While Haven and Santini were occupied, she quietly asked Helene Bourbon, "How goes the hunt?"

Helene laughed softly. "Constance's nest is getting fat. I've got a snack put away for later. Constance would like permission to take the hunt to a second night. They may not be able to get all the cult members tonight."

"Depends on how the rioting plays out," Char answered. "I'll talk to her later, if we have time." She studied the contours of the small houseboat moored at the end of the dock across the street. It was one of an upscale little community, and looked no different than the other floating houses around it.

The boat showed no outward sign of the chaos that raged inside. The place had exploded not half an hour ago, but not on any physical plane. No one on any of the neighboring boats in this crowded marina had a clue that anything had happened. Maybe a few had headaches or were having nightmares. But only the truly magic-allergic population of Seattle had any inkling of the truth, and most of them were too busy rioting or becoming vampire kibble to investigate the explosion.

She had to squint hard and concentrate all her vampire senses to see through the residue of evil energy that floated around the boat like a black fog.

"If there were any magical defenses on the inside, the energy blast would have destroyed them."

"Hope you're right, sweetheart." Haven said as he and Santini joined the two women.

"The demon's in there," she said. "I can feel him."

"You two are lucky to be mortal," Helene said. "The hunter and I can smell him, too."

Haven's expression told Char that he was uncomfortable with Helene's easy acceptance of him as one of them. She hid her own smile. "What have you got, Jebel?"

His shotgun was in a holster on his back. "A Husqvarna," he said, holding up the thing in his hands. "You said I need something to take off the demon's head. This ought to do it. It's a chainsaw," he explained when she continued to stare. He rubbed his thumb over a button on the base of the chainsaw. "Electric starter."

"Charming." Well, he'd told her he'd been shopping. "Not as elegant as a sword, but it'll do the job." She hoped he didn't plan to turn around and use it on her once the demon was decapitated. It could prove a challenge to disarm him. Which was something she'd worry about if she had to. "All right," she said to the assembled crusaders. "The plan is—Jebel and Santini go in the front—and Helene and I go in the back."

"Brilliant strategy." Haven sneered. "You go to military school to learn that?"

"We taking orders from her?" Santini asked Haven.

"The *back* is on the water," Haven pointed out. "You going to swim to the back door?"

Char and Helene exchanged a look. "Jump over the top of the boat?"

Helene studied the slight pitch of the houseboat's roof. "These things usually have a back porch on the water. Let's do it."

Haven began to protest, but Char paid no attention. She and Helene moved back to the far side of the street, gave each other a swift look. Then Char ran forward, with the nest leader keeping pace as they picked up speed. Jebel Haven was a blur as she raced by him, gathered herself, and jumped.

"Did you see that?" Santini asked after the women flew by. They weren't *really* flying. At least Haven didn't think they were.

"No," Haven answered. "Cover me." He hefted the chainsaw and moved as swiftly as he could toward the houseboat entrance. Maybe Santini should be leading the way, but Haven always took point. He could barely see the magic-shrouded houseboat, but he knew the door was there. That was the important thing. If it was there, he could kick it in.

Damn magic.

• • •

"I'm glad I wore my Nikes."

Char grabbed Helene's arm to steady her. Helene had a manic grin that was more Santini than staid nest leader. The woman's breathy whisper was barely audible, but it wasn't the sound of her voice Char worried about. Their landing on the rear deck of the boat had not exactly been the most silent and stealthy of maneuvers. In fact, Char thought the bad guys inside must think that a herd of elephants had just made an amphibious landing on their back porch. Oh, well, it would serve as a diversion for Haven's frontal assault.

She shook her head, said, "Shhh," then kicked in the glass door in front of her. If one was going to make a dramatic entrance, one might as well go all the way over the top. Or through a broken glass door into an unlit room in this case.

Char didn't need any light to sense the two women on the bed, both very much alive, thank the goddess Char didn't quite believe in. Body heat, mental signature, and scent pinpointed the prisoners' location. That, and Della's whispered, "Over here!"

"Take care of them," Char ordered Helene. She drew the .22 Haven had loaned her. Tearing out throats and ripping out hearts might be more fun, but she remembered that the point was not to leave any more evidence than necessary of strigoi involvement at the scene of a demon execution. She hadn't forgotten her reason for recruiting Haven, even if some other details had fallen by the wayside. With luck, no demon would ever investigate this site, but if they did, she hoped Daniel's mental signature would be strong enough to overlay her and Helene's brief visit to the scene.

"About time," Char heard Della say. "Where's Santini?"

"Careful. Don't cry," Helene said. "I'm here. You're Novak, aren't you?"

Uh-oh. Char couldn't remember if she and Helene had discussed Char's decision to let Daniel's mother live. Char held the gun at ready but glanced back from the door at the other women.

Which was a mistake, because the door banged open the instant she took her attention from it. She turned, caught a glimpse of gesturing hands, as a ball of fire flew toward her face. Fire was fast, but Char was faster. She dove, rolled, and came up again on the other side of the room.

A horrible growling roar came from the other room. Wood splintered. Maniacal laughter filtered through shouts of rage and pain.

Haven and Santini had arrived.

The sorcerer spun to face her, wild-eyed and mumbling. He was small and bald, scraggly bearded, and an altogether sorry-looking piece of humanity to have caused such horror. Char flashed fangs at him but wouldn't sink to biting such useless filth.

The sorcerer began to gesture and mumble again. The temperature in the room rose as his hands began to glow.

"Fireballs?" Char sneered. "That the best you got?"

His eyes were full of brash, mad confidence. The energy between his hands pulsed white hot. "What have you got, bitch?"

"This." Char raised the gun and quite calmly shot him between the eyes.

The energy dissipated, surrounding the sorcerer with a faint, fading glow as his body fell forward onto the deck. Char waited until all the life and light was gone, then nudged the body with her foot to make absolutely sure. Physical weapons were always far more efficient at dealing death than mental ones, which was why there were so many of them. When magic-users forgot that even a small-caliber bullet worked faster than a spell, this sort of thing was bound to happen.

Char kicked the body again, hard this time. "Rot in hell, idiot."

Della came up and added a kick of her own. Char put the gun back in her belt, stripped off her jacket, and put it around the naked woman's shoulders. The noise from the other room was deafening and disturbing.

"Shouldn't you be in there?" Della asked. "Helping fight the demon?"

Char deliberately turned her back on the closed door, just as a heavy body crashed against it. "They're big boys," she said. "They can take care of themselves." It was up to her to deal with Helene and Agent Novak. Oh, yeah, and Daniel. "Where the devil's Daniel?"

The room had already been a wreck when they'd broken in. The creature hadn't noticed them for a split second because its muzzle was buried deep inside somebody's skull. Haven got a glimpse of a naked male body laid out on a dining table. The hilt of a knife stuck out of the corpse's back. Blood dripped, entrails hung out, and this putrid-green-shit-brown scaled horned *thing* was feasting on the dead man's brains.

Then the *thing* looked up, dripping blood and gore from a face full of yellow, crooked fangs. Glowing red eyes under a forehead bristling with a dozen spiky horns focused on them. The demon bellowed and leaped at them.

Damn, it was fast!

Haven was glad Santini had brought the flame-thrower. A sheet of fire caught the demon in the chest and slowed it enough for the two of them to spread out away from the door. Some stuff in the room caught on fire as flames sprayed out around the demon. Smoke and the stench of searing scales filled the air. The demon spun around, grabbed the corpse, and threw it at Santini.

Haven dropped the lightweight chainsaw long enough to pull the shotgun from the holster on his back and send a double blast into the creature after it hurled the body. Santini dodged the corpse, then the table that was thrown after it. The demon turned on Haven, screeching and bellowing. Huge, horny claws swiped at Haven's mid-section. Haven jumped back, barely in time to keep from being gutted.

Fast. Damned fast.

Crossbow bolts from Santini bounced off the creature's scaly hide but stung it enough to distract it. It turned back toward Santini, diving at his legs. Santini jumped over the overturned table. He fired up the flame-thrower again from behind the flimsy barrier of the tabletop.

Haven coughed and his eyes stung from random fires

smoking up the room. He snatched the chainsaw and, pressing the starter, ran forward and swung the whirring blade at the monster. It bit through scales, into flesh, down to bone, and through. Green and yellow gore spurted from the demon's wound. Demon blood smoked, and the drops of it that hit Haven's face stung like hell. The pitch of the monster's screeching changed to a howl of pain.

It lunged for him, but Haven kept coming at it with the chainsaw. Damn, it was hard to kill! Haven hadn't had this much fun in months! He *hated* it when the monsters were easy to kill. This one, now, this one was a challenge.

"Thanks, sweetheart," he said, and continued to hack the demon apart piece by barbecued piece. After a long, gory, scary time, the chainsaw finally bit into the demon's throat.

The head was still screaming when it flew across the room. All the severed body parts twitched and moved around for a few seconds after that. But as soon as the head stopped screaming and the glow faded from the evil red eyes, Haven decided the thing was dead enough for federal standards and turned the chainsaw off.

Haven's arms ached and shook, he had burns and bruises, and the smoke seared his lungs, but he and Santini exchanged high fives and triumphant looks. Adrenaline pumped through him, and he let out a crow of delight. "All right!"

He stepped over demon parts to the doorway to the back of the houseboat. Santini hurried after him. Now it was time to get back to vampire hunting.

• • •

Helene knelt on the floor in front of where Novak sat on the bed. She held the woman's hands, and they were looking deeply into each other's eyes. Helene spoke to the mortal woman, her voice soft, coaxing. Novak nodded, ever so slightly. A tear rolled down her cheek, but there was light and life in her eyes. Helene spoke again. Novak's breath caught in a funny gasping sort of sigh. She almost smiled. Helene touched a finger to Novak's cheek, traced the line of the woman's tears. The air between them sizzled.

Char looked away, down at the body of the sorcerer. A small amount of blood from the wound pooled beside his head. She wouldn't have fed it to her cat. She turned her back on him, met Della's gaze. "I hate amateurs."

Della moved away from where she'd had her ear to the front room door. "Getting quiet in there."

The roar of the chainsaw had stopped. The demon was no longer screaming. Jebel Haven would be here in a moment, and all of a sudden her heart beat faster and her stomach knotted with worry for him. What if he'd been hurt? Or wounded terribly? Had her knight perished slaying the dragon for her?

Then the door opened and he swaggered in with barely a bruise on him. Fireworks shot through her at the sight of him. Fireworks and heat, and her worry turned to—

Oh, no, not that!

You will not even think the L word, she informed herself sternly. She did not run into his arms.

Della, however, let out a whoop of joy and ran into

Santini's embrace. This served as diversion enough to pass an awkward moment when Char's and Haven's gazes met, and they *almost* reacted like a pair of lovers reunited after surviving a hell of a firefight. She knew that he thought about it, and knew that he knew that she thought about it, but they left it at that.

"Everybody okay in here?" he asked her.

"We're all fine."

He barely glanced at the sorcerer's corpse as he came up to her. He gestured toward the oblivious Helene and Novak. "What's with them?"

Char's face and throat went hot. She blushed, which was something vampires, even shy and semi-innocent ones such as herself, didn't do easily or often. She cleared her throat. "Them? Well . . . It started out with Helene asking her about Daniel. And, well, the poor woman was justifiably upset, and Helene's quite good at comforting and counseling and—" Char's voice trailed off as Novak leaned forward and kissed Helene on the mouth.

Haven cringed and turned away. "She's with the FBI. She can't do that."

"And I suppose Daniel's the product of a virgin birth?"

"Yeah, but—they're women."

"They're bonded. It happens that way sometimes with us. Gender doesn't matter when you look into someone's eyes and—bam!—instant soul mates. The more crass among us refer to it as love at first bite."

It saves a lot of problems, Char thought. *Novak needs to be detached from her involvement with the federal government. Helene could probably use the services of a woman trained in criminal profiling in socializing a house full of unstable young vampires. They could both use the companionship, or they wouldn't have reacted to each other so strongly, so fast. And this way, if all worked out right, both Daniel's maternal figures could share raising him.*

"This is so . . ."

Helene leaned back and grew fangs. Haven raised his shotgun. Char grabbed his arm, pulled it down, and held it down. Helene bit her own wrist, enough to bring up a bead of blood. She held her hand up to Novak, who smiled and began to suckle.

". . . sick," Haven finished.

"Romantic," Char corrected.

Haven was not unaware that Charlotte was stronger than he was. The hand on his arm was small and beautiful, and it was steel hidden in velvet. And she was *smiling*, smiling all over, with her lips and her eyes and her body language, smiling in that goopy, scary way women had when they watched weddings and held babies.

Why didn't she look evil? Why didn't she act like a monster? He glanced toward the front room. A wisp of smoke curled in under the door. The *thing* in there looked and acted like what it was. Monsters should all be like that.

He stopped looking at the women by the bed. "Where's Daniel?" he asked Char.

The woman with Santini—Della—answered, "Gone. The scarecrow took him. I remember blacking out.

Thought I was dying. The vampire kid was gone when I woke up. Lots of howling and shouting from the bastards that were holding the kid prisoner. Boy's waking up," she added. "Getting over teething. He recognized his mom and wouldn't touch companion blood. He wanted the scarecrow to get him out."

"That was what the magic was for," Char said. "I bet Daniel's companion made the sacrifice to cover their escape."

Haven checked his watch. "About half an hour ago." Was that all? Time compressed when adrenaline flowed. A half hour? He tried to call up a mental map of the city.

"Where'd they go?" Char asked. She released her hold on his arm and rubbed her chin thoughtfully.

Haven said, "Boat's on fire."

Char glanced at the door, saw the smoke. "Oh, good," she said. "Best way to dispose of any evidence." Then what he'd said sank in. *The boat was on fire. Oh.* Was that the sound of approaching fire engines in the distance? "Right." She turned around, clapping to get attention. "Helene! Move it! We have to get these people out of here."

There followed a few minutes of frantic activity that involved dodging flames and a certain amount of smoke inhalation. They got everyone out through the heat and blinding smoke, and then Char had to draw shadows around them so they could dodge a growing crowd of neighbors and get away from the docks. A fire truck, police car, and an emergency vehicle arrived as the survivors fled the burning boat, which added to the confusion.

When Char finally stopped to take stock and count heads, she noticed that Haven wasn't with them. When she went back to look for his Jeep, she saw that it wasn't there. She sighed, aware that she wasn't the only one who'd used the fire as a diversion.

"What are you going to do?" Helene asked.

Char hadn't realized the nest leader had followed her. She looked at Helene Bourbon. "It's all right."

Some of Helene's frantic worry returned. "The mortal's gone after Daniel, hasn't he? Where?"

"Yes. It's all right," Char repeated. "I know where he's going. Get the others back to my place," she added. Char left the other mortals in Helene's capable hands and took off running. She could only hope that her guess was right.

Chapter 25

WHEN YOU LIVED on the street, you learned things. Sewer entrances, where holes in the walls of subbasements could be found, things like that. You found routes and roads underground, places to hide. You always needed places to hide, living on the streets. You needed to hide from everybody. The Disciple knew how to hide. And the Angel knew where he wanted to be. Both underground. They were made for each other, him and his Angel. They'd live underground now, just the two of them. He'd take care of the Angel, bring him everything he needed, and the Angel would love him.

There was a place he used to sleep, a room made of brick, surrounded by tons of earth and the city overhead. He'd left a stash of candles there, and he lit them all as soon as he settled the Angel on the floor of their new sanctuary.

A stream of water glistened in the candlelight as it ran down one of the walls, formed a pool, and drained away beneath the floor. They'd gotten in down a corridor that had been an aboveground street a century ago, through an opening that had once been a window, half-buried now. This part of the city's underground hadn't been opened to tourists yet, though it could be reached from the more public, shored-up, and safer corridors, if you knew just what holes to wriggle through.

The Angel sat on the floor and held his head in his hands. The trip had tired him. The Disciple wanted to make someone pay for that. "I'm hungry," the Angel said.

"I know," said the Disciple. He turned to go back through the tunnel. "Stay here." The Disciple grabbed up the jagged glass remains of a broken bottle. "I'll bring you someone to eat."

The one thing Haven was sure of about vampires was that they always went underground. Maybe some were smarter than others, but vermin hid in the dark. The trick was learning how to find and follow their trails. He'd been learning about magic the last few days, learning about when darkness was made rather than being real. He knew that Danny boy had escaped from the houseboat wearing a cloak of darkness. He'd learned a new way to look at the night. The dark magic left a kind of negative energy hanging in the world as it passed. Jebel Haven followed a wisp of black magic away from the lake like a hound on the scent. But he would have guessed where the vampire and the sicko that looked after him went even without the scent that led him through a sewer to a hole in a basement wall and finally into a corridor in the buried part of the city beneath Pioneer Square.

They always went to ground in the most obvious hiding places.

Thanks for the lessons, though, sweetheart, he thought. *Thanks, sweetheart*. Not for the first time he'd had the thought tonight, Haven realized. Damn the woman—monster—girl. Nice girl. No. To think like that negated everything he needed to believe. Had believed?

Wanted to believe. Why did he want to believe?

She was right. Ambiguity sucked.

"But sometimes you have to live with it," he murmured and pounded a fist in frustration against an old stone wall. Debris tumbled down from overhead, leaving Haven choking from a cloud of disturbed mold and dust. His lungs already ached from inhaling smoke, and his eyes stung as well. He didn't appreciate this added discomfort, which he'd brought on himself.

He'd spent his whole life bringing shit down on himself—until he'd discovered the vampires.

His purpose and salvation was in killing vampires, he reminded himself. He couldn't have gotten to the women on the houseboat with Char there—and not just because she was stronger and faster than he was. He suspected he hadn't tried to do them because he couldn't bear to see the look on Char's face when he killed the lady vampire and her new girlfriend. But Danny boy was a different story. He'd get Danny tonight, worry about the others tomorrow, he told himself, blinking hard to clear his vision in the near darkness of the underground.

But his vision didn't clear, and it only got darker. It was damp down here, and cold, and getting colder by the second. "Shit," he muttered.

Then Haven heard the mumbling.

A spell. Shit. Somebody was putting a spell on *him?*

"Fuck that," Haven growled, brought up the shotgun. The attack came from behind.

Broken glass slashed across Haven's shoulder and down his arm. It was enough to throw off Haven's aim as he turned and fired.

"Why didn't I drive?" Char muttered between panting breaths. "No, I had to let Mr. Macho take his Jeep tonight."

It hadn't been that long of a run, but she wasn't used to this sort of exertion. Besides, she alternated cursing with crying the whole way, not to mention dodging rioters. Expending all that emotion was more tiring than the exercise. She leaned against an old stone wall, breathed in mildew, and swore silently at Jebel Haven some more. The man was stubborn and fanatical and was going to kill Daniel just because he thought he should. Just out of *habit!*

"Well, I won't have it," she muttered as she followed him along the dark, magical trail. "He's had his chance. He's done his job. The next time I see the man, he's dead. Period. It's over. Finished."

The darkness got darker with each step she took deeper into the labyrinth of the buried streets. Her determined fury grew deeper with each snarled word, with every inch she drew closer to her quarry. Until her diatribe was suddenly drowned out by a cry of pain and the thunderous discharge of both barrels of a shotgun.

Char's fury shifted focus in the roaring echo that

bounced off the old walls. She shouted, "Jebel!" Pulling her dagger from its sheath, she ran.

The air reeked with blood and magic when she reached them. Sick, sick hunger hit her like a wall of flame. The men were on the ground rolling around like a pair of frenzied animals in the dark corridor. Haven's shotgun was on the ground. The horrible battle before her was being fought to the death with mortal hands and teeth and will.

Insanity rose off Haven's opponent like steam. Jebel's determination to survive, to kill, was rich and red and controlled and slashed like a laser. Neither man noticed Char. Neither man was aware of anything but the other. Their intensity was painful against her psychic senses.

Char put away her dagger and jumped into the fray anyway.

The bastard was *strong* for all that he was nothing but gristle and bone and unwashed human stench. And slippery as water. Every time Haven thought he had a good grip, the wraith slipped out of it and came at him another way. Haven was hurting the man all right, but he was being hurt, and the bastard was a determined little fuck. There was no stopping until somebody was dead, and that was just fine with Jebel Haven.

He kept on fighting—until, abruptly, there was nothing there in the darkness for him to fight.

Haven didn't know why the weight of his attacker was suddenly absent, but he sprang back into a low crouch the instant he felt the other man move. He spun and kicked, aiming for a darker piece of darkness across the corridor. His foot caught nothing but air. He spun again at a low cry behind him. He kicked again, contacted flesh with a hard thud. Heard the loud crack of breaking bone. A whimper this time.

A plea. "Angel . . ." A prayer spoken low and raspy.

Haven moved toward the voice. The magical darkness began to blow away, enough for him to make out not one, but two figures on the ground. One of them was Char. She held Haven's attacker in her arms.

"His spinal cord's broken," she said and stood, still holding the limp body. The man in her arms groaned when she turned.

Haven followed when she strode determinedly off. "Where are you taking him?"

"I smell candle wax up ahead." They came around a corner, and Haven made out the faint, warm glow from a hole low in the wall. "There," she said. "Daniel's in there."

Haven had had a pack with his toolkit when he was attacked. He'd lost it during the fight. His shotgun was back along the corridor, too. Not that he was completely unarmed now, he never was, but he'd be happier if he went to meet vampire Danny Novak better equipped.

"Why?" Char asked.

Haven pretended that she hadn't just read his mind or emotions, and he didn't say anything. She let it go. The man in her arms groaned again. "He's going to die," she said.

Haven was all in favor of that. He didn't know why she'd brought the vampire's minion with her. And it also occurred to him that maybe he hadn't been the one who'd broken the man's spine.

"Char?"

They'd reached the half-sunken opening, and she ignored him to lower the limp body through what might have been a window a hundred years ago. She followed the body inside, and Haven followed her. The candles gave a cozy glow and a small amount of warmth to a small, filthy, littered den.

Haven got a good look at the vampire in the corner as Danny Novak lifted his head. He was blond and blue-eyed, handsome but for the prominent front teeth. He looked a lot like his mom.

When Char grabbed the injured man again, it wasn't gently. She dragged his body across the small room and tossed him in Danny Novak's lap. "This is yours," she said.

She stood over the young vampire, harsh and angry, and Danny slowly looked up and up to meet her gaze. She was not a tall woman, but from that angle Haven thought she must look pretty impressive—like an avenging angel or a judge.

"Mine?" Danny Novak asked. He didn't seem to notice that he was stroking the other man's hair.

"Your companion," she said. "He's insane. Dangerous. Filth. He's a killer and the willing pawn of killers. This is not good, Daniel, and it's your fault."

The boy blinked slowly. "Me?"

"Do you know what an Enforcer is? What I am?" Danny stared at her for a while, but he finally nodded.

She nodded decisively back. "Why did you do this, Daniel?"

"Do?"

"Why did you make him your companion? You don't have that right. You're too young."

"He's my companion? Somebody told me about companion—" Danny's stunned expression turned to one of disgust. "Him? Blech. No."

"Your blood fills him. Smell it."

"My blood? Yeah. I fed him, but not 'cause . . . I don't want a companion!"

"Then why did you share your blood with him?"

"He took care of me. The others kept me sick, wouldn't let me go." Danny kept stroking the man's hair. "They made it dark around me." He blinked. "Like I had fog in my head . . . not so bad now."

"The spells they used to imprison you are wearing off. And you seemed to manage to survive teething on your own. It won't be so bad after this, Daniel. If you make it to morning."

"Big if," Haven added. Char didn't act like she heard him.

The dying man opened his eyes and ate Danny with his gaze. He didn't move, though. Couldn't move. And his breathing was ragged and growing weaker.

"He wouldn't eat," Danny explained to Char. "He was always hungry, but he wouldn't eat. I didn't want him to die. You can't let someone die if you can do something to help them. Unless they're evil, and it's a hunt." He sounded like he was repeating a catechism lesson.

Char nodded at his answer, satisfied. It made Haven

think briefly of her as Sister Mary Charlotte, mother superior of some weird order of fanged nuns. *Unless they're evil and it's a hunt.* Haven rubbed his jaw. What kind of monsters lived by rules like that? "Monsters aren't supposed to be ethical," he muttered.

Char continued to ignore him. "He belongs to you, Daniel," she said, gesturing at Danny's companion. "There's another lesson you have to learn right now. A very important lesson. A very simple one. And that is, if you make a mess, clean it up." She took a step back out of the corner. "He's served you the best way he could, as damaged and warped as he is. He deserves to die, but *you* have to make it the best death you can." Finished with what she had to say, she gave him one long, hard look, then turned her back on him and took one more step away.

Danny boy looked after her for another confused moment, then down at his companion. The man stared back with complete worship in his fading eyes. Danny smiled gently at him, and breathed a soft, comprehending, "Oh."

Haven saw the shift in Danny's features, saw Danny's lips pull back, the bright white fangs grow. He should have been repulsed, but the change made Danny Novak *beautiful.* He looked like an angel when he lowered his head to the man's throat.

Haven stayed where he was, next to the entrance, and watched. What he saw was a vampire feeding, but this time he thought it was *right*. Acknowledging the rightness of a vampire draining the blood from an already dying human disturbed him, but Haven would have been more disturbed if that particular sick piece of human shit lived to fight another day.

And since when did he use words like *disturbed*? Pissed off. He would have been *pissed off*. Char had messed up his mind *and* his vocabulary, not to mention totally trashing everything he believed in.

"You'll get over it."

His gaze shifted from the feeding vampire to meet her eyes, and he wondered how long she'd been looking at him, into him, while he watched that *creature* take a human li—

"He's dead," Char cut him off.

"You sure?" Haven demanded. "Is he going to wake up as an undead in a couple of minutes?"

"That isn't how our kind of vampire is made. It isn't an infection with us—none of that hillbilly animated dead corpse crap in our family tree. Besides, Daniel's too young to make a blood-child."

"You're sure?"

"I'm sure. Let it go, Jebel. I feel sorry for that poor man in some ways. I think he was always dead. Some people can't be saved. Some shouldn't be. You were," she added. "Finding out about the underneath world was the best thing that ever happened to you. It gave you purpose, Jebel. Some of us need a higher purpose to be truly alive. But once you go through that first hidden door . . ." Char shrugged. "You can't step back and close it, and you aren't the type to bang around in the vestibule forever. You're the sort who eventually goes looking for doors to the wider underworld. That's when it gets tricky. The doors are there, but they have guardians."

"Like you."

"Yes. The truth is out there," she added with a smile that showed a bit of fang. "And it will eat you."

Welcome to the underneath world, all right, Haven thought. He shrugged. "Maybe I won't bother with the doors. Maybe I'll blast my way in."

"It's already too late for that, Jebel. You know about us, but we know much more about you. That's my fault, I'm afraid. I check for people who do the same sort of research I do." She made a small gesture, which included a whole world. "Welcome to the underground, Mr. Haven. Tourists aren't allowed; you have to live here."

Or die here. That was too obvious to be spoken or even implied.

"Or maybe you're just imagining it," she said.

He shook his head. "You're not a very good liar, Charlotte. You came down here to kill me." He pointed at Danny boy. "To save him."

"Or kill him. I had to have a face-to-face with him before I could make a decision about whether he was victim or villain. Could have gone either way." The boy vampire in the corner made a startled noise, but she paid no attention to him. She continued to concentrate on Haven as she wiggled her hand slightly. "If I decided Daniel disobeyed the Laws, if I believed he'd been a willing accomplice of the sorcerer in killing those people, then his life was forfeit. I think he's innocent of murder. I've decided not to kill him."

She didn't consider Danny boy's draining the life from his human protector murder? She called it justice. Haven tried to tell himself he was being warped by this

crazy woman's ideas of justice, but that didn't stop him
from agreeing with her.

Haven crossed his arms; the gesture was almost as
casual as it looked. "You haven't denied that you came
here to kill me."

"Could have gone either way," she repeated. She
sighed loudly, and it echoed around the little room.
"You're right, I'm not a good liar. The truth is, I have
orders to kill you because you're likely to become a
threat to my people."

"I'm flattered."

"You're tough and you're tenacious. I think you do
necessary work, but I see my boss's point about stopping
you before you got too close. Didn't mean I wanted the
job of executing you. I came to Seattle to find Daniel to
avoid having to carry out that assignment. But since fate
doesn't let people with our sort of gifts off the hook, of
course you showed up in Seattle, too."

"And you used me to kill a demon."

She tried to look shocked and surprised. She didn't
fake those very well, either.

"I did notice you weren't in on that fight. I've seen
you vamped out to the max, sweetheart. You could have
taken him."

Char looked furious for a moment, then embarrassed,
then she laughed—quite sincerely. "You're too quick on
the uptake for your own good, Jebel. You're right; I
can't kill demons."

"Only allowed to kill other vampires, sweetheart?
And humans who get in your way?"

"Something like that. Having you show up was very

useful for me . . . so I used you. But you enjoyed the challenge of killing a demon, didn't you?"

Haven started to protest that that wasn't the point, that she'd *used* him. Then he thought, *What the hell?* "Best night I've had in years," he admitted. "Except for last night in the alley," he added as she started to get a look of female outrage. "Best sex I ever had. So . . . last night . . . was . . . the best. Night." *It was, wasn't it? Damn.* And she hadn't bit him or put a spell on him or anything, had she? She'd just been herself. "Wait a minute, why am I trying to pacify a woman who's going to kill me?"

She shrugged. She didn't look very happy about what she said next. "I don't want to kill you."

Char's heart was breaking as she looked at the mortal—the man, the lover, the hero—across the room. His injuries didn't show up in any stark detail in the candlelight, but she could sense the unshielded heat and throb of pain, both physical and psychic alike. She should thrive on drinking in all the raw reality of his personality, but she never had been that kind of girl. "Some of us are monsters," she heard herself explaining to him. "Immortality can make people careless and callous, decadence sets in like rot. We need to hunt. My kind thrive on draining emotion, and fear is an easy emotion, vampire fast food. But it doesn't have to be—" Char made a helpless, frustrated gesture. "Just because you have to be a predator doesn't mean you can't be an ethical one. You, of all people, should understand that."

She was talking too much, thinking too much, all of it to avoid what had to be done. Truth was, if she was going to live by her own moral compass, she had no reason or right to kill Jebel Haven. He had done nothing to harm her people. Potential threat, yes, but—

A fist of dread clamped around Char's heart as she saw a way out and stepped to one side of the room. She was no longer between Jebel Haven and Daniel Novak. Daniel's eyes were closed, his head back, stoned and sated on blood. Vulnerable. He wouldn't see an attack coming.

Haven's attention focused sharply on Daniel rather than her. His faux relaxed posture changed. Haven drew not one weapon, but two, a gun in one hand, a wickedly pointed wooden stake in the other.

Jebel Haven had come here to kill a vampire.

She could not allow a helpless vampire to be killed.

Please, Jebel, Char thought, and she prayed to deities she didn't quite believe in. *Please make this easy for me.*

She held her breath, turned her face toward the shadows, and put her hands behind her back to cloak the appearance of fangs and claws, and waited.

And waited.

Haven didn't move. She expected him to, she prayed for him to. A candle burned out, taking some light and warmth from the underground chamber. Her senses registered the dampness of the place, the musty, dusty, bloody, decayed smells beneath the pervasive aroma of burning wax. Mostly, Char was aware of Jebel Haven's tense heartbeat, the heated scent of his bruised skin over taut muscles, and the singing, adrenaline-drenched blood beneath the surface. She was even more aware of the burning in her head, her gut, and her heart. And of how much she didn't want to kill him.

But she would. She knew she would. One step toward Daniel, and she would.

"I can't."

Char opened her eyes. She hadn't realized they'd been closed. She met Jebel's dark brown eyes, as full of anguish and self-disgust as her own. "You can't what?"

He smiled a little at her indignation. His deep voice was rough when he said, "I can't make it that easy for you, sweetheart."

She noticed that he'd put away his weapons. "Damn it, Jebel! How am I supposed to kill you if you don't do anything wrong?"

"I can't kill him," he said. He pointed at Daniel. "*He* hasn't done anything wrong. You said so. Besides," he added, "we wouldn't want him to miss Blessing Day, would we?"

Frustration welled up in Char. It made her want to howl. She didn't know whether she wanted to kiss the mortal or shake him in frustration. "But—"

He laughed at her. "It's not my fault if you've widened my perspective on the nature of good and evil."

"But . . . !" She gestured wildly. "What the devil am I supposed to do with you if I don't kill you?"

And the answer was obvious and inevitable and came as such a shock that she had to sit down, because her legs wouldn't hold her at the moment. "Oh, dear."

"Charlotte, you're blushing."

She put her hands on her cheeks. "Oh, dear," she said again, and things became obvious to her. Machinations. Plots within plots. Haven wasn't the only one who'd been used. Had *he* been lurking around in the shadows watching? Had he sent the other vampire after Haven to get her jealous? To make her *do* something? And it had worked. "That son of a bitch."

"Charlotte, I'm shocked at your language."

She looked into Haven's eyes, and those eyes were laughing at her, but with affection rather than mockery.

"Who's a son of a bitch? Your boss?"

She nodded. "I don't think he wanted me to kill you at all. I think . . . that he wanted me to get out more." *And to recruit you,* she thought. *Damn it, Istvan, why couldn't you do this yourself? What about Jimmy Bluecorn? What about . . . ?*

Jimmy was long gone. Pining for him wasn't going to bring what they had back. Thinking there was only one great love in her life was all very sentimental and romantic, but it was only an excuse to remain alone. And think too much. A child of the Nighthawk line was reborn to act, and Haven certainly brought out her inner hunter. He was born to be a hunter himself, mortal or immortal. He'd managed to fight the good fight nicely on his own so far. She owed him the beginning of his immortality.

Haven came over to her and helped her to her feet. She was glad that her claws were sheathed when he took her hands. He didn't let them go once she was standing. "What do we do now, sweetheart?"

She knew that he knew very well what the answer had to be. Knew and accepted it. "Right now," she said primly, "we are going to make sure Daniel is safely returned to his family."

He was standing very close to her. His hands were

on her hips. Attraction charged between them. "Aren't you going to bite me? At least a little?"

She put her hands on his shoulders. Oh, yes, it was very tempting. "I'm not a love at first bite sort of woman."

She and Jimmy had known each other for a year before he tasted her. It had been at a Queensryche concert. The band had been playing—No. She wasn't going to think about Jimmy anymore.

"Just because we've had sex in a back alley doesn't mean I'm cheap and easy. I will make you my companion at an appropriate time and place. And I think champagne, chocolate, violins, and possibly engagement rings should be involved."

"Will it be heaven?"

"Yes. Whether you think you deserve heaven or not."

"When?"

"*After* an appropriate amount of time has passed."

He was puzzled, impatient now that he'd accepted that he wanted her brand of forever. Then he asked, "Can we still have sex?"

"Frequently." She wanted to have sex right now. She glanced back at Daniel. "But not in front of the children." She made herself draw away from Haven to go and hoist the sleeping vampire over her shoulder.

Haven moved to help her haul Daniel through the room's entrance. He took point when they started down the corridor. "After we give Danny boy to his mom— moms—then what?"

She thought for a moment about what *she* really wanted to do with her life. All she ever wanted was to be a superhero. "I think I'll move to Tucson," she answered. "Help you with your work. There are a lot of evil beings, supernatural and otherwise, that need killing. I can teach you about them. We can expand the business, call the firm, Haven, Baker, and McCairn, Psychic Detectives. How about that?"

Haven stopped and turned to face her in the shadow-filled corridor. His face was clear to her, and his expression pleased. She'd just offered him everything he wanted: complete access to the underneath world. "Baker'd like playing hero," he told her. "Santini'll have fun. Yeah," he admitted, ducking his head. "I like it."

Char wasn't certain if Santini would be coming with them. But she decided not to get into that.

"Good," she said. "But first we have to stop in Portland to pick up my cat."

"Cat!" he said, disgusted. "I hate cats!"

She shifted Daniel's weight on her shoulder and moved to walk ahead of Haven. "You'll get used to him," she said as Haven followed after her. "In fact, you're going to love night hunters with sharp claws and teeth by the time I'm done with you."

Glossary

Blessing Day Also known as Blessing of the Knives. Strigoi winter solstice holiday celebrated on the new moon before the winter solstice.

Bloodbond The spell that enthralls slaves and companions to their vampire masters

Bloodburn The instinct to Hunt

Bloodchild What a vampire calls a mortal they've changed

Bloodfever Another term for bloodburn

Bloodmother Vampire's female maker

Blood Parent A vampire that has changed a human into a vampire; a Nighthawk who has changed a vampire into a Hunter

Blood Promise Strigoi treaty, sealed in blood

Bloodsire Vampire's male maker

Coin Gold coin imprinted with an owl symbol unique to each nest; symbol of authority

Companion Someone chosen to be a vampire's lover

Curse, The Vampirism

Dhamphir Child born of a vampire father and mortal Romany mother

Dream Riding Telepathically eavesdropping on someone's thoughts and dreams

Enforcer of the City Vampire appointed by the Strigoi Council to police a territory

Enforcer of the Laws Vampire cop

Fledgling Young vampire

Fosterling Young vampire living and training under the protection of a nest leader

Gift, The Psychic ability

Goddess Some vampires believe they were created by a curse because of sins against the Goddess

Go into the night Strigoi saying, can mean either someone has joined the strigoi community, or that someone is dead

Hunt Sanctioned taking of human prey, regulated by enforcers

Hunter Members of the Nighthawk line, and courtesy title of enforcers

Mindrape Forced telepathic intrusion into another's mind

Nest A group of vampires, companions, and slaves that live and Hunt together

Nest Leader Senior vampire in a nest; teacher and adoptive parent of younger vampires

Nighthawk Another term for Hunters/Enforcers

Owl Bait Term of affection

Silver Dagger Symbol of Enforcer authority

Strig A vampire who lives outside the protection of the Laws; a loner

Strigoi The vampires' name for themselves

Strigoi Council The secret society that rules vampire society

Teething Slang for the period young vampires spend making the complete change from mortal to strigoi

Transient Mortal psychic unable to form a permanent mental bond with a vampire

Underneath World Strigoi term for all the supernatural cultures and creatures that live out of view of the mortal world